Mystic Turmoil

Kelli Marie

ISBN-13:978-1725065307
ISBN-10:1725065304

I dedicate this book to my family. Thank you for always encouraging my dreams

Prologue

Jordan

I KICK ONE OF the metal bars around me in frustration. My foot stings, but it doesn't compare to the pain of uncertainty that is rattling around in my head. I've been stuck in this cell for days, with my only companions being the guard that brings me food once a day and the gloating traitor, Xavier. Four days have passed since we returned to the castle after Xavier betrayed us. Four days since I've seen Cara. He has her, and there's nothing I can do; I'm helpless.

The ground beneath my feet is starting to show the signs of my anxiety. I spend most of my days pacing wearily and watching the main door of the prison. How could I have let this happen? How did I not see that he was going to betray us? I was supposed to protect her. My hand runs through my hair, sending it in all different directions. I was never supposed to fall in love with her. She was never supposed to be mine. I was only supposed to—

I turn as the main door of the prison opens and blinding light streams into the cell block. There are about a dozen cells and, lucky me, I'm the only one in them. Just as quickly as the door opened, it closes, and my eyes once again adjust to the dim light of the cell.

I sigh, "That time again, is it?"

"Hello to you too, Jordan." Xavier has the gall to smile, as though we are old friends. I just want to punch him.

"Where is Cara?" I've asked this every day.

"*My* fiancé is doing quite well, baker. You know that I would never hurt her."

I snort and lean against the bars with a nonchalance I do not actually feel. "You already did."

Xavier shrugs, "It was a necessary evil. But she will come around soon enough. She will realize that what I did was for us and our future." His eyes shine in their intensity. "She is my world and nothing will stop us from being together, not even her."

I run my hand over my face and sigh. How did I never notice how insane he was? His love for her was obsessive, but I thought it would keep her safe. I realized too late that it was dangerous, and we fell right into his trap. Thank goodness she never told him that she chose me. I have a feeling that I would no longer be breathing if that were true.

"She asks about you too, you know," Xavier comments offhandedly. When I don't rise to the bait, he continues, "It got me thinking. Why does she care so much about you? I know you two are close, and that you were there for her before me, but there is something more. There is something different now in the way she asks."

"It's called concern, Xavier. You should try it sometime." I am displaying a bravado I don't feel.

Xavier smiles, unworried. "We shall see."

He turns to leave, but I reach through the bars to grab at his arm. He shakes it off, continuing to the door. I'm getting desperate; I don't want him to leave yet. I need more information about Cara. I'm like a man starved for water and any drop of information will satisfy me.

"You were right, you know." My words stop his progression. He doesn't turn around, but I know I have his attention. A plan develops in my mind that I hope will protect Cara for now. "You were right about my feelings for her."

He turns swiftly, irritation hardening his features. I take that as my sign to continue. "I've loved Cara since the day I met her but she only ever had eyes for you. She always wanted you, Xavier. She only wanted friendship from me, no matter how hard I tried."

Xavier moves faster than I expected, pulling me by the neck and ramming my face against the bars of the cell. His eyes are wild as he leans in close. "I never should have allowed Cara to befriend you. You are nothing. The only reason you are still alive is because of her. As soon as she comes to her senses you are a dead man. I will kill you myself. Cara is mine and she will always be mine."

"You're right," I gasp out, "Cara is yours. I know that now."

"What makes you so sure now, baker?" he sneers.

"I finally told her how I felt when we were in the Mystic City. She told me that she was with you and that we could only be friends."

Xavier pushes me back and my lungs finally fill with air. He smiles smugly. "Nice try, but that will not save you. Trust me when I say, you will be dead by the end of the week."

He storms out of the prison and I am shrouded in darkness once again. I slump to the ground in relief, hoping that my plan worked. Xavier thinks I was trying to save myself but my only care is to keep Cara safe. If Xavier believes Cara still loves him it will keep her safer longer. I rest my forehead against my knees and conjure up an image of Cara in my mind, the only thing giving me strength. I sigh. If we get out of this mess, Xavier's threats of killing me will be the least of my problems. Little does he know, I'm already a dead man. My father will not let my mistakes go unpunished.

Chapter 1

Cara

MY DRESSER FLIES ACROSS the room and slams against the wall, shattering into pieces. I am back in my old quarters in King Rolland's palace. Everything is destroyed, thanks to me and the wind element. The first day I sat in silent shock, and no matter what Xavier said or did, I said nothing. My whole world had been shattered, and my mind could not take the pain that came with that realization. Xavier had betrayed us. He had led his father straight to the Mystic City. They set fire to the sacred city and murdered my brother, Kaden, right in front of me.

Finally, on the second day, anger broke through my sorrow. I threw Xavier up against the wall but he just smirked. "If anything happens to me, Jordan dies," is all he said. My temper flared and Xavier wisely made his exit. That was two days ago, and he has not been back since.

I take in the carnage that was once my beloved room but I cannot manage a feeling of remorse. This place was a lie, just like everything else in my life. The King and Queen who raised me are behind my parents' murder. Xavier, my fiancé, the boy who I always thought would protect me is in league with his father. He led him straight to the Mystic City. How did I not see this? How was I so blind?

A knock sounds on the door and it cracks open enough to allow in a shaggy blonde-haired head. Xavier eyes the room in a glance and finds me in the corner, with what is left of my bookcase.

"Are you done?" he asks. When I don't reply or make any move to attack him, he braves a few more feet into the room and closes the door behind him. He gestures to the room. "Did this make you feel better?"

"What do you want?" I barely recognize my voice; it seems so long ago that I last used it.

"Can't a man check on his fiancé when she is obviously upset?" He looks so much like the Xavier I used to love. He appears apologetic and worried, but I am no longer fooled.

I release a dry laugh, "You're out of your mind if you think I am still going to marry you."

His calm mask slips slightly but he recovers quickly. "My love, I know you are upse—"

"I thought you loved me."

"I do love you."

"What you did is not love, Xavier. And if you think it is then you have a very twisted sense of it." I turn away from him but he is undeterred.

"I will admit that the plan was never for me to fall in love with you. But I did and here we are."

"I don't understand any of this."

He wraps his arms around me, gingerly. "All you need to know is that I love you and I will take care of you."

I push him away. "Where is Jordan?"

This time his mask does slip and annoyance flashes in his eyes. "I never should have allowed you to befriend him."

"You don't control me, Xavier."

"It's cute that you think that."

The air shifts around the room as my anger rises. Xavier eyes me warily but stands his ground. Tears of frustration gather in my eyes.

"How did I never see what a monster you are?"

"You will come to see that I did everything I did for you."

"How is any of this for me? You betrayed me. You destroyed the Mystic City. You killed my brother! In what twisted way is any of this for me?!" The frustrated tears leak down my cheeks and fall into the carnage that was once my bookshelf. Pages from torn-up books drift between us as we stare each other down.

Before he can answer me, the door to my room creaks open and a nervous servant peeks inside. "Your Highness, the King is requesting your presence in the throne room. He said to bring the Princess as well."

"Tell him we'll be there shortly," he replies without taking his eyes off me. The servant nods and closes the door.

"I'll make you a deal, my love. We'll meet with my father and, afterward, you will join me for dinner, where we will discuss everything. If you behave appropriately, I will allow you to see your precious baker after dinner. Do we have a deal?"

"You will let me see Jordan?"

Xavier extends his arm, offering me his hand. "If and *only* if you behave appropriately with my father, and allow us to have a civilized dinner where you are not trying to kill me."

"You have a deal." I breeze past his outstretched arm and head to the door. I hear his sigh of annoyance but he says nothing as he follows me out of the room. We make our way through the spotless white halls of the palace. Guards flank us on either side, but we all know that they are just for show. I could take them all out with a quick gust of wind. I smirk to myself at the image that brings.

When we reach the throne room doors, Xavier grabs my elbow to stop me. "My love, I need to warn you. My father is not like you remember. He changed a lot after we left."

"I'd say, but then again I never really knew any of you to begin with."

"My love, I'm still—"

"I don't want to hear it right now, Xavier, I just want to get through this meeting with your father." I push open the throne room doors and stop short.

Nothing has changed in the throne room itself; it is still as pristine and beautiful as I remember it. The sparkling white walls are covered in colorful tapestries, and the vibrant red carpet that leads to the throne does not have a speck of dirt on it. What stops me short is the line of people along the wall of the throne room. I count eight individuals all chained hand and foot. Guards flank them on either side with guns aimed, poised to fire. A familiar face with short black hair catches my eye but Xavier takes hold of my arm and begins pulling me towards the throne where his father waits.

King Rolland sits upon his golden throne like one of the ancient gods. His posture speaks of a power and a confidence that I only wish I could feel. His clothes are immaculate, as usual, but gone is the loving father figure I once knew. Gone is the man who raised me as one of his own. In his place is a cold, unrecognizable monster. He sneers at our approach and eyes me with disdain.

"It's about time. Still having problems controlling her, Son?" Rolland laughs at his own joke.

Xavier squeezes my arm and I take that as a signal to keep my mouth shut. I find it funny that he thinks I will listen. Little does he know he killed the meek little girl I once was when he betrayed me.

"No one controls me."

"So, she speaks? I heard you were not saying much of anything, girl? Decided to finally grow a backbone?" Rolland's mocking tone incites my anger. The air around me begins to shift.

Xavier feels the change in the air and pulls me close to him. He nuzzles my ear and whispers, "Remember our deal, my love."

I glare at the King but take a few deep breaths to calm my temper. Xavier steps in front of me and addresses his father.

"What is it that you needed, Father?"

Rolland snorts. "Still protecting her, Son? You are such a soft fool for falling in love with her."

"My feelings for her will not interfere with your plans. I have told you this many times. Now, what is it that you needed?"

Rolland struts down from his raised dais and makes his way over to us. He motions for Xavier to move aside and stops in front of me. He grips my chin roughly and pulls my face close to his. "You have no idea how nice it feels to finally show you who we really are. Our little act was so exhausting." he smiles, but it does not reach his eyes. "My son's love for you does complicate things but, in the end, I will still get what I want."

"What is it that you want?" My cheeks are beginning to hurt from his tight grip.

Rolland ignores my question as he walks me over to the prisoners along the wall. Xavier makes a sound of protest at his manhandling but Rolland ignores him. He moves my face from side to side slowly so I can take them all in.

"Do you know any of these Mystics, Cara?"

"Don't call me that."

Rolland raises an eyebrow. "Is that not your name?"

I wrench my chin out of his grasp and rub my jaw. "I want nothing to do with the name your traitorous family gave me. My name is Maia."

Rolland stares at me for a second and then begins to laugh. "Where was this spirit when you were growing up? It's delightful."

"Betrayal tends to do that to a person."

"If you say so, Maia," he draws out the name mockingly, "Now answer my question, do you know any of these Mystics?"

I survey the group of eight in front of me and stop at the black-haired Mystic that caught my eye earlier. Myka. He is the husband to Layla's mother, Sage. I look around frantically but see no sign of Layla. How is he here? Where is Layla? Is she okay?

"No." I don't know what Rolland's plan is, so I won't expose my friend so easily.

"Father, she knows the one on the far right. His name is Myka."

I shoot Xavier a death glare as Rolland motions for the guards to bring Myka forward. As he draws closer, I can see that his right eye is swollen and his lip is busted.

"What have you done to him?"

The King motions to his guards again and the one to Myka's left punches him in the stomach. Myka lets out a cry of pain and doubles over. Xavier grabs me around the waist to stop me as I try to lurch forward.

"That is for lying, girl. So, who is he to you?"

Xavier's arm tightens around my waist in warning. "He is my friend," I grind out through clenched teeth.

Rolland pats my cheek. "Now, was that so hard? Do you know any more?"

I shake my head. Rolland looks to Xavier for confirmation, and I feel him nod.

"Very well. Guards take the rest outside and take this one to a cell. I will be in need of him later." The guards lead Myka away and take the seven remaining Mystics out of the throne room.

"Father, you still haven't told us why you wanted us." Xavier looks unsure as he eyes his father.

"Son, I really am sorry about this. An example needed to be made. I must ensure that no one will ever betray me again. She will die with the other traitors." Rolland leads us out of the throne room. Xavier is silent by my side, but I can feel the uncertainty radiating off him. It worries me.

Rolland stops us just as we are about to exit the palace. "I expect you to act as I have raised you. Do you understand? "

The King opens the giant palace door before Xavier can answer. The sunlight is blazing and I cover my eyes while I wait for them to adjust. When they do, I wish that they hadn't. Before us is a crowded courtyard filled with the people of Myridia. On the far side, a firing squad awaits as the seven Mystics are lead out.

"No." I grab Xavier's arm. "Xavier, please, this is an execution. Xavier, stop this."

"My people of Myridia!" Xavier ignores me as the King begins addressing the crowd. "Today is a day that I do not like being King. For you see, it is on days like today that I need to make very difficult and heartbreaking decisions. A traitor was in our midst, and they have finally been rooted out. This traitor is someone very close to me and it saddens me that they would turn to such violence. It is the ones closest to us that can hurt us the most." The King wipes a fake tear off his cheek and a bad feeling creeps up my spine.

"Before you are seven traitors who conspired against the crown and attacked my son and I as we were returning from rescuing our beautiful Cara just days ago. She had been kidnapped by the Governor of New Port, but she has been safely returned to us. These traitors attempted to finish the Governor's plan and knew our exact route."

The King grabs me and pulls me to his side tightly. He smiles down at me fondly. "I am not too proud to admit that we never would have made it if it were not for Cara here. My good people, I must be honest with you. I have kept a great secret from you. The girl that stands with me today is a Mystic." A collective gasp ripples through the crowd. "I know, I know. I apologize for the deception, but we needed to protect her identity until she was old enough to defend herself. The people of Estera would do anything to get their hands on her. She is that precious to us."

I look out at the crowd in disbelief. Some of the faces are of shock, others of understanding. Multiple women are crying and staring adoringly at the King, and it seems the entirety of Myridia is hanging on the King's every word. How are they believing any of this? None of this is true! I try to push away from him but he tightens his grip.

The King continues his speech, "And this is what leads us to today. These seven traitors attacked us but someone had to have let them know our route. Someone had to have let the Governor know who Cara was, which led to her kidnapping. This person betrayed us and tried to turn our future queen over to our enemies!"

The King motions to the guards at the edge of the courtyard. They pull a hooded figure out of the shadows, lead them to the line of Mystics along the wall and chain them to it. At the King's signal, a guard removes the hood and cries of despair come from all corners of the court yard.

Standing before the crowd in a dirty, tattered robe, is the Queen of Myridia.

Chapter 2

"NO!" XAVIER GRABS FOR me as I break out of the King's grasp. I evade him and use the wind element to send myself soaring over the crowd to the Queen's side. Exclamations of shock and awe sound behind me but I ignore them as I take in the frail woman in front of me. I drop to my knees in front of her and grasp her chained hands.

"Anya." The childhood nickname for the mother who raised me once again crossing my lips. When she had told me the truth and the part that she played in my parents' murder, I had told her she would never hear me call her that again. But, I was wrong. She will always be my Anya; she will always be the woman who raised me.

She lifts her head and tears gather in my eyes at the sight of the bruises that cover her face. "Anya, what have they done to you. I'm so sorry. I never wanted any of this. I'm so sorry."

Guards grab at me and try pulling me away from the Queen. I hold onto her hands as tightly as I can. Silent tears make their way down her cheeks. "This isn't your fault, Cara. I love you; you will always be my daughter. I regret nothing." Her voice is barely recognizable.

Xavier appears next to me and takes my face in his hands. The guards have stepped away and left the three of us alone. Tears are gathering in his eyes as well but he does not let them fall. "My love, you are making a scene. You need to come with me now."

"Xavier, how can you be okay with this? He's going to kill her. She's your mother."

Xavier looks down at me despondently, pain etched in every outline of his face. "I have no choice." He wraps his hands around mine and begins to separate them from his mother's.

"Go with him, Cara, it will be alright." The Queen squeezes my hands one last time and releases them. Xavier throws his arm around my shoulder and I bury my face in his shirt. We walk through the shell-shocked crowd as sobs rock my body. Rolland's face is murderous when we reach his side. Rage radiates from his body, but he faces the crowd with a melancholy expression.

"My people, look at how distraught our Princess is. The shock of finding out who betrayed her has sent her into despair. She must have justice! That venomous woman has hurt us all. She is a traitor and deserves to pay for her crimes!" The silent murmurs that had flowed through the crowd have now turned into a tumultuous outcry. Cries for blood and vengeance reverberate off the palace walls. The King's speech has incited the mob.

"Cara, don't watch." Xavier whispers and pushes my face deeper into the nook of his shoulder.

Tears are flowing down my face and sobs wrack my body. "Please, Xavier, stop this. Please stop it. They are all innocent."

"Shh, it's going to be over soon."

I break down into uncontrollable sobs as my pleas turn into mindless babble. Xavier holds me as the King gives the signal and the sounds of the firing squad echo through the courtyard. The cries of the condemned mix in with those of the inflamed crowd. But, just as soon as it started, it is over; silence descends upon the courtyard. The Queen and the innocent Mystics are dead.

After the execution, the King excuses himself to his study, leaving Xavier and I alone. If he is upset over what happened he doesn't show it. I'm beginning to think that the pain I saw on his face earlier was imagined. I stare out the window at the dispersing crowd. They were so eager to see their Queen die. *Funny how they care so much about me now.* I think bitterly to myself.

"Guard," Xavier's voice breaks through my reverie, "take Cara to the prison cells so that she can visit with her friend. Give her five minutes and then take her to her new rooms, next to mine."

"We aren't having dinner first?" I ask quietly.

"No, I think we've had enough for today. Now, go, before I change my mind." With that, I am dismissed and Xavier walks away from me.

I follow the guard through the halls until he stops in front of a set of steel doors. "You have five minutes. I will knock when it is time to come out. Don't make me come in and get you," he gruffly informs me.

I push open the door and squint through the darkness.

"Didn't I already have to see you today?" a voice says ahead of me.

"Jordan?"

"Cara! Is that really you? Light the lantern by the door."

I light the lantern and a soft flame bleeds light into the darkened space. Jordan stands before me, behind a set of steel bars. He's covered in dirt from head to toe and he smells like manure, but nothing stops me from running up to the bars and pulling his face to mine and kissing him.

Fresh tears run down my face, but, unlike the ones before, these are happy. His fingers wipe the tears away and his lips follow as he kisses my face in adoration. We both drop to our knees and grip each other through the bars, holding one another the best we can.

"How are you here?" he asks quietly, as though he's afraid I'll disappear.

"Xavier gave me five minutes to see you."

"Is he treating you well? Are you hurt?"

"No, I am not physically hurt."

Jordan must have sensed something in my voice because he pulls back and examines my face. "What happened?"

"They just executed the Queen and a group of Mystics. The King made up an elaborate story about me being kidnapped because I'm a Mystic, and that the Queen was behind it all. He ordered their execution by firing squad. He killed her because she told me the truth about him. It was revenge."

"Oh, Cara. I'm so sorry. I know you and the Queen were not on the best of terms, but I know you still cared for her. What happened to her was not your fault."

"It's just so hard to believe that she's gone. That the King would do that to her. He was her husband and he killed her."

"I know. There are a lot of things we do not understand." Jordan lifts my chin up with his finger and pushes my hair back from my face. "I love you."

I manage a half smile. "I love you too."

We sit in companionable silence, just holding each other but I know our time is ticking away. "Are you okay?" I ask.

"I'm doing alright. I'm in here alone, except for the guard that comes once a day to give me food and Xavier."

"Xavier comes here?"

"Yes. It is our daily ritual. He comes and taunts me and I try to learn as much as I can about how you are doing."

"I'm so sorry I got you into this mess, Jordan. This is all my fault."

"No," I feel him shake his head against mine. "This is Xavier's and King Rolland's fault. They did this. You are not to blame. This whole thing was set in motion before you could even talk. *You* are *not* to blame."

Jordan pulls out of my arms and faces me. He grabs my hands and holds them to his chest. "Buttercup, I need you to listen to me. I told Xavier that I expressed my feelings for you in the Mystic City and that you dismissed me saying you are with him. I told him that you are in love with him."

"Why would you do that?"

"I did it to protect you. If he knew you were about to leave him for me he would kill me and likely take his anger out on you. He thinks you are just mad at him for what he did. As long as he believes you still love him and do not love me, you are safe." He kisses my knuckles. "I know it will be hard, but I think you need to pretend that you still love him."

I pull my hands out of his grasp in shock. "What are you talking about?"

"I've been thinking about it a lot. If he believes you forgive him and finally see reason he may get sloppy or make mistakes. His love for you blinds him sometimes. You are his obsession. It could open a door for you to escape."

"I won't leave without you."

Jordan reaches through the bars and grabs my cheeks. He pulls me into him for a rough, passionate kiss. "You can and you will, you stubborn girl. All I ever wanted was for you to be safe and I will do anything to keep you safe. If you see an opening you take it, do you understand? Promise me."

I stubbornly shake my head, "I won't. I will do as you ask and pretend to forgive him, but I will not leave here without you. I've already told you I refuse to live in a world without you in it."

"Cara, please."

"No, I would never ask you to do what you are asking me to do. I won't do it. You would never leave me behind and I will never leave you behind. So stop asking me to."

Jordan sighs dejectedly and kisses my forehead. "You're right. I'm sorry."

He rests his forehead against mine and we stare into each other's eyes. I fidget nervously with my locket. "Do you think Kaden is alive?"

"I don't know, Buttercup. The King stabbed him and he wasn't moving when they took us away."

"I just feel like I would know if my brother were dead. I feel like I would sense it."

"Then hold on to that. Hope is important. You are my hope."

"What do you mean?"

"I hope for our future together. Just you and me and Titan."

I let out the first laugh I've had in a week, thinking of Jordan and his beloved wooden spoon. It feels good. Even with everything that happened today, it feels good.

"You are——" I'm interrupted by a loud knocking and my laughter stops. "I have to go. The guard instructed me to come out when he knocks."

Jordan places one last lingering kiss on my lips and then pulls away from the bars. Not knowing when I will see him again, I watch him as I slowly back out of the chamber, only looking away when I step out of the steel doors and into the bright corridor.

The guard says nothing as he strides down the hall, expecting me to follow. I follow him even though I know the way. My thoughts turn back to my conversation with Jordan. Can I pretend to still be in love with Xavier? I know a part of me will always love him. No matter what he has done, he was my first love, my fiancé, and my confidante for as long as I can remember. But can I pretend that the love of my life is still him, and not that beautiful boy alone in his cell? For Jordan's sake, I'm going to have to try.

"This is your room." The guard's gruff voice interrupts my thoughts.

"Oh," I glance to the door on our right. It's Xavier's room. He wasn't kidding when he said it was next to his. "Do you know if Xavier is in his room?"

He ignores my questions as he reaches around me and pushes open my door. "A guard will be posted outside your door at all times. You do not leave this room without being escorted by the Prince or a guard. Is that understood?"

Without waiting for me to reply, he corrals me into the room and closes the door. The room is massive, of course, and I can see a beautiful balcony behind a set of large glass doors. I run to the doors, passing the enormous bed and a door that I assume leads to an even larger closet. I turn the handle of the glass doors and then nothing. I jiggle the handle and pull, but the doors remain closed. They locked them. I stare longingly outside at the vast forest beyond. I had a taste of freedom and will do anything to get it back.

The sound of glass shattering breaks through the silence of the room. It sounded as though it came from that door I passed. I make my way back to the door and quietly open it. To my surprise, on the other side of the door is not a closet but Xavier's room. Our rooms are connected; I make a mental note to find a way to block the door.

Once I get over my shock of having adjoining rooms, I locate the source of the breaking glass. The remains of a drinking glass are littered across the floor and liquid runs down the wall where it must have collided. Xavier is on the other side of the room, chest heaving, with another ready to be sent flying.

"Xavier?" He doesn't acknowledge that I spoke, too lost in his thoughts. I slip into the room and tentatively make my way towards him. "Xavier, look at me."

Finally realizing that someone is in the room with him, Xavier raises his gaze and I can see the tears that are gathered in his eyes. Recognition flashes across his face and he almost drops the glass that he was about to throw. My heart breaks at the sight of him. He once again looks like the boy I fell in love with, his mask of indifference gone and in its place a broken boy who just lost his mother. I know I shouldn't, but it's hard to erase years of feelings, and I wrap my arms around him. He's so much taller than me, which is one thing I have always loved, so he rests his forehead on my shoulder as I rub his back. He makes no noise but silent tears wet my shoulder, and I let them.

Sometime later he raises his head and pulls away from me. He looks lost as he sits down on his bed and looks down at the ground. "I went to speak with my father," he pauses, but I say nothing, giving him time, "he didn't want to tell me he had planned this because he thought I would stop it. He was right. I would have; I would have tried to talk him out of it. He knew that I wouldn't interfere in front of everyone. But he made the right choice. She needed to be punished; she was a traitor."

"How can you say that? She was not a traitor."

"She almost ruined Father's plans by telling you everything. She got what she deserved."

I slap him across the face and the sound echoes across the room. "She was your mother, Xavier! How dare you say she deserved to die!"

He touches his cheek gingerly, shock written across his face, but I'm not done. "I know you, Xavier, or at least I did. The boy I knew would not be okay with his father killing his mother. The boy I knew would not be justifying his father's actions. She was your mother! The woman who raised you and gave you life. How can you be so blasé about this?"

"I trust my father."

"Your father is a monster." As soon as the words leave my mouth, I know I have made a mistake. His mask slips back into place and his face hardens. Gone is the broken boy of a second ago. In his place is the Xavier I now know.

"I think it's time you went to your room."

"Xavier, it's okay to be upset that your mother is dead."

"Cara. I said go."

"I don't understand you. You want me to forgive you, but you are pushing me away."

The glass Xavier was holding flies past my head and shatters on the wall, next to the other one. "I said go!"

This time I listen and I leave the raging prince alone.

Chapter 3

TWO DAYS PASS BEFORE I see Xavier again. He comes strutting into my room without a care in the world, over to my perch by the window and kisses my cheek.

"Good afternoon, my love. How are you today?"

"Where have you been? I've been stuck in this room for two days," I say without looking away from the window.

"Why? Have you missed me?" I can hear hope and glee in his voice.

"No, I just don't appreciate being locked up for two days while you're off doing whatever you want. If you're trying to win me over you're doing a terrible job of it."

Xavier sighs, "I can see that you're still mad at me." He sits down next to me and turns my face towards him with his finger. "My love, I am sorry for the way that I acted the other night. You were trying to help me and I lashed out at you. It was a moment of weakness."

"It was not weakness. You were grieving the loss of your mother."

"I had a lot of emotions being thrown around in my head. My mother was a traitor, now that is the end of it. Accept my apology so we can move on."

I bristle at his tone and turn away from him. Pretending to love this version of Xavier is going to be a lot harder than I thought. He is giving me a headache with the way his personality changes every hour.

"I have a special dinner planned for us tonight," Xavier comments, "I feel it might be a good opportunity to discuss our future together."

"What future?"

"Oh, don't play, my love. I saw the way you looked at me the other night when you tried to comfort me. You still love me, you are just in denial. You will come around soon and when you do we can finally be together."

"What do you mean?" My insides churn with anxiety.

"Why, our wedding, of course."

"Our wedding? What do you mean our wedding? I already told you that I am not marrying you, Xavier."

He brushes off a piece of lint on his shoulder. "And I'm telling you that you will come around. Now, let's find you something nice to wear to our dinner tonight." He claps his hands together and heads for my closet. He comes out a few minutes later with a long red gown, simple yet elegant. He lays it out on the bed for me.

"I love you in red. I think this dress will be perfect for you. Plus, it matches the present I have for you." He walks back over to me, lifts up my right wrist and encircles it in a slim bracelet. It's similar to the one he gave me after he pushed things a little too far during our first training. Instead of a silver bracelet with white diamonds, this one is black with two red crystals.

"They are called Red Stars," he comments as he watches me examine the bracelet. "They are very rare. Legend has it that in ancient times, long before any humans came to be, there was a race of giants. They populated the Algarian mountains and Forgotten plains. The giants were violent and destructive, and they destroyed everything that was around them. Their Princess, though, was kind and gentle, and she hoped that with her rule, she could teach her people a new way of life, without violence or destruction. She succeeded to some extent, some of the giants started to follow her ways, including a young giant who she fell in love with. The two of them fell deeply in love and were wed. Together they worked to better the lives of the giants. But the Princess' father, the King of the giants, the most brutal of them all, did not like what she and her mate were doing. He liked the violent way his kingdom was run and hated the way that his people began to follow his daughter and her peasant mate.

Consequently, the King incited a mob, feeding them lies about the Princess and her mate, which drove them into a frenzy. In the dead of night, the mob pulled the pair out of their bed and dragged them into the middle of the village. They killed her beloved before her eyes and she held him as he took his last breath. The mixture of her tears and his blood embedded into the earth and became the Red Stars. In her grief, her father finally got his wish and she turned into the violent beast he desired. She lashed out at the incited mob, taking out every giant that had taken her love from her. The village streets swam with their blood. Her father, realizing what he had done, pleaded for mercy but it was too late. The gentle Princess was gone, replaced by a raging monster. His plan worked too well and she became his undoing. She murdered the King and then sent the giants into an epic war that destroyed their race forever. In the end she became the most violent queen to ever rule the mighty giants."

I sit in shocked silence as Xavier finishes his story. I shake my head to clear it. "Why would you tell me this story?"

"So that you can understand that anyone can change, given the right push. Don't make my father have to push you, my love, because he will to get what he wants." He kisses my wrist just above the bracelet. "Now, get ready. I will be back later to take you to dinner. I will send in a maid to help you with your hair."

He leaves and I stare at the closed door for far too long. His story weighs heavily on me. If something were to happen to Jordan could I become like the Princess in his story. Do I have the potential of becoming a destructive monster if I were pushed too far? I don't ever want to find out. I will get Jordan and I out of here even if it kills me. I will never become like the monsters in Xavier's story.

A maid I don't recognize enters my room and nervously curtsies. "I'm here to do your hair, miss."

"Where are my usual maids? I'm sorry but I don't recognize you."

Her eyes dart around the room, avoiding me. "I'm sorry, miss, but they are gone. I will be your new maid."

"What do you mean, 'gone'? Where did they go?"

The maid starts wringing her hands. "Miss, I shouldn't say."

"What is your name?"

"Alexia."

"Alexia, I won't hurt you. Please tell me what happened to my other maids?"

Tears begin gathering in her eyes and once again she is looking at everything but me. Her gaze finally settles on me, after some time, and I can see the fear that runs deep. "Please do not tell him that I told you. I don't want to end up like them."

"You are safe with me. I will not hurt you."

"When you left, everyone who was associated with you was executed for treason. Your maids and any guards that regularly guarded you. The King was convinced that anyone who had contact with you either failed in their duty or assisted in your kidnapping. A new batch of maids, including myself were just brought in, in preparation for your return. I will not fail you, miss, nothing will happen to you on my watch."

"Did you know about the other maids before you got into the palace?"

Alexia shakes her head. "No, we were told that there were openings and I took one. It is a far better life than I had. I had to leave my family, but I can send them money. It wasn't until a few days ago that I learned what happened to the other maids. And now I am terrified I will mess up and the same thing will happen to me. My family needs this money." Alexia breaks down in tears.

I turn away to give her a moment of privacy and to collect my thoughts. Rolland probably killed the old staff to ensure that the true story of my escape never was heard by the people. Guilt engulfs me as the number of people killed on my account weighs down on me. If I had never left, the staff here in the castle never would have died, the Mystics would still be safe in the Mystic City, and the Queen would probably still be alive. So many deaths because I wanted a taste of freedom. So many deaths because I wanted to find my people.

No. I shake my head and look over at the sobbing maid. This is all Rolland's fault. Jordan was right. This was all set in motion before I could even talk. This was caused by the King's greed and his thirst for power. I steel my heart against the assaulting guilt. None of this is my fault. We are all just pawns in Rolland's game. He caused all of this to happen and everything that has resulted since is on him. Xavier's story and its warning come back to me again. I will not become the giant Princess. I will not allow myself to be a pawn in the King's game. I will do what I was born to do, I will save my people. I will save all of Myridia from their tyrant king.

A few hours later, Xavier arrives to take me to dinner. Alexia did a wonderful job of fixing my hair. It now cascades down my back in soft blonde waves, with just a small amount pulled back behind my ear with a brooch. I must say, the red gown looks spectacular on me but I won't give Xavier the satisfaction of knowing that.

"You look amazing, my love; your maid really outdid herself," he comments as he takes my arm and leads me out of the room.

"Her name is Alexia."

He waves off my comment and we continue walking in silence until a thought occurs to me. "Did you know that your father killed all my maids and guards?"

"Yes, he informed me when we returned from the Mystic City. But it is nothing to worry about, as you can see they were easily replaced."

"They were people, Xavier, and they were killed for no reason."

"They were servants. Their deaths mean nothing."

"Is Maxwell okay?" I ask. Maxwell is Xavier's personal butler and probably the closest person that Xavier could consider a friend.

"Of course he is. He did nothing wrong."

"Good, I'm happy that he was not taken from you. I know how much he means to you."

Xavier says nothing as we enter the dining hall. My heart constricts as I think about all the family dinners we have had in this hall. A family who I thought loved me. The Queen's seat is empty as though she never existed. He leads me over to my chair and pulls it out for me. Normally he would sit next to me, at the seat to the right of his father, but tonight he sits across from me, next to his mother's empty chair. If its vacant presence bothers him, he doesn't show it.

As soon as he is seated, a servant comes out and places napkins on our laps and fills our drinks. The Prince instructs the servant to bring out the food as soon as it is prepared and reminds the servant to remember his instructions.

"What instructions?" I ask, once the servant has left.

"I have instructed the staff to cut our food for us before it arrives at the table. I took the liberty of being sure all sharp objects and cutlery were removed before we dined. I can't have you trying to murder me over dinner."

I let out a very unladylike snort. "I don't need a knife to hurt you, Xavier, you know that."

He eyes me cryptically. "We'll see."

Before I can ask him what he means, the servant returns with our first course, a tray of fresh cheeses and bread. I pick at it as Xavier talks about random court dealings. It isn't until he says the word wedding that I actually pay attention to what he is saying.

"There you are, I was wondering what would bring you back into the conversation," he comments.

"You act like I care about all the court dealings."

"You should care, they are soon to be your people. You are to be their Queen, you should be aware of the royal court."

I crumble the bread that I was holding in my hand. "Why are you doing this? Why are you forcing me to marry you?"

Xavier actually looks perplexed. "I am not forcing you to marry me. You will come to agree in due time."

"I have already told you I will not marry you, Xavier."

He reaches across the table, grabbing my hand, stroking his thumb along my knuckles. "Our love is special. You will come to see that soon enough. You will understand that you are the air I breathe, and you are mine. There is no one out there for you but me."

Those words, *You are the air I breathe and you are mine,* he has spoken them to me a hundred times. I always viewed that as a sweet sentiment, a declaration of his love. I never noticed the hidden menace behind them; the hidden danger. I had so many warning signs, but I was too blind to see them.

"If I were to agree to marry you, what would happen to Jordan?"

"That depends on you, my love."

The servant returns and replaces our cheese with our main dish. It smells divine and I feel my stomach grumble. Xavier raises his eyebrow knowingly and I ignore him as I pick up my utensil and eat. Xavier instructs the servant to leave us undisturbed until he is called for again. We eat in silence as I mull over his words. Xavier is so confident that I will come around and marry him. Is he really that blinded by his love or is he that confident because of something I do not know. Once I have eaten my fill I push my plate away and look up to meet his expectant gaze.

"Ready to talk now?" he asks.

"Why are you so confident that I will come around? You betrayed me, Xavier, you helped kill my brother. You assisted in destroying the Mystic City. How many Mystics do you think died because of what you did?"

"Their deaths were a necessary evil for us to be together." He puts his hand up when I start to object, his eyes flashing with annoyance. "Let me finish. How am I supposed to explain myself when you are always interrupting me?"

He pauses and waits for my continued silence. Satisfied that I will not interrupt him again, he continues, "My father had this elaborate plan that he would raise you as his own and then mold you into the weapon he needed. As you got older it became evident that you were not easily manipulated and that you would not take orders very well. You were, and are, a very stubborn and headstrong person. So he had to change his plans. His next scheme was to tell you the truth and then torture you into submission. But I decided to step in and came up with the strategy of seducing you. We thought that if you fell in love with me, we would then be able to mold you into whatever way we wanted."

"What about the objects he would use to try and control me? Your mother." I choke up at the mention of the Queen. I take a deep breath and continue, "She told me that he was trying to use items to control me. Like that lavender ring you gave me on my birthday."

"Those were foolish dreams of his. He had heard of legends of ways to control people with items but it has been eighteen years and he has yet to figure out how. I went along with it when he asked, but I knew his plans in that regard would never work, until recently."

"Until recently?" I can't help the bad feeling that is creeping into my body.

"We'll get to that later." He waves off my concern. "So, as time went by, our plan backfired and I ultimately fell in love with you. At first this upset him, believing my feelings for you would blind my judgment. It has caused many arguments between the two of us. But, I proved him wrong, time and again. My love for you has never blinded me, it just strengthened my resolve. We are meant to be together. And he grew to understand that. Then my mother had to go and ruin it all, and our plan had to change once again."

"So, if your mother had never told me the truth, what would have happened?"

"We would have been wed as planned and eventually I would have given you the books, giving you the history you so desperately craved. Together we would have found the Mystic City, but not before I had poisoned your view of the Mystics. By the time we got to them you would have wanted their destruction. You would have believed they abandoned you and left you to be raised by humans. We would have destroyed the Mystic City together and then set our sights on Estera. Together, with Father, we would have ruled over all. Nothing would have been able to stop us." He sighs dramatically. "But, sadly, that will not happen and now we are stuck in a whole new mess."

"Mess?"

"Father is doubting my ability to control you. He says you are unruly, disobedient, and ungrateful. You should have seen him after the stunt you pulled at the execution." Xavier grabs my hand and runs his fingers along my knuckles lovingly. "My love, he has figured it out. Or, at least, he thinks he has."

"Figured what out?"

"How to control you. He has found the secret to controlling you."

I pull my hand out of his grasp. "If he has, then why hasn't he used it yet?"

Xavier stands and comes to my side of the table. He turns my seat around and kneels in front of me. The way he looks at me makes me believe he really does love me. "I am holding him off, but I don't know if I can for much longer. My love, I don't want him to use whatever he has to control you. I don't want to lose the woman I love. If he uses what he has, you could change, you could become a different person. Please." He cups my cheeks and pulls me in for a kiss. "Just tell me you'll marry me and you'll follow our orders, and it will all go away. He'll be convinced that you are under our control. You can remain as you are. Don't force his hand, Cara. Just obey and I will take care of you. You and I can be together. Nothing has to change between us."

In need of space, I try to push him away with the wind element, but nothing happens. I try again but I feel nothing, no movement in the air.

"Wh-What?" I stand, which sends Xavier tumbling to the ground. I try again to summon the wind element but nothing happens. "What is going on?"

"My love, sit back down. I can explain."

"What did you do to me?!" I am barely containing my hysterics. Then it dawns on me. "This is why you had the knives removed."

"I didn't know how you would react." Xavier takes his seat again. "Please, let me explain, sit down, my love."

"What did you do to me?!"

"I'm afraid it's my fault, dear." A sultry voice says from behind me. I turn as a woman I don't know enters the room. She appears to be around the same age as me, maybe a year or two older. Her hair is red, almost like fire, and it flows down her back in tight curls. Her piercing green eyes seem to be laughing at me as she takes in my situation. Her black knee-high boots click on the floor as she makes her way closer to us. Xavier seems annoyed by her arrival but says nothing as she takes a seat next to him and rests her feet on the table we just finished eating at. Her very short and tight black dress rides up her thighs so much that I'm sure Xavier is getting an eyeful.

"Who are you?" I look to Xavier for help but he is conveniently quiet.

"My name is Seraphine." The fiery redhead helpfully supplies while she pulls a piece of meat off Xavier's plate and slips it between her blood-red tinted lips.

"What did you do to me?"

"Nothing," she smirks but it does not reach her eyes, "but I did supply the means to taking away your powers."

"Xavier, what is she talking about?"

"Oh, don't talk to him. Talk to me, dear. I've been waiting for this for a long time." Seraphine snaps her fingers and a goblet of wine appears in her hand, which she sips. She stares at me over the rim of the glass, expectedly.

"You're a witch," I gasp out.

"Very good, little Mystic, I am."

"How? I don't understand."

"Oh, there is a lot you don't understand." She laughs and the sound is silky and provocative. The woman before me oozes confidence and power, and she knows it.

Xavier finally having enough of this game turns to the witch. "Seraphine, don't you have something else you should be doing?"

"But, Xavier, this is just so much more fun. Watching your poor beloved try to figure out who I am and what is going on with her powers is just delightful. Your father will understand why I am late when I tell him that."

"You are making matters worse. I have it handled." Xavier pushes Seraphine's feet off the table and they fall to the ground. She just smiles in amusement and puts her feet back up. Xavier goes to push them off again but he must see something in her expression because his eyes widen and he retreats back in his chair.

"Now, where were we?" she says as she sips from her goblet and turns her attention back to me. "Ah, yes. How have your powers gone?"

Seraphine places her goblet on the table and elegantly rises to her feet. She sashays over to me and picks up my wrist with the bracelet on it. "This little bracelet here is why you cannot use your powers."

"The Red Stars?"

"Yes." Her green eyes captivate me and I cannot look away from her. She terrifies me and intrigues all in the same time. Who is this woman and why is she helping Rolland? "The Red Stars are the only things in our world that can block a Mystic's power. And unlucky for you my people live on the only land that they are found."

She releases my wrist and I immediately try tugging the bracelet off. It won't budge. She smiles at me in fake sympathy. "Sorry, dear, but the only way that bracelet is coming off is if Xavier or I remove it."

"Why are you doing this?" For the first time since my power manifested I feel weak. I came to depend on them; they gave me a sense of security, now they are gone.

Seraphine pats my cheek. "That's a story for another time. As Xavier mentioned, I have places to be." She smiles again but this time there is something sinister behind her eyes. I see Xavier tense from his place at the table. "I look forward to us getting to know each other more, Cara. Though I have a feeling you won't enjoy it as much as I will."

And with those parting words Seraphine exits the dining hall and her alluring laugh echoes back to us.

Chapter 4

I PULL AT THE bracelet for the hundredth time and growl in frustration as, once again, it doesn't come loose. What is keeping this thing together? Fury rips through me as yet again Xavier has betrayed me. How dare he put this on me and take away my powers.

After the encounter with Seraphine, the mysterious witch, Xavier took me back to my room and left saying he would be back later. I bombarded him with questions the entire walk back but he ignored them all. I let out another growl of frustration and throw my pillow against the door. To my surprise the door opens and the guard peeks his head in.

"Is everything okay in here?" he asks.

"I want to speak to Xavier now," I demand.

The guard looks behind him and then steps into the room, closing the door behind him. "He said he would be back soon, Princess."

"I want to talk to him now." I step back putting some distance between the guard and myself. A guard has never entered my room before by themselves. "Go and get him."

The guard puts his hand out in what he must feel is a reassuring way. "I'm not going to hurt you."

"Get out of my room."

"Maia."

"What did you just call me?"

"I am a friend. My name is Ben. You have many friends here." He comes closer but stops a good distance away from me. "The Mitera sent me. She is watching over you."

"The Mitera? I don't understand. Who is that?"

"She is our leader. She—"

"What is going on here?" Xavier stands in the doorway, with his eyes taking in the picture of me in my room alone with a guard.

"Your Highness, I heard a commotion inside the room and investigated. The Princess was visibly upset, so I was just checking the room to make sure it was secure," Ben explains, smoothly.

Xavier eyes Ben skeptically and then slides his gaze to mine. "Cara? Is this true?"

Intrigued by this guard and this 'Mitera', I go along with the lie and nod. "Yes, I was throwing things against the wall. I was understandably upset over what happened earlier." I couldn't help throwing in that comment.

"That is why I returned so soon. I couldn't leave you like that." Xavier turns back to Ben, "You are dismissed, I will be with her for the rest of the evening."

Ben bows and goes to move past Xavier but he stops him before he can exit the room. Ben winces as Xavier squeezes his arm. "Do not let me catch you alone with my fiancé in her room again, do you understand?"

Ben nods and Xavier releases him. Xavier dismisses him with a wave of his hand and he is gone. Xavier locks the door behind him.

"Was that really necessary? You should be happy that he was doing his job and ensuring my safety."

Xavier stalks over, and as he nears I can see the possessive fury that lies behind his eyes. He cups my cheek. "You are mine.

You are never to be alone with any man but me. I share you with no one."

I knock his hand away from my face. "Xavier, he was checking to make sure I was safe. He wasn't doing anything wrong."

"My father's guards think they can get away with anything. They know the rules. They know who you belong to."

I let out an exasperated sigh. There is no use talking to him. "Since I don't have my powers right now, can you please unlock the balcony? I want to feel the fresh air."

Xavier watches me for a second, like he can't believe that I am not arguing with him, but then his face breaks into a smile. "Of course, my love, anything to make you happy."

He takes a key out of his pocket and slides it into the lock. I push the door open before he can take the key out of the door. The blast of fresh air breathes life into me. There is a cool breeze and the sun is high in the sky. I take a deep breath and let it out slowly, and it feels like welcoming home an old friend. Being separated from nature has made me feel incomplete and hollow, and I finally feel whole again. Even with my connection to the elements cut off, I still feel my connection to the earth around me.

"Thank you," I murmur, forgetting for a second all the reasons why I should not be thanking the man standing next to me.

Xavier encircles his arms around me and hugs me from behind. He nuzzles my ear. "I told you, anything to make you happy. I live to see that smile on your face."

I try to push his arms off me but he just tightens his embrace. "Come on, my love, don't ruin this for us both." I don't miss his threatening tone.

Not willing to give up my little taste of freedom, I relax against him. I hear his sigh of contentment and we fall into silence. I close my eyes, enjoying the breeze running across my face, and imagine that it is Jordan holding me. It is the feeling of Xavier absently rubbing my wrist that brings me out of my stupor.

"I'm sorry it had to be this way," he says and lightly touches the bracelet.

"No, you're not."

I feel his chuckle against my back, "You're right, I'm not. You know me too well. I'm not sorry I had to do it. But I am sorry that you had to find out the way you did. I planned to break the news to you a little gentler than Seraphine did."

"Who is she?"

"It's not something that I can tell you right now. You will find out about her when the time is right."

"Can you tell me about the Red Stars?"

"I don't know much about them, honestly. I knew of them, like I told you earlier, they are a rare jewel. I just never knew the special quality they possessed, Seraphine brought them to the palace with her. All I know is that they stop you from using your powers; they block your connection to the elements. She explained it all to Father." He kisses my cheek. "They are for your protection."

"My protection?"

"Yes, everything I ever do is for you. They will protect you from doing something foolish. We don't want another display like at the execution."

"So, I am to be your prisoner for the rest of our lives? You'll keep me locked up and my powers restrained?"

"I will do so for as long as is necessary, my love. I suppose that depends on you." He rests his chin on my shoulder. "I forgot how beautiful this view was."

"Yes, it is," I respond wistfully. "I miss the forest."

"I don't know why. You almost died there, twice. First that rhifter and then those arachpids." He shivers in disgust. "Those things were dreadful."

"Being in that forest was the first time I ever felt free." I pull out of his arms and this time he lets me. I walk to the edge of the balcony and hop up onto the railing with my feet hanging over the edge. We are extremely high up, even with my powers I don't think I would have the ability of getting down. Xavier comes up beside me but instead of sitting on the railing he leans against it so he is facing me.

"So how did you do it?" I ask.

"Do what?"

"Help your father follow us. I never suspected anything."

"It wasn't easy for sure. Especially once we got into the mountains. It took Father's men a week to figure out how to get across those canyons. It would have taken longer if it hadn't have been for Seraphine. For the most part they were trailing us, but when they fell behind I would leave some clues."

"Seraphine? When exactly did she arrive here?"

"Right before we left. It's how Father realized the books were missing. She asked about them and they were gone."

"Why did you kill Jeremiah? I know it's not because of the reason you gave me in the Mystic City."

"I gave him a choice and he chose wrong. I wanted him to report back to my father, he refused, so I killed him. Either way, I got the result I needed, Father knew where we were."

"He was a good man. He didn't deserve to die." I wish I still had the shoes he had made me when we traveled through Frea, something to honor his memory, but they were lost along our journey.

Xavier shrugs, "He made his choice."

I turn away from him and focus on the setting sun. It is coloring the horizon in a beautiful display of reds and oranges. The colors blur as my vision clouds with tears. It isn't until the sun dips below the horizon that I acknowledge Xavier's presence again.

"And the Governor?"

"That one was easy. He deserved to die. Father has been looking for an excuse to get rid of him for years. While we were in Murr, Father caught up to us and I informed him we were heading to New Port. When we ran into the trouble with the Governor, his men pretended to be the Governor's guards and helped Jordan and I escape."

"Your father's men could have helped us more. You had me kill those men. Jordan was right, I was just a weapon to you."

"I'm tired of hearing that baker's name on your lips," he sneers.

"He's been my best friend since I was a child." I absently play with the locket around my neck. "You can't just make him go away, Xavier."

The smile he gives me scares me. "Want to bet? With a snap of my fingers he would die."

"You kill him and you will lose any chance of me ever cooperating with you."

"And that, my love, is the only reason he is still alive."

I shake my head in disgust. "Why not just let your father use whatever he has to control me? It seems like it would solve all your problems."

"Like I told you at dinner, it could change who you are. What he wants, you will want. It could change you into a person

I would not know. I'm not willing to risk it. I fell in love with you, not a personality-less shell. You are a challenge but I love a challenge."

"What you feel for me is not love, it's obsession."

"They are the same thing, my love. You are the air I breathe. I told you I would burn the world down to keep you and I did. You are mine and I will do anything to keep it that way. No one will keep us apart, not you or Father." He grabs my chin and once again I see the possessive fury in his eyes. "Say it, my love, say you are mine."

"No."

Xavier just smirks as if he expects nothing less. "One day you will say it, my love, and when that day comes you will finally understand my love for you."

"You are insane."

He laughs and pushes off from the railing and holds out his hand. "Come, we have wedding plans to prepare."

I eye the darkened horizon, wearily. Xavier sighs, "I will keep the door unlocked so you can come out here again. Please don't make me regret it."

I take his hand and we venture through my bedroom and into his, through the connecting door. He leads me to his bed where he instructs me to sit. He grabs a stack of papers from his desk and joins me, spreading them out in front of us.

"What is all this?" I scoot away from him, putting some distance between us.

"Wedding details. And before you say you are not marrying me, let me explain what happens if you don't." He counts off on his fingers. "One, your baker dies. That will be first and foremost. Two, I will not be able to hold Father back any longer and he will take over your control. Three, as payment for your stubbornness he will probably send you after the remaining

Mystics and have you kill them yourself. You were mad at me for making you a weapon, he will make you the ultimate weapon."

"When do you plan for us to get married?"

Xavier smiles and I see a glimpse of the boy I fell in love with. "By the end of the month."

"That soon?"

"It isn't soon enough."

I settle in as he begins a long discussion about wedding colors and people who will be attending. How many times did I wish for this day as we were growing up? How many times did I look forward to sitting on this very bed and going over the plans for our special day? I watch his face as he goes over plan after plan. He reminds me so much of the Xavier I used to know. His boyish charm is showing and his youthful enthusiasm is almost contagious. I know deep down he really does love me, or at least he believes he does. I don't know what is scarier. But, even if his feelings are real they are jaded and dark, corrupt. How did I miss the warning signs for so long? Was I that desperate to be loved that I allowed myself to fall into his version of love?

"You're not listening to a word I'm saying, are you?"

"Honestly, no."

Xavier sighs and puts whatever he was trying to show me aside. "Is this how you're always going to be?"

"What do you want from me, Xavier? You've taken away my freedom and my powers, you constantly threaten to kill Jordan, your father killed the woman who raised me, and my people are either dead or scattered. Please tell me how I am supposed to be acting?!"

Xavier blinks at me, like he wasn't expecting my outburst, then he nods, "You're right, I'm sorry."

I'm struck speechless for a second so I blurt out, "I'm sorry?"

"I haven't been considerate of your feelings, my love. You need time, I understand that, but time is not a luxury that we have right now. My father wishes to move forward with his plans and I can only do so much to hold him off."

Xavier pushes his items aside and scoots up on the bed, resting against the headboard. He motions to me to join him and I reluctantly do as he asks. He wraps his arm around me and pulls me close, with my head resting on his chest. My heart thumps loudly in my chest, bringing up old feelings and emotions. I used to feel so safe in his arms; I knew that he would never allow anything to hurt me. Even now, with everything going on, after everything he has done, that safe feeling remains. He will never allow anything or anyone to hurt me. Confusion and guilt ripple through me. How can I still have these feelings towards this man who has betrayed me over and over? How can I have feelings for him when I obviously love Jordan?

Xavier kisses the top of my head. "I know what you are thinking."

"Yea, what's that?"

"You are feeling guilty that you still love me after everything that has happened. You are feeling guilty for feeling safe with me even though I have brought you pain." He takes my silence as confirmation and pulls me in closer. "No one will understand you like I do, Cara. No one will ever love you like I do. The sooner you understand that, the easier it's going to be. I will never let anyone hurt you. You are mine and nothing will ever change that."

"Even your father?"

"No, my love, not even my father will come between us. We are meant to be together." He starts to rub my back soothingly. "Everything is going to be okay. You will always be safe with me."

Between the soothing motion on my back and the steady rise and fall of Xavier's chest, I slowly begin to doze off. My last thought before I fall asleep is that pretending to love this version of Xavier is not going to be as hard as I thought, and that terrifies me more than I'd like to admit. What if I stop pretending and fall back into his snare?

Chapter 5

"I FIGURED I'D FIND you out here."

I look back at Xavier from my perch on the balcony railing. His shaggy blonde hair is sticking up in every direction and his eyes are still heavy-lidded from sleep. I woke up early this morning, still nestled against him like it was the most natural thing to do. Needing space away from him and my confusing emotions, I retreated to the safety of the balcony.

"I needed some air."

"You should have woken me." Xavier jumps up on the ledge next to me and lets out a loud yawn.

"I needed some time alone. Plus, you were sound asleep. I don't even think an arachpid attack could have wakened you."

Xavier kisses my cheek. "Well, it's easy to sleep soundly with you next to me."

"Sorry for falling asleep on you."

"Never be sorry for that, my love. I wasn't. It just means you felt safe." I'm saved from thinking about that too closely by the sound of my bedroom door slamming against the wall. A few seconds later the red-haired witch, Seraphine, makes her way onto the balcony.

Xavier groans in annoyance, "Could have sworn I locked that door, Seraphine."

She smiles, unapologetically, "You did. But locks are nothing to me." Today she is dressed in a black and red form fitted lace dress that barely reaches her knees, where it meets those same black knee-high boots.

"So, what is so important that you couldn't wait until I was fully awake?" Xavier asks.

"Nothing, actually. I was just bored and I had so much fun meeting your Mystic pet yesterday."

"Excuse me? I am no one's pet." I snap.

Seraphine eyes me up and down and just smirks. I decide then that I do not like this woman. I don't know who she is or why she is helping King Rolland, but I do know that she is pure evil.

"Cara, why don't you go inside and freshen up so that I may talk to Seraphine," Xavier suggests and gets down from the railing to face her.

Not really wanting to be anywhere near the witch, I gladly take his suggestion and exit the balcony, stopping just inside the door. I peek out through a slit in the drapes.

"You really need to stop interrupting my time with Cara, Seraphine," Xavier growls.

Seraphine sticks her lip out in a fake pout. "I don't know why you want to be with her when you could be with me." She runs her finger down his chest.

He pushes her hand off him. "I've already told you that I have no interest in you. I have feelings strictly for Cara."

The witch sighs dramatically. "Yes, you have made that abundantly clear, but you can't blame me for trying."

"So, what is it that you really wanted?"

"Your father sent me."

"I wasn't aware that you were his personal messenger now. Do you also polish his boots?"

Seraphine's eyes flash with anger and Xavier flies back, landing in a heap against the railing. She stalks over to him and pulls him up by his shirt. I cover my gasp with my hand. "Let me make one thing very clear, prince, I work for no one. The only reason I am here is revenge. I will work alongside you and your father for as long as I deem necessary, and not a minute more." She drops him unceremoniously back on the ground.

Xavier gets to his feet, brushing dirt off his clothes. "You have an anger problem."

"And you're a lovesick fool."

Xavier shrugs. "Can't argue with that. Now what did Father want?"

"He wants to ensure that you are progressing with Cara. Is she cooperating?"

"It's kind of hard to get her to cooperate when you keep interrupting us and making her upset. I'm walking a very thin line with her right now and you keep coming in and screwing it up."

"Perhaps she needs some motivation."

"You are not allowed to touch her. She is under my protection," Xavier snarls.

Seraphine rolls her eyes. "I won't touch her, you fool. I have other effective ways of motivating her. Perhaps a demonstration of what will happen if she doesn't cooperate and your father gains control of her." She taps her finger on her chin. "Yes, I think that it is a splendid idea. Rolland will love it. Let's plan for this afternoon, shall we?"

I scramble away from the door as Seraphine starts towards my location. I slip into the bathroom just as she enters my room. I let out a sigh of relief and slide to the floor against the door. Who is this mysterious witch and who is she seeking revenge against? She seems to really hate me but I've never met her before.

A knock on the door makes me jump. "My love, I have some things to take care of. I will be back later. If you need anything let the guard know outside your room."

"Okay."

I listen for his steps until he leaves the room. I rest my forehead on my knees and close my eyes. Tears prick my eyes but stay safely behind my eyelids. I feel so torn up inside. Xavier is messing with my emotions. I know this, yet I still feel myself falling for the same tricks. When he acts like he did last night and this morning it's easy to forget the man he truly is. The man who betrayed me and is restraining my powers. What if by playing along with this game and pretending to be in love with him I end up back in the same situation again? What if he traps me in his dangerous love and I'm unable to get out? I don't want to be with him anymore, but I can't escape the feelings that he evokes. No matter what, he makes me feel safe. He will protect me from anything.

That thought makes my head shoot up. That's it. I know what I need to do. Xavier will never allow anyone to hurt me. I need to use that to my advantage. With my new-found plan in my head and new sense of hope I pull myself off the ground and prepare for whatever "motivation" that Seraphine has planned.

Hours later Xavier arrives to retrieve me and I follow him down the hall. His face is stern and his body tense, and that worries me.

"Is everything okay?" I ask. Xavier either doesn't hear me or ignores me because my question goes unanswered. We walk in silence for several minutes before I try again. I stop walking but Xavier is seemingly lost in thought and keeps walking.

I take a deep breath and decide to put my new plan into effect. "Xavier, I'm scared."

That stops him and he turns, concern etched on his face. "What's the matter, my love?"

"I overheard your conversation with Seraphine earlier. What is she going to do to me?"

Xavier is in front of me before I can blink. He grips my shoulders. "Nothing. I will protect you. No one will ever hurt you."

"But I heard—"

"No. One. Will. Hurt. You." He punctuates each word with a shake of my shoulders. He releases me and runs a hand through his hair. "Though I can't say the same for your friends."

"What do you mean?"

He grabs my hand and we begin walking again. "Just remember that this was not my idea."

Xavier leads me down a set of stairs into a part of the palace that I have never been. Here, the walls are dark and there are no windows. There are cobwebs along the ceiling and the air is stale and musty.

Xavier pushes open a set of steel doors to find King Rolland and Seraphine. The two are standing beside a giant circular enclosure that is made of thick steel bars. Inside the enclosure, leaning against the bars is Myka.

"Myka!" I run past Xavier, not paying any heed to Rolland or Seraphine. Myka looks up at my outburst and comes to my side of the enclosure. He reaches through the bars and clasps my hands. I notice a similar bracelet to mine encircling his wrist, but instead of two crystals his only has one. His face is beat up and from what I can see of his arms; they are also bruised.

"Myka, what have they done to you?"

"They've been trying to get me to tell them where the remaining Mystics are. I haven't been cooperating." He winces as he tries to give me a smirk.

"I'm sorry, Myka, I'm so sorry." I look behind me, but Xavier and his father seem to be deep in a heated conversation. I drop my voice into a whisper, "Are Layla and Sage safe? How did you come to be here?"

"Layla and Sage are safe. I was able to get them to safety before I was captured. I went back to find you after we separated and the King's men got me." Myka squeezes my hand. "Are you alright, Princess, are they treating you well?"

"Don't worry about me." I give him what I hope is a reassuring grin but I'm pretty sure it comes off as a grimace.

He pulls me in close, his concerned eyes taking everything in. "You have to be careful. I heard part of their plan. You—"

"What a beautiful reunion." Seraphine leans against the bars next to us. I was so focused on Myka I didn't even hear her approach.

"Why is he in here?" I snap at her.

She grins and I'm starting to understand that this particular smile is pure evil, and leans in close. I can hear Xavier and Rolland arguing behind us. "Do you realize I could break your neck so easily right now, before anyone could do anything."

"Xavier would kill you."

Seraphine laughs. "How brave you are with your prince protecting you. I wonder how you would be if he weren't around."

"Take this bracelet off and you'll find out."

She taps my cheek. "Maybe someday, little mystic."

I smack her hand away. "Don't touch me." I seriously hate this woman.

"Seraphine!" Xavier appears next to me. If looks could kill, the witch would be dead where she stands. "I believe I told you to never touch her."

Seraphine sighs, "Looks like our fun is done, little mystic, your princely guard is back."

She whips around so fast that her fire red hair hits me in the face. Xavier growls in warning but she doesn't acknowledge it as she returns to Rolland's side.

"What is going on, Xavier?"

He grabs my arm and leads me over to his father and Seraphine, who is practically draped on his arm. The King glares at us as we approach. Seraphine whispers something in his ear and he snickers. The way he looks at her fills my stomach with disgust. How easy it was for him to move on after he killed his wife.

A door opens on the far side of the room and two guards enter with a figure between them. It takes me only a second to realize that it is Jordan. Without a thought, I make a break for the little group but Xavier grabs me around the waist and holds me back. I push against his embrace but his iron grip is strong. The guards lead Jordan to the enclosure and open a small door on the side. They push him in and he staggers, landing face down on the dirty floor.

My eyes frantically search over his figure. For the most part he seems unscathed. He's just as filthy as he was the last time I saw him but his beautiful face still fills my heart with joy. He's still okay, and that's all that matters. I watch as Myka leans down and helps Jordan to his feet, and they embrace.

Rolland eyes the entire display with distaste while Seraphine appears to be amused by the struggle going on between Xavier and I. He finally releases me and I make another attempt at getting to Jordan. I don't get far, though, as I run into what feels like an invisible wall and fall to the ground.

"Does she ever stop?" I hear Seraphine ask.

"No, but I would appreciate it if you didn't use your magic on her. I can handle her." Xavier leans down and helps me from my place on the ground.

Seraphine looks skeptical. "Yep, sure looks like it."

I rub my sore nose. "What did you do?"

She shrugs. "Just a simple spell to block your path."

"I hate her," I grumble under my breath to Xavier.

"Don't worry, the feeling is mutual." Seraphine throws back at me as she makes her way towards my friends.

Xavier sends me a stern look to stay put and I decide that this is one of those times I'm going to pick my battles.

Jordan and Myka watch Seraphine warily as she approaches. When she reaches the outside of the cage she beckons Myka to her. He folds his arms across his chest and stand his ground. She chuckles softly, "We can do this the easy way or the hard way. It's up to you. Personally, I enjoy the hard way."

Myka continues to stay where he is and Seraphine just shrugs. "Fine, have it your way."

She enters the enclosure and sends Jordan back with what I assume is the same spell she used on me. He remains immobile in mid-air against the bars and her invisible wall. She stalks towards Myka, but he holds his ground, and it isn't until she reaches him that I realize she has immobilized him as well. She grabs his hand and looks down at his fingers.

"What is this?" she asks innocently, referring to the green vine that is wrapping around one of his fingers. He struggles against his invisible bonds. She slips the green vine off his finger.

"Don't touch that," Myka snarls.

"A token from a love, perhaps?"

Myka struggles against his invisible bonds but his attempts to move get him nowhere. Seraphine leaves the cage with the ring in her hand.

"Rolland, dear, I just need a drop of your blood," She says as she approaches us.

Rolland removes a blade from his sleeve and pricks his finger. Seraphine guides his hand to the ring and smears the tiny drop of blood on it. She winks at him and sashays back to the cage. As she walks away I can hear her mumbling what sounds like a spell.

Bad feelings creep up my spine. I grip Xavier's hand. "What is she doing?" When he doesn't answer me right away I shake him and repeat my question.

Rolland is watching the entire interaction with amusement and laughs at my growing panic. "What you are witnessing is what will happen to you if you continue to be disobedient. Personally, I would rather it be this way, but my son prefers you the way you are."

Realization hits. "No, don't do this to him. Please." I watch in horror as the ring in Seraphine's hand glows and the blood on the ring fuses into it. I turn to Xavier as panic grips me. "Please, Xavier, stop this. He is my friend."

"I'm sorry, my love, there is nothing I can do."

"You said you would protect me! That no one would hurt me."

"No one is hurting you."

"You are! By allowing this to happen you are hurting me!" My voice is getting shrill. I run to the enclosure and fall to my knees. Seraphine is standing above Myka's frozen form.

"Myka, it's going to be okay. I promise, I'll find a way to fix this." Myka turns his head and the uncertainty in his eyes makes my heart break.

"Tell Sage—" His words are cut off as Seraphine slips the ring back on his finger and his body goes rigid. He closes his eyes and when he reopens them they are black. Silence fills the room as we wait in trepidation, unsure of what is to come next. Seraphine exits the enclosure and locks the door behind her, releasing both Jordan and Myka from their invisible bonds. Jordan collapses to the ground but Myka is staring lifelessly in my direction.

"Myka?" I try.

"Don't bother, he cannot hear you," Seraphine comments, "the only person he hears now is Rolland, unless he is instructed otherwise."

She reaches down and pulls my head back by my hair. "This will be your fate soon, little mystic. It's only a matter of time," she whispers in my ear, "Xavier can only protect you for so long."

The next second her presence is gone and I hear a scuffle behind me.

"Would you two stop it? I'm eager to try out my new toy," Rolland exclaims.

Xavier and Seraphine separate but not before Xavier lets out a few choice words.

Xavier picks me up off the ground and holds me against him. I lean heavily on him, for either support or safety, I'm not sure which one anymore. Jordan is looking back and forth between us with concern in his eyes.

Rolland approaches the enclosure and contemplates the silent figure inside. "So, he is completely under my control?"

"Yes, he should be. By adding your blood to his token from a loved one, it ties him to you." Seraphine replies.

"So that's the key then, the token?"

"Right. The spell won't work unless you have a person who is in love and they have a token of their love. That love fuels the spell."

"How is this possible? I don't understand," I ask.

Seraphine picks at her nails. "It's a simple spell but requires a few important elements. Rolland believed that he would find the answers in our ancient books but they are not very clear on this spell for many reasons. It's usually pretty frowned upon, it's dark magic. Taking away a person's self-control, their personality, their free will, it's a little taboo."

"You are a monster."

"Oh, darling, you have no idea." She flashes her teeth at me.

Rolland rubs his hands together. "Let's test this out. Seraphine, how do I begin?"

"Say his name and give a command."

"Myka, rise and come to me."

Myka rises from the ground and walks to the edge of the bars, next to Rolland. Rolland looks upon him in childlike glee.

"Do you know who I am, boy?"

"You are my master." The voice that comes out of him is gravelly and foreign, nothing like the soft-spoken soldier I knew.

"And what is your purpose?"

Myka hesitates and Seraphine clicks her tongue. "Fascinating. It appears he is trying to fight it. He must have a strong will. But it will break soon enough; he is no match for my magic."

Hope fills me. "He's still in there?"

"To some degree, yes. He will remember everything from before and will be able to perform basic functions without command. But when given instructions by Rolland he will have no ability to refuse his command. He is now linked with Rolland; whatever Rolland wants, he wants."

"Is he in pain?"

Seraphine shrugs. "Probably. If he's fighting my magic, it's going to fight back."

"And what if it wins?"

"*When* it wins, he'll be trapped inside his own mind. Able to see, hear, and comprehend everything but unable to do anything about it," she laughs.

Seraphine's head snaps back as I punch her in the face. Xavier moves quickly and places himself between her and I.

Seraphine wipes a small trickle of blood from her chin. "That was a lucky shot, little mystic. I guarantee you won't be that lucky again."

Rolland gets between us. "Can we get down to business? I would like to see him in action."

It's in that moment that I remember that Jordan is still in the cage with Myka. Now it all makes sense why they brought him here and why Xavier was so tense.

"Myka, I command you to turn and fight the friend beside you," instructs Rolland.

"No!" I run for the enclosure door and try to pull it open. My muscles strain and sweat pours down my brow but the door doesn't budge. Myka barely hesitates as he stalks towards his prey and my heart stops. "Myka, no! Myka, stop, fight it!"

But my cries fall on deaf ears as I watch on in horror. Myka reaches Jordan and rears his arm back, catching Jordan in the jaw. Jordan falls to the ground but rolls out of the way just in time before Myka's foot finds his stomach. As soon as he gets to his feet Myka rushes him and slams his body against the bars, landing a few punches along the way.

Jordan pushes Myka off him and sends him back a few feet. Jordan's strength is serving him well but Myka is smaller and more agile. He charges Jordan and sidesteps at the last second, getting Jordan in his ribs. Jordan grunts in pain but continues moving as Myka stalks him. Myka attempts to attack again but Jordan catches him by surprise and is able to land a solid kick to his midsection, sending Myka spiraling to the ground. Taking advantage of his reprieve, Jordan leans doubled over, with his hands resting on his knees, drawing large amounts of air into his lungs.

"Jordan, look out!" I cry out desperately, but I am too late.

Myka has risen quickly and slams his shoulder into Jordan's gut. Jordan lands roughly on the ground, gasping for air. He rises, his movements stiff. He rolls out his shoulders and rushes Myka this time and they trade blow after blow. It isn't long before both are bleeding from their faces and their punches become more and more sluggish.

I drop to my knees in front of Rolland, throwing my pride away. "Please, stop this. I will do anything you ask. Please."

Rolland eyes me with a mixture of disdain and satisfaction and I feel true terror grip me. "Myka," he says quietly.

Myka stops, arm in mid air, about to throw a punch to Jordan's nose, and turns to his master. Jordan takes this moment to put some distance between himself and Myka, limping away to the other side of the cage. He is favoring his left leg. I think it might be broken.

Rolland strokes my cheek and smirks, insanity reflects in his eyes. "Myka, kill him."

"No!" My scream rips out of my throat as Myka turns back to Jordan. Tears stream down my face as I once again attempt to open the door to the enclosure. Blood drips from my hands where the metal bites into my skin.

"Father! Stop this. You have proven your point," I hear Xavier demand, but I am too far gone in my terror to care.

"Jordan! Jordan!" I am screaming his name at the top of my lungs, begging and pleading to anyone who will listen to save him. I cannot lose him.

Myka's fist connects with his face again and blood sprays from Jordan's nose. Blow after blow, the sound of bones breaking echo along the walls, each crack mirrors the sound of my heart breaking. He's dying; I can feel it. He is dying and there is nothing I can do.

Pain rips through me at an alarming rate and my body feels like it is burning from the inside out. The world is splitting apart; I can feel it shaking. Is this what it feels like when you lose the one you love? Is this how the giant Princess felt as her mate lay dying in her arms. I hear my name and shouts of alarm but they sound so far away. All I can see is Jordan; all I can see is his bloodied face as Myka delivers yet another punch. He reaches out to me, calling me; he needs me. I can't help him. I can't save him. A blood-curdling scream, primal and raw, tears past my lips as red-hot pain ripples through my body again.

Blinding light fills the room, blanketing the world in white. My body burns and it dawns on me that the light is coming from me; my body is emitting it. I place my luminous hands on the bars of the cage and watch them quickly melt away, within seconds the large enclosure is barely a puddle on the floor.

Someone gasps behind me and mutters the word, "Prakera."

Myka is still beating Jordan, completely focused on the command of his master, oblivious to the destruction around him. I hold out my arm and the possessed Mystic flies across the room, landing in an unconscious heap on the ground. I drop to my knees next to Jordan. He is completely unrecognizable, his face a bloody and destroyed mess. I lay a hand on his face, knowing instinctively that I will not hurt him, even after what I just did. He leans his face into my warmth.

"Cara." his voice is just a whisper. I lean in close to hear his final words. Tears gather in my eyes, just on the edge of falling. "I love you," he whispers and his eyelids begin to fall.

I cup his cheeks with my hands and lean my forehead against his. My tears go over the edge, trailing down my cheek. I can no longer hold them back. They fall from my face in tiny glowing orbs, mixing with the blood that covers his face, and I can't help but wonder if our story will be told like the legend of the Red Stars. The cry that I release shakes the walls and ceiling; tiny specks of debris rain down on us. Jordan jolts beneath me and I pull away in alarm. Is this the end? I touch his face again, wishing that I could have given him a better life. He did not deserve this. To my surprise, his skin is warm and tiny lines of glowing light are moving below his skin. He jolts again and lets out a gasp for air. He's breathing!

The glowing lights beneath his skin spread throughout his veins, and before my eyes his open wounds begin to close. One by one the wounds seal of their own accord, not leaving a single scar on his ivory skin. Beautiful cerulean blue eyes greet me as I once again take his face in my hands. "You're alive," I breathe the words for fear that they are not real.

"I'm alive," he croaks out with a small smile. He reaches a hand up to cup my face but something behind me catches his attention and his eyes widen. I turn to see what has him so alarmed, but all I know is darkness.

Chapter 6

"**Y**OU DIDN'T HAVE TO hit her so hard."

Voices filter into my subconscious as I slowly come out of the darkness. The next thing to come to me is pain. My head throbs and my body feels like it is anchored to the ground. I am drained and exhausted, my eyes unable to open.

"If I hadn't, the whole ceiling would have come down on us."

I attempt a scowl but my face does not cooperate with the command. I know that voice. It is that witch, Seraphine.

"Why didn't the Red Stars work? You said my blood was the only thing that would remove the bracelet and give her back her powers," Xavier questions.

Seraphine sighs. "Obviously she is more powerful than we thought and she overpowered the jewels. We will just have to add more Red Stars to her bracelet."

"What was that display of power? She's never done that before."

"I wouldn't have believed it if I hadn't witnessed it myself. It was Prakera. That hasn't been seen in thousands of years. Not even the Auroras that came before her possessed such power," Seraphine replies, almost sounding in awe.

"What does that mean for us?"

"I'm still trying to figure that out."

I can feel myself slipping under again. The voices sounding further and further away. My body is no longer able to sustain. But I try to fight it; I have to hear more.

"We need to get more Red Stars on her bracelet before she wakes up," Xavier says.

"I will go and get them, and deposit the boy in his cell," Seraphine replies.

My heart soars. Jordan is alive. He is okay, but Seraphine's next words break my internal celebration.

"You better watch her, prince, her feelings for that boy are more involved than she's led you to believe."

"I will handle her, Seraphine, just take care of the Red Stars." Annoyance is heavy in Xavier's tone.

Unable to hold on any longer, the voices fade and I slip back into darkness.

The next time I wake I am lying on my bed, being blinded by the light streaming in through the balcony window. I cover my face to block it and notice the new bracelet on my wrist. Instead of two Red Stars there are now at least a dozen encircling it. I give it a tug as an experiment, but of course it doesn't budge. I sit up in my bed and glance around the room. I am, surprisingly, alone.

How long have I been out? I rise from the bed, looking down at my clothes. Thankfully, I am no longer in any bloody clothes. I really hope it was my maid that undressed me and not Xavier or Seraphine. I wander into the bathroom, half expecting to find my skin still glowing, but it's back to its normal pale color. What was that power? Is that the fifth element that everyone has been waiting for? I literally melted those bars on the enclosure. And then Jordan's wounds somehow healed. Did I also do that?

I open the door to return to my room and stop short; I'm no longer alone. That didn't last nearly long enough.

"You're finally awake," Xavier says. He is sitting in one of my armchairs with a blank expression, his mask fully in place. I can't read him and it scares me.

"Yes," I tread carefully over to him and sit opposite him in another chair. "How long was I out?"

"About a day and a half."

Shocked, I just nod in acknowledgement. That must have been a tremendous amount of power that I used to have drained me so fully.

"Do you remember what happened?"

"Yes. Your father ordered Myka to kill Jordan. I stopped him."

Xavier smirks, but there is no warmth to it. "Don't be coy, my love. What do you remember?"

"I remember trying to get the door to the enclosure open and not being able to. My skin started glowing and I melted the bars. I pushed Myka back." I pause. "Is Myka okay?"

"He is fine. Continue."

"Jordan was dying, I felt him slipping away. The next second I knew his wounds were healing and he was alive." A memory nags at my consciousness as I nervously play with the bracelet around my wrist. "Is he alright?"

"Yes," is all he says, and I know that he is purposely not elaborating. "Do you know what that power was, my love?"

"No, I had no idea what was happening. One second, I was trying to open the door and the next it was melting. I just remember feeling helpless. I don't know how it happened or what it was."

"It is called Prakera."

"Is it the fifth element?"

"Somewhat. Seraphine tells us that it is an ancient power, not seen for thousands of years. It has not been seen since the first ever Aurora. According to Seraphine, the fifth element is usually something different, less powerful."

"How does she know so much about the Mystics?" *And I know so little,* I think to myself.

Xavier shrugs. "She has her ways." He leans forward and stares intently at me. "She did reveal a rather interesting development though."

"What's that?" His gaze is making me uncomfortable and I squirm a little in my seat.

"Prakera has many properties. To put it simply, it is pure energy, and that's why you were glowing. You became pure energy and you used that energy to melt the bars of the enclosure. But here's the part that really bothers me. Do you realize you are the one who healed Jordan?"

"How?"

"Your tears. When you were crying, your tears dropped onto his skin and you healed him. Seraphine tells us that the only way the tears work is if there is a true need by you for them to work. If there is no real need or if you have already used too much energy your tears are useless."

"What are you insinuating, Xavier?"

"Is there something you are not telling me, my love?" He reaches over and drags my chair closer to him. He puts both of his arms on either side of mine, trapping me. His imposing presence suffocates me. "Because I would hate to think that you were keeping something from me."

You better watch her, prince, her feelings for that boy are more involved than she's led you to believe. The memory surfaces again and Seraphine's words come back to me. My heart begins to race as panic fills me. If Xavier thinks I love Jordan he will kill him. I need to convince him otherwise or Jordan could be lost to me forever.

"Xavier, if you are thinking that I healed him because I love him, you are wrong. I needed to save him because he is my best friend. I didn't want anything to happen to him." Bile rises in my throat at my next lie but I have to continue. "I love you, Xavier. You and I are meant to be together."

Surprise and disbelief color his gaze. "Why the sudden change? The other day you were saying you would never marry me. I believe the word you used to describe me was insane."

"I heard you when everything was happening. You were trying to get your father to stop. Even though you would like nothing more than for Jordan to die, you tried to stop him from dying. You knew it would hurt me to see that and you tried to stop it. You were doing it for me, putting my happiness before your own. It made me realize how much you love me and how lucky I am to have you." I kiss his cheek, appearing demure. "You are my protector, and you know what is best for me. I'm sorry it took me so long to realize that."

I can see the turmoil behind Xavier's eyes. He wants so badly to believe me, but he is suspicious of my words. I can only hope that his love for me wins out. He stares at me for what feels like hours as I hold my breath in anticipation.

Finally, he nods his head like he's made a decision, and when he pulls my face in for a rough kiss, I know that his love for me is winning out. He growls possessively as he devours my lips. When we pull apart he is panting. "You have no idea how much I've wanted you to say that, my love, but I can't bring myself to believe your words just yet."

"Xavier, I mean every word. I love you and you love me. You are the air I breathe and I am yours. Only yours." This time I pull his face in for a kiss to help my words. He doesn't respond at first, confused by my new behavior. It isn't long though before his arms encircle me and we embrace. It takes everything I have to continue with this charade. Jordan's life depends on it.

We pull apart and Xavier abruptly stands up. He runs his hand through his shaggy blonde locks as he paces the floor. "Do you really mean it, Cara?" My heart almost breaks at his hopeful tone. This Xavier in front of me right now is the one I fell in love with. This is the Xavier who loves me and truly cares for me. He has shed his tough exterior and stands before me a vulnerable man. I could destroy him right now but I would be destroying myself and Jordan as well.

"Yes, Xavier, I do."

"I need you to prove it."

"How? I won't let you kill Jordan. I may not love him but I still care about him deeply. He is my friend."

"Agree to never see him again. Don't even ask. I don't even want to hear his name on your lips. It'll be like he never existed."

"Xavier. That isn't—"

"I will promise not to hurt him or allow anyone else to hurt him but he is gone from your life. You are mine and I will not have you 'caring' for another man."

"What will happen to him? Will you have him rot in your cells for the rest of his life?"

"That will no longer be your concern. Do we have a deal, my love?" He eyes me intently, watching my every move. This is a test; if I refuse it proves that I am not true in my word but if I accept, I may lose Jordan forever. The only relief is that he will be alive and safe.

"You have a deal. Do I get to say goodbye?"

"No. I will inform Jordan of your decision." He gives me a small peck on the lips, "Now, do we still have an agreement?"

It kills me to say it but I have to hope that we will someday be reunited. I nod my consent and Xavier's face breaks out into a boyish smile.

"Perfect, now you're all mine." He kisses me again and this time it is passionate and triumphant.

"I guess this is how you are handling it," Seraphine's voice interrupts. Xavier stiffens and pulls away, sending her a deadly glare.

"What do you want, Seraphine?"

"Just came to check on your darling princess." Seraphine sits down in the chair that Xavier used to occupy. "I was actually hoping I could have a word with her."

When Xavier makes a move to sit, Seraphine says, "Alone."

I don't want to be alone with this witch; I don't trust her. I squeeze Xavier's hand and hope that he understands what I am trying to say.

"I won't hurt her, Xavier, I just want to have a little chat."

Xavier hesitates for just a second. "I have a matter to take care of anyway." He kisses my cheek and I hear him whisper, "behave."

I watch him leave until he closes the door quietly behind him.

"I know what you are doing, little mystic."

"I have a name and you know nothing."

"Oh, I know a great many things. You think I don't see that you are manipulating the prince? Making him believe that you love him so you can protect that boy that is in his cells. He is blinded by his love for you and it makes him stupid."

"If you think you know this, then why not tell him?"

"Because it will make what comes next so much more amusing." She twirls her finger along the arm of the chair, absently.

"What comes next?"

"You will have to wait and see."

"I don't like you," I comment as she stares at me.

Seraphine chuckles. "I don't like you either."

"Why? What did I ever do to you?"

Seraphine snaps her fingers and her goblet of wine appears in her hand. She takes a sip before answering. "You personally? Nothing, yet. Your family though, that's another story."

"My family?"

"You see, our mothers were best friends growing up. From what I hear, even back then your mother was very cunning and had a way of manipulating people to her will." She sneers at me. "From what I've seen of your behavior you are not much different. She pulled my mother into her lies and deceit even at an early age."

"My mothe—"

"Quiet," Seraphine calmly speaks and suddenly no sound is coming out of my lips. She smiles maliciously as my eyes widen in alarm. "That's better. Now, where was I? Oh yes, your mother, As I said, Alera and my mother, Melinda, were the best of friends. My mother's parents were killed at a very young age and she was sent to live with Alera's family, to be trained as a queen. They were like sisters and were inseparable. This was a time when humans, witches, and mystics all lived together in peace.

Unlike mystics, witches begin to gain their powers at the age of thirteen. When Melinda gained her powers, she began to pull away from Alera, spending more time with other witches as she learned about her new abilities. Alera was jealous and would trick Melinda into using her powers to help her get her way in many things. This continued for many years until they turned eighteen and Alera was finally Melinda's equal.

It was at this time that Alera met Gaven. The two fell madly in love and were wed the next year. They rose to power, with the help of Melinda, and soon became king and queen of all the mystics. Throughout it all, Melinda stood by her side but Alera was greedy." She pauses when I raise my eyebrow. "Don't give me that look. Alera wanted power and when she didn't have the means to gain it herself she turned to Melinda to do it for her. Melinda was the queen of her own people yet she was constantly coming to the rescue of Alera and the mystics. Your parents were not strong enough to lead so they continued to exploit my mother every opportunity they had.

When the war broke out between Myridia and Estera, your parents once again came crawling back to Melinda. They needed protection they said; their people were dying." Her face twists in disgust. "If I had been in charge I would have let you all die, but I was just a child. Alera begged her friend to help them, using their friendship against her, manipulating her into doing her bidding. Melinda, of course, agreed; She loved Alera greatly and would have done anything to help her. So Melinda brought together her council of witches and they created the barrier and enchantments that protected the Mystic City.

With all the mystics safely inside the Mystic City, Rolland came for the witches. It was not long after Alera and Gaven had been killed, and he came with an army. He brought his wrath down on the witches for foiling his plans and helping the mystics escape his reach. He started by taking our ancient artifact, cutting us off from our powers. Then he burned our homes, killed most of our people, and banished what was left of us to the forgotten lands. All because your mother had to take advantage of a good friend."

Tears fill my eyes at her story. Could it be that my parents were not as wonderful has everyone had led me to believe? Saving their people was their first priority, but at what cost? Their request cost the witches their lives and their homes.

Seraphine waves her hand and I gain the ability to speak again. "How do you know so much about these things?" She ignores my question. "I'm sorry for the part that my parents played in your people's pain but what about Rolland? How can you work with the man that killed so many of your people?"

"I have my reasons."

"So, you take revenge on me and *my* people, but he gets to go free?"

"I didn't say that."

"You say it by working with that monster."

Seraphine shrugs nonchalantly. "Rolland and I have a symbiotic relationship. I offered to help him and he gave me back my powers. It's a win/win for me."

"So why does he need me if he has you?"

"Because I am no one's weapon. I take orders from no one. His plan is his and mine is mine."

An awkward silence descends upon us as we stare each other down.

"What happened to your mother?" I finally ask, breaking the silence.

For the first time, pain flickers across Seraphine's face but she quickly catches it. "She disappeared several years ago. I woke up one morning and she was gone. I can only assume that her grief over losing her people finally overtook her and she took her own life. Your parents' greed killed my mother."

"They were best friends, you can't put that blame on my mother. Your mother was helping her friend because she cared about her."

"She exploited the relationship she had with my mother and manipulated her into putting herself and our people in danger for her selfish reasons."

"My mother couldn't have known that Rolland would retaliate like that!"

Seraphine moves faster than I can follow, and she slaps me across the face. "Do not make excuses for your deplorable mother. She knew enough."

My cheek is throbbing but I refuse to show the woman before me any weakness. I return her hateful glare with one of my own.

"That boy in the cells, do you love him?" Her nonchalant tone and abrupt change of subject surprise me and I don't immediately answer. She returns to her chair and crosses her leg over her knee. "I'll take your silence as a yes. Does Xavier know?"

Again, I say nothing and Seraphine lets out a dry laugh. "Oh, what a delightful web of lies you've spun. It must make you feel so wonderful having two men fight over you like this. How pitiful you are, just like your mother." She stands to her feet. "I think I'll go pay this friend of yours a visit."

"No." I surge to my feet and block her path to the door.

"Or what, little mystic? As long as those Red Stars encircle your wrist, you are powerless to stop me."

"I will find a way. Do not touch him."

Menace fills Seraphine's gaze as she lifts her hand and suddenly I am flying backwards into my chair, being held down by a gust of wind. My mouth hangs open as Seraphine walks past me to the door. Before she exits she says, "Yes, that is wind you are feeling, little mystic. You wonder how I know so much about mystic history? Well now you do. I am half mystic."

With those words she releases the element and slams the door behind her.

Chapter 7

DAYS PASS WITHOUT ANY more interactions with Seraphine. This makes me rather happy, but also worries me to no end. With her parting words about Jordan, I fear for his safety where she is involved. Unfortunately, after my deal with Xavier, I am unable to ask if Jordan is safe, so I secretly worry in nervous silence.

Since that day in which the Prakera powers appeared, Xavier has barely left my side. He is a constant in my life; when I go to sleep, and when I wake, he is there. Today is no different as we enjoy a picnic in the garden, my once-serene getaway. I smile up at him and touch his hand, playing the perfect part of doting fiancé. I know there is a little part of him that doubts my intentions; I can see it in his face when he thinks I'm not looking. However, as the days go by and I pass every test he throws at me, I see the doubt draining from him.

"It's a beautiful day out today," He remarks, lacing his fingers with mine.

I lean my head back and soak in the sunshine. The warmth on my face is a welcome embrace. "Yes it is; thank you for bringing me out here. You always know how to make me happy."

I've stroked his ego and his chest puffs out with pride. "Anything for you, my love."

He kisses my cheek and we fall into a comfortable silence as he runs his hand absently along mine. He seems lost in thought today, which is a welcome break from his constant babble about our upcoming wedding.

My thoughts once again return to the conversation I had with Seraphine a few days ago. What if she's right and my mother used her friendship with Melinda to manipulate her into doing whatever she asked. What if she wasn't the kind person that everyone made her out to be? I've been lied to before; my whole life has been a lie, so why not that too. Seraphine could be completely justified in wanting revenge against me.

"Your Highness?" Myka's voice breaks our quiet sanctuary and I stiffen. Every time I see his face or hear that gravelly voice I am filled with guilt. I got him into this mess and now he is trapped as an unwilling servant to King Rolland. And if Seraphine is to be believed he is still in there somewhere imprisoned within his own mind.

"Yes, Myka?" Xavier replies.

"The King is requesting your presence in his study."

"Tell him I'll be right there." Myka leaves and Xavier squeezes my hand. "He could have sent any guard for that. He only sent Myka to rattle you. I will talk with him, you are cooperating, there is no reason for him to antagonize you."

It's true; I was cooperating. As much as it hurt me, I complied with every command they had given me. We had dinner with the King two nights ago and I was civil; I sat demurely through many different court proceedings; I even acted the still-grieving, but enraged, victim of the traitorous Queen during an official announcement to the people of Myridia. To all appearances I was a willing and eager participant in the King's game. I was behaving and acting perfectly for my captors. It all felt so normal and mundane, putting me on edge.

This can't be all there is, there must be something going on behind closed doors that I am missing. My gut tells me they are waiting for something. What it is though, I have no idea.

Xavier stands and reaches down for my hand. "Come, I will escort you back to your room so I can meet with Father."

I'm not ready to leave this place, my beautiful garden. I don't take his offered hand. "Please, can I just stay out here a little longer, Xavier? I'm not ready to go back in yet."

"My love, you know the rules, you are not to be out of your room unless escorted by a guard or myself."

I gesture to the guard standing by the door to the castle. "There is a guard right there. I'm not going anywhere."

"I don't know or trust that guard. He's one of the new ones that Father brought in."

"Xavier, really, where am I going to go?" I feel my irritation peaking. "Just let me enjoy the sunshine and I will wait for you here. Have I given you any reason not to trust me the last few days?"

Xavier hesitates, probably torn between wanting to make me happy and wanting to keep me locked up for himself.

I stand and wrap my arms around his waist, resting my head just under his chin. "I'm not going anywhere, Xavier. I'm yours and yours alone."

I know I have him when I feel him sigh. He kisses the top of my head. "Please don't make me regret this."

Maybe Seraphine is right. I am surprisingly good at manipulating Xavier and getting what I want. It's almost too easy.

I kiss his cheek. "Thank you. I promise I'll be here when you return."

He grabs my arm as I go to sit back down, and his eyes are deeply ladened with warning. "I mean it, Cara, you better be here when I return."

I shiver at his tone and I'm reminded again of how unstable he is. I'm playing a dangerous game with him. No matter how much I think I may be affecting him he is still unpredictable and deadly.

I attempt a shaky smile as I lay back on the blanket. "Of course."

He gives me one more stern look and then disappears into the castle. I sigh in relief at finally being alone. Xavier's presence isn't always unpleasant but it can be extremely suffocating. I stretch out across the blanket and stare up at the blue sky, finding shapes in the clouds. I feel more relaxed right now than I have in weeks. Being back in my garden, alone in nature, is making me more at peace. It isn't long before I notice my eyes getting heavy and I begin to doze off.

"Pst, Princess."

I jolt awake and find no one around me. I search my surroundings, trying to find the source of the voice. "Who's there?"

Ben, the guard who came into my room, comes out of the bushes and crouches down next to me. I look over his shoulder at the guard that is standing by the door and notice that he is gone.

"He got sent on a quick errand, so we have about five minutes until he returns," Ben remarks when he sees my glance.

"Who are you and what do you want?" I sit up and face him.

"I mean you no harm, Princess. In fact, I am here to help you. As I told you, my name is Ben. I am a soldier in the Kamora."

"The Kamora?"

"It is the rebellion against King Rolland. It is led by the Mitera, she is our leader."

"What does a rebellion want with me?"

"We know what you are—you are the prophesied Aurora. You have the power to save us from the tyrant king. With your help we can once again bring peace to this land. We want humans, mystics, and witches to live in harmony once more. The Mitera has been watching you; she has always been watching."

"Who is this Mitera?"

"She will reveal herself to you in her own time." Ben checks around him and leans in closer. "Princess Maia, you have to remain strong. The Mitera is working on a plan to get you out of the King's clutches. There are many within the castle that support our cause and we are all working on a plan."

"Does this plan involve Jordan and Myka?"

"Yes, Princess, your friends will be saved as well. Though the witch's spell has complicated things with Myka. The Mitera has a plan. You must be prepared for when the time comes."

"How will I know?"

"You will know, trust me. But until that time comes, the Mitera needs you to do something for her." He waits for my nod. "The King is up to something. The Mitera is concerned about his plans now that Seraphine is involved. You need to find out what the King's plans are so that we can stop them. There are too many meetings behind closed doors, too many whispers. He is planning something big with her and it could be our end."

"Do you think Xavier is involved?"

"No, and that is why the Mitera is concerned. Xavier is being left out of these meetings, which means that the plan involves something that may hurt you. Rolland knows that Xavier will never allow anything to harm you."

"So how am I supposed to find out this information? Xavier is always with me."

"In five days the King is holding a banquet in Seraphine's honor. She is being welcomed into court and being presented as his future bride."

I knew there was something going on between them. "Seraphine doesn't seem like the marrying type," I comment.

Ben smirks. "She's not, which is another reason the Mitera is concerned. She thinks Seraphine may have an ulterior motive, but that is a concern for another day. On the day of the banquet we will create a diversion and you will slip into the King's study to locate any plans he may have."

"And once I have these plans, you will help us escape?"

"Yes, Princess, you and your friends will be safe." The guard by the door is returning to his post and Ben slips back into the bushes, barely exposed. "One more thing, I need you to give me your necklace."

I touch the necklace in my pocket, the only thing I have left of Jordan. Xavier seems to have forgotten about it and I have kept it that way by hiding it in different places when he is around. Today it is safely in the pocket of my dress. "Why do you need my necklace?"

"You must trust me." He holds out his hand, expectantly. "You will get it back."

I grip the necklace tightly, hesitant to give it up. It is all I have.

"Princess, I have to go. Please, the necklace," Ben implores. Hoping my trust is not misplaced, I slip it out of my pocket and drop it into his waiting hand. He disappears fully into the bushes but I hear him say, "You are not alone."

"Did you enjoy your time outside?" Xavier asks after he retrieves me from the garden and is escorting me to my room so we can prepare for dinner.

"I did. Thank you. Did you enjoy your meeting?" I smile up at him sweetly.

"Seraphine is a pain. I don't know what Father sees in her. If I had known she was going to stick around this long I would have never agreed to her help."

I chew at my lip, nervously. "Xavier, you don't think she is planning to hurt me, do you?"

Xavier raises his eyebrow. "Why would you think that?"

I shrug. "Just a feeling I have. I just can't shake the feeling that something is wrong. That she is hiding something. Did you know that she is half Mystic and is the daughter of Melinda, the witch Queen who created the protection around the Mystic City?"

"Yes, I did. She told us when she arrived."

"So then why doesn't she want revenge against Rolland, why just me? And why does Rolland even need me anymore? He has her. She seems to be a pretty powerful witch. Something doesn't feel right. I think they are keeping something from you."

Xavier hesitates as he opens the door to my room, allowing me to enter. Doubt flashes on his face but he covers it quickly. He pulls me into his arms and hugs me. "Cara, my love, you have nothing to worry about. I will protect you and will never allow anything to happen to you. As long as you are with me, you are safe."

"But—"

"There is nothing going on. Father has just been preoccupied with Seraphine and they are working on their plans for attacking Estera and beyond."

"Beyond? I thought this was just a feud between Estera and Myridia."

He kisses my head. "No, Father plans to take over everything. He wants to rule every kingdom. Estera will be just the beginning. And with you and the Prakera, nothing will be able to stop us."

"Xavier, I don't want to hurt people."

"Shh." He rubs my back. "Don't worry about it yet. When the time comes we will discuss this further. Now get ready for dinner."

I pull away from him but he grabs my arms and pulls me back to him again. He pulls my face into his and kisses me, until he is forced to come up for air. He rests his forehead against mine. "You are the air I breathe and you are mine."

"I know, Xavier, I love you too." Bile rises in my throat every time I have to force those words.

"I forgot to tell you. Father is having a banquet in a few days that we are expected to attend." He remarks.

"What is it for?"

"To introduce Seraphine to the court and to announce their engagement."

"Their engagement? You can't be serious. First of all, your mother literally just died, and second, you can't possibly believe that Seraphine wants to marry your father."

"I don't know what to tell you. It is his choice. Nothing I say will change his mind. He seems pretty smitten with her."

"Xavier—"

"Cara, just drop it. My father's relationship with Seraphine is none of our business. We will attend the banquet as requested and we will support his decision. I don't want to hear anything else about it. Now go get ready for dinner." He gives me a pat on the butt, shoving me towards the bathroom. He disappears into his room as Alexia enters to do my hair.

"How would you like your hair tonight, miss?" she asks.

"I don't care," I remark as I take a seat, "Just something simple."

She nods and gets to work fashioning a simple updo. I fidget with the Red Star bracelet absently. I miss my locket and I wish I knew why Ben asked to take it. It's never left my side since Jordan gave it to me. Despair fills me at the thought of Jordan. There isn't a day that goes by that I don't worry about him. I just hope that Xavier held up his end of the bargain and he is safe, and not in the clutches of that evil witch.

"Miss, are you alright?" Alexia's voice breaks into my thoughts.

I give her a reassuring smile. "Of course, I'm sorry, just lost in thought."

She glances at the door to Xavier's room. "You looked so sad there for a second. Were you thinking about your friend?"

I glance up at her in shock. "How do you know about him?"

"Please don't be mad. I know I overstepped, I just overheard a conversation."

"I'm not mad, Alexia, just tell me what you heard."

She once again glances at the door and lowers her voice. "The Prince and that woman, Seraphine, they were arguing in the halls about you and him. She called him a blind fool. She said that you love the baker and he is too stupid to see it. She wanted to prove her point by using something on you, I wasn't sure what she was talking about. The Prince adamantly defended you, which seemed to just infuriate Seraphine."

"When did you hear this conversation?"

"While you were unconscious, several days ago. But is it true? Do you love this other boy?"

Unease fills my belly, why would Alexia bring this up out of the blue? Something feels off. I don't know who to trust in this place anymore. I shake my head as she applies the finishing touches to my hair. "No, Alexia, I don't. I love Xavier."

She almost looks relieved when I say that but it could all be in my head. "I would appreciate it if you didn't spread this conversation anywhere else. I am faithful to my future husband and I will not have others doubting me."

My voice is more stern than I intended and Alexia stammers an apology, effectively chastised. If this was a test from Xavier, then I passed. If it wasn't, then I may have just lost an ally. As Alexia quickly makes her way out of the room I try not to feel guilty. I can't trust anyone and I have to protect myself.

Xavier enters the room dressed in his dinner clothes. He looks around, surprised. "Your maid already left?"

"Yes, my hair didn't take long."

He kisses my cheek. "No matter what it looks gorgeous."

Pushing the weird interaction with Alexia out of my mind, I smile up at him sweetly. "Just give me a moment to change and we can go."

He pulls me into his arms as I stand. "You know, we could just have dinner in here, just you and I." He nuzzles my ear and places a kiss just below it.

"Isn't your father expecting us?"

"Yes, but he will understand if you and I need some *alone* time." His voice is suggestive.

I try to laugh off his words, awkwardly. "Xavier, we get plenty of alone time."

He groans. "How long are you going to make me wait?"

"Xavier, I've already told you that we are not taking that final step until we are married. It is my decision."

"But, we love each other and it feels right."

I push away from him, putting some space between us. "No, it doesn't feel right. My decision is marriage and that is the end of the discussion. And before you try to tell me that it's because you think I'm not fully committed to you, just remember that I had this stance before you betrayed me."

Xavier looks annoyed as he crosses his arms along his chest. "It just doesn't make sense why you would wait when we both know we are meant to be together."

"It is *my* decision, Xavier. Respect it." I disappear into the closet and grab the first dress I see, too irritated to really care how I look. I change quickly and join Xavier back in my room. He is staring moodily at the ground when I return. I sigh inwardly, I need to fix this or it could turn into something worse.

I grab his hands and bring them to my lips. "Xavier, my love. Please, haven't I shown you enough how much I love you? Haven't I proven time and again that I am yours and only yours? Why do you need this final act of affection so badly?"

He looks at me and I see turmoil in his eyes. Once again something is causing him to doubt me, but for once I have a suspicion what. "What did Seraphine say to you?"

The turmoil turns to surprise. "What do you mean?"

"Every time you doubt my faithfulness to you it's because of something that witch said. What was it?"

"Nothing in particular, this time. I just thought that if we made that final step then it would prove her wrong and shut her up." He rubs my hands.

"Xavier, I want our first time to be special, and that means our wedding night. If Seraphine has a problem with that she can talk to me. We love each other and we don't need to do that to prove it."

Xavier searches my gaze for several minutes and then must see what he is looking for because he nods. "I'm sorry, she just has a way of getting into my head."

I kiss his lips. "I know. But don't let her get to you. That woman is pure evil and she has nothing to do with our relationship. Now let's go to dinner."

He smiles boyishly. "I do so love it when you get fiery." He holds the door open for me and we head to the dining hall, hand in hand.

Chapter 8

THE NEXT FIVE DAYS go by in a blur as preparations for the grand banquet begin. Xavier brings in a seamstress to design a dress for me and Alexia talks non-stop about her plans for my hair. It seems her excitement over the banquet has helped her get over her chastisement.

"Do the people know that Seraphine is a witch?" I ask the morning of the banquet as we are eating breakfast on the balcony.

"No, everyone believes that the witches are long gone. Father's already admitted to having a Mystic in his palace, it would not be a good idea to reveal he had a witch as well."

"Isn't he worried about people finding out?" I take a bite out of my pastry and muse that whoever is baking pastries now has nothing on Jordan. I miss his cocoanos.

"The only people who know that Seraphine is a witch are you, me, Father, and a few of Father's trusted guards. No one would risk his wrath to tell that secret."

"I suppose you're right."

"Don't get any ideas, my love."

I look innocently at him over my cup. "I would never dream of it."

A commotion in my room draws our eyes inside, effectively ending our discussion. Xavier moves to investigate and returns with a chuckle.

"It appears it is my time to leave. Your seamstress is here with her army of women to prepare you for the banquet." He kisses the top of my head. "Have fun, I will be back later to escort you. I look forward to seeing you."

"Xavier?" I call out as he makes his way to the door. He turns back to me, "I'll miss you."

His face lights up and he sprints back to me, enveloping me in a passionate embrace. A throat clears behind us and we both look up to the find a stern-looking seamstress.

He gives her one of his best charming smiles. "Apologies, can't help myself."

She waves him away while smiling good naturedly, no longer able to control her stern look. From what I've learned about the seamstress, she has a big heart and genuinely cares about everyone.

"Come, dearie, we have a lot of work to do," she says once Xavier has left the room. She holds out her hand and I take it. For the next several hours I am plucked, tweezed, pampered and made up. I haven't had this much attention since my eighteenth birthday, which seems so far away now. So much has changed since that day. Not much time has passed but it feels like a lifetime ago. At that time, I was young and naive, so blind to the secrets around me, and so hopeful for the future. Now I don't know what the future holds.

"What do you think, dearie?" the seamstress remarks as she motions towards the mirror.

In the mirror is a woman I barely recognize. My blonde hair is tightly braided to the side and swoops down my bare shoulder. The dress that clings to my body is ruby red, the color handpicked by me, to please Xavier. He loves me in red; he's told me many times, and I hope to use that to my advantage. It is an elegant dress made of lace and other materials that help it cling to my body and then flare out towards the bottom. I chose a form-fitting dress instead of a massive ball gown in the hope that it would help me move more quickly through the King's study.

"Wow." Xavier is in the doorway, staring at me with a look of pure admiration, exactly the effect I was hoping for. "You look…wow."

I laugh at his dumbfounded face. "Can't say I've ever seen you speechless before."

"Can't say I've ever seen you more beautiful." He remarks. He turns to the maids and seamstress. "Thank you, ladies, for making me the luckiest man in the world."

They giggle, eating it all up. I contain my eye roll and giggle along with them, playing the part of a girl thoroughly in love. I close the distance between us and Xavier's eyes never leave mine. He touches my bare shoulders and I see his eyes dip to the low-cut neckline. I smile at him demurely and he smiles wolfishly.

"You really are stunning tonight, my love. I will be the envy of every man there."

"I highly doubt that." I comment, as he tucks my hand in the nook of his elbow. "You forget Seraphine will be in attendance."

"Seraphine is nothing compared to you."

I feel my heart warm a bit at his words and I have to take a second to remind myself that we are playing a game and, in the end, only one of us can win. He is my enemy, no matter how sweet he is.

Xavier walks past the dining hall and I look at him quizzically. "Where are we going?"

"The banquet is being held in the throne room. It's more spacious and intimidating, according to Father."

"Intimidating? Who is Rolland trying to intimidate?"

"Most of the men attending tonight are town leaders. He wants to make sure they stay in line."

I gnaw nervously at my bottom lip as we enter the throne room. This definitely makes my sneaking away a lot harder. The dining hall was much closer to the King's study than the throne room. I will now have to be gone for a considerable amount of time.

A man approaches us and shakes Xavier's outstretched hand. "Your Highness, how wonderful to see you again."

"Edgar, nice of you to join us. Have you met my fiancé, Cara?"

"No, I haven't had the pleasure." He takes my hand and kisses it. "My name is Edgar and I am the new leader of New Port. You are as beautiful as the stories say, Princess."

"Stories?" I'm genuinely perplexed.

"Xavier hasn't told you?" He raises an eyebrow at him, but Xavier just shrugs. "Ever since the King announced what you were and you showed that display of power, you are all that anyone talks about. You are a legend among the people and you have given them a hope they haven't had in decades."

"A hope? I don't understand."

"For a better life. When the Mystics were around this land prospered. There was plenty of food and every mouth was fed. The Mystics helped maintain peace and, with their powers, helped those most in need. I'm sure the King has started discussing these plans with you."

Xavier wraps his arm around my waist, tugging me closer. "Of course, he has, Edgar, stop fishing for information."

Edgar lets out a booming laugh. "Can't blame me for trying, Your Highness. I am from a fishing port, after all." He winks and walks away, greeting someone else.

When we are safely out of his earshot, I pinch Xavier's side to get him to release me. "What was that all about?"

"It's true; the stories of you have grown as of late, but you will not be reduced to gardening for the peasants. The hope keeps them loyal for now, at least. We'll have to come up with a better plan down the road."

"If it means better lives for them, I will do it."

"You will do no such thing. You are to be Queen one day. You will not lower yourself to such a demeaning task."

"But Xavier—"

"End of discussion, Cara." Xavier's tone is final and I know better than to push him.

I plaster a smile on my face and kiss him. "Of course."

It isn't long though before that smile melts off my face as Seraphine walks into my line of sight. Tonight, she is wearing a floor-length all-black gown. The front is simple and hugs her curves to perfection. As she turns I can see that the back of the dress is a different matter entirely. The back is a work of art; a network of straps that expose her back, showing just the right amount of skin.

Every man's eyes turns to look at her as she sashays past on her way to us.

"Xavier, why don't you look dashing?" She flashes her white teeth at us in an elegant smile. The perfect picture of a future royal. "Isn't this so extravagant? Rolland really spared no expense."

"Shouldn't you be near Father?" Xavier comments and Seraphine's smile slips a little in irritation.

"I am not some trophy for him to have on display."

"Yes, but it is a banquet announcing your engagement. So, I would assume you would be on the arm of your future husband."

Seraphine waves off Xavier's concern and smiles mischievously as a servant approaches to hand her a glass of wine. It doesn't take me long to realize that said servant is none other than Jordan. He looks much better than the last time I saw him. He is cleaned up, his hair has been trimmed, and he's dressed in clean servant's garb; And he is very much alive.

My whole body reacts to his appearance. My heart quickens and it takes everything in me not to run to him and pull him into my arms. Xavier's irritated growl is what finally pulls me out of my gawking.

"What is the meaning of this, Seraphine? I strictly told you that he was to remain in his cell until I decided what to do with him," he snarls.

"And I told you that I don't take orders from you. I needed a new servant to keep up my appearance of being a normal human and there was one just lying around."

"Jordan is not a servant." I snap and then realize my mistake when Xavier grips my arm.

"I told you I never wanted to hear his name on your lips ever again," he grits out, his eyes seething.

"You promised me he would be safe, Xavier."

We are starting to draw some attention from the surrounding people so Xavier leads me out of the throne room into the hall with an amused Seraphine not too far behind. He whirls on her as soon as the door to the throne room closes and pushes her against the wall.

"Explain yourself, witch."

Seraphine's eyes snap and her nostrils flare. Her voice is deathly calm as she says, "Get your hands off me, prince."

He hesitates only a second before he releases her and backs up to a safe distance. "Put him back in his cell. I won't ask again."

"Why? Because you are afraid I am right? That your perfect little fiancé is playing you for a fool."

"Parading him around in front of her proves nothing, Seraphine."

"It proves enough, did you not just see her reaction when she saw him?"

"Xavier." I touch his arm gently. "Don't listen to her. Remember what you said, she is just trying to get to you. Don't let her affect you."

Xavier's face is twisted in uncertainty. Seraphine is too good at this game; I am no match for her. How could I ever think I could outsmart her?

"Go back to your room, Cara." Xavier says.

"What?" I couldn't have heard him right.

"I said, go back to your room. This is not the night for this drama and I won't have you longingly watching him as he serves Seraphine."

"Xavier, I don't love him."

"But, you care for him and that is enough. Go back to your room and we will discuss this later. It's just easier if you go." He opens the throne room door for Seraphine and they enter together, leaving me alone in the hallway.

I start walking back to my room, in somewhat of a daze, until I suddenly realize I'm alone. Xavier didn't leave me with a guard; he left me to walk back to my room alone. This was the mistake I have been waiting for. I pick up my pace and head towards the King's study, determined to find the information that Ben requested. As I round the corner to the study I slip off my shoes and hide them behind a potted plant. I need to make as little noise as possible. Not a single guard is in sight as I creep to the study. As my hand lands on the handle of the door, though, it swings open, revealing a surprised guard.

He recovers quickly. "Your Highness, what are you doing here?"

"Oh, the King asked me to get something for him. It's a gift for Seraphine in his study." The lie slips easily past my teeth. I am getting surprisingly good at lying.

He holds the door open for me and allows me to enter. I gnaw nervously on my cheek. The study has not changed a bit since the last time I was in here.

"Go ahead and get the item and I will gladly escort you back to the banquet." The guard remarks with a smile.

I touch his arm lightly. "Oh, that isn't necessary. I know you are probably busy, I can find my way back."

"I insist, Princess, I would hate for something to happen to you on my watch."

Realizing I am not getting rid of him any time soon, I look around the room for anything that may help me. My eyes settle on a bronze statue sitting on the King's bookcase.

"Do you know what you're looking for?" the guard asks.

"Yes, it should be on his desk." I remark, making my way towards the bookcase and tripping on the chair sitting next to it, grabbing the statue on my way down.

The guard runs to my side. "Princess, are you alright?"

I almost feel bad for the concern I hear in his voice. "Yes, thank you." He helps me to my feet and when he turns his back I smack him on the head with the statue. He crumples to the ground, unconscious. I let out a sigh of relief I didn't realize I was holding. I drop the statue on the ground, bolt to the desk and begin ruffling through the papers on Rolland's desk. Nothing is looking promising, court dealings and maps of the surrounding lands.

My hand passes over a drawing of the Mystic City and my breath catches. The drawing and words are in Xavier's handwriting. This representation of his betrayal reopens the wound of that day. All the death and carnage still fresh in my mind. My fingers touch the town square where I shared a dance with Jordan and watched as my brother was stabbed to death.

A groan from the floor interrupts the memories evoked by the drawing. The guard shifts but stays safely unconscious. I take one last look at the drawing and then shove it under another pile of papers. After several minutes of finding nothing on his desk, panic begins to set in. What if I can't find what I am looking for. What if he didn't write down what his plan was, would he risk Xavier finding out about it? A thought occurs to me and I drop to my knees quickly, pulling out the drawer. I find the secret compartment where he hid the Mystic books and pop it open. Inside is a small journal and I let out a small sound of glee as I pull it out.

I thumb through the pages, skimming as I go, looking for anything that might tell me what Rolland's plan is. Most of the pages of the books are filled with spells and incantations. There are numerous drawings of pieces of jewelry. One picture draws my attention and I realize it is the engagement ring that sits upon my finger. I move past the drawing in disgust and continue flipping through the pages. It isn't until the final pages of the book that I finally find what I am looking for.

Horror fills me at the words on the page. A lengthy description on how to transfer a Mystic's powers to someone else. They are planning to steal my powers. That is why Rolland has been wanting the fifth element to manifest so much. He is planning to use Seraphine to take my powers away from me!

"I don't believe that belongs to you, little mystic."

I drop the book in surprise at Seraphine's voice. She is standing in the doorway with her hands on her hips looking entirely too pleased with herself.

"You are planning to take my powers from me? How is that possible?"

Her face transforms with her evil smile. "An ancient spell, passed down through generations of witches."

"You can't do this." Panic is beginning to set in as she begins to advance on me.

"I can and I will. Rolland will get your powers and you will die."

"How can you help that monster! He is a murderer!"

Seraphine lashes out, slapping me and sending me crashing to the ground. "No, little mystic, I am the monster."

"Seraphine, what is going on in here?"

She tosses the book to Rolland. "I found her snooping in here. She found your book."

Rolland turns his murderous gaze on me. "How long until you are ready to perform the spell?"

"A few more days, the potion needed to perform it takes several weeks to mature."

Rolland growls in frustration and pulls me up by my hair. "Once again, you have ruined my plans, you little brat." He shoves me back to the ground and turns to Seraphine. "My son cannot find out about our plan. He will never allow it to happen."

"She will tell him the first chance she gets. I can only keep her quiet for so long with my magic. Perhaps we should finally do to her what we did to Myka."

Rolland eyes me from my place on the ground, with disgust. "My son will never allow it."

"We will do it without him knowing. It is the only way our plan will still work. If she is under our control she will not be able to tell him our plan. I can do it right now." Seraphine makes a move to grab me and I scoot away from her.

"Don't touch me. You will not do that to me."

"You have no choice, little mystic. You sealed your fate when you decided to go snooping around." Seraphine raises her hand and I raise with it, controlled by her magic. She drags me closer to her as I struggle against her invisible bonds. She leans in close and whispers, "Now we will see how honest you have been about your feelings for your prince. No matter what, you are about to lose everything. I'm going to thoroughly enjoy this."

"No! Stop!"

"Shut her up, Seraphine, she is making way too much noise. Xavier will not be far behind us. We have been gone from the banquet for longer than we should."

Seraphine silences me like she did when she was telling me the story of our mothers. I watch helplessly as she removes my engagement ring and rubs her blood along its rim. She begins whispering quietly over the ring, speaking the incantation that will put me under her control. Helpless tears fill my eyes, how did it come to this? How did I let myself get into this situation. I should have been more careful.

"Father, your guests are getting—What is going on?" Xavier enters the study and stops short when he sees me in Seraphine's clutches.

Rolland swears and turns to his son. "We found her snooping around in my study. She was looking for something. I thought you had her under control, Son?"

"I did."

"Obviously you didn't. You allowed your love for her to blind you and she used that to her advantage. Now we are doing what we should have done from the beginning. We are putting her fully under our control."

"You cannot do this. She is mine." Xavier's eyes fill with possessive fury. "Seraphine, stop this."

"It's too late. I'm sorry, Son." Rolland says, motioning for the guards who just entered to hold Xavier as he tries to rush to my side.

His cries fill the air, as he struggles against the guards. "Father, stop this. I love her, you can't do this."

Seraphine finishes her spell and the ring begins to glow. She smiles knowingly at me while my panic-filled eyes follow her motions. She slips the ring onto my finger and I fall to the ground as pain rips through my body. The skin that touches the ring burns and my mouth opens in a silent scream. Inside my mind, a war is raging with the spell fighting for control. It fights against my subconscious, trying to batter it down into submission. I wither on the ground as the world melts away, I barely feel Xavier's comforting hands on my shoulders or hear his whispered reassurances. All I hear and feel is pain.

Just give up, little mystic. The pain will end. The slithery voice feels like it is everywhere.

I don't love him! The spell shouldn't have worked. I yell back.

The slimy voice cackles. *Some part of you does love him.*

I shake my head. *Stop it. No. I don't, I don't.* The inky blackness is closing in. My cry of despair vibrates off the walls of my mind.

Jordan. I whisper his name like an incantation. I'm never going to see him again. I've failed him. *Jordan, I'm sorry.*

The spell lashes out again, but it somehow feels weaker. *It's too late, you can't stop this. Just give up.*

No! I love Jordan! I love him, only him. Again, I feel the pain of the spell pushing against me but this time it doesn't hurt. I didn't imagine it, it is getting weaker. Its power comes from the token of a loved one but my love for Xavier is not strong enough to sustain it. My love for Jordan is overpowering it.

I don't love Xavier. I love Jordan. I scream into the darkness.

You lie. I feel something slimy move past my ear. *If you did not love him, I would have no power here.*

I can feel you growing weaker. You will not control me. My love for Jordan will overpower whatever remnant of love that may still exist for Xavier. I begin chanting his name and the darkness begins to retreat but its threats still linger in my mind. It taunts and mocks, still trying to convince me that I cannot win. I push against its words and its haunting power until finally the darkness is gone and I open my eyes to the sight of Xavier's concerned face.

"Xavier?" I choke out. My throat is scratchy and I feel like I've been running for hours; I am exhausted.

"You see, Xavier, I was right. She doesn't love you." Seraphine says from behind him. "There is no way she could have fought off my spell if she did."

Terror fills me at this realization. Seraphine was right. I am going to lose everything. She wanted this to happen.

Xavier looks conflicted as he glances between Seraphine and me. He doesn't know what to believe. Once again, I can only hope that his love for me wins out. My internal battle with the spell has weakened me and I don't have the strength to fight this one too.

His eyes settle on my face. "She is strong. She could have fought it off herself. You've seen her power."

"And what power does she have now? Her powers are blocked. My spell is powered by love and the only thing that can stop it is an even stronger love." Seraphine's voice is suggestive.

Realization colors Xavier's eyes and he pushes me away. "Jordan."

I shake my head weakly. "No, Xavier. It's not what you think."

He stands to his feet, running his hands through his hair. His face is a blend of pain and fury. "You made me believe that you loved me."

"Xavier, I do love you."

"Stop lying!" His outburst makes me jump. "Guards, get her out of my face. She can rot in the same cell that her baker used to occupy."

"Xavier, please listen to me. You don't understand—" Xavier's hand slapping me across the face stops my words.

"One more venomous word out of your mouth and I will kill Jordan right now in front of you."

Seraphine's face is filled with glee as the guards pick me up off the ground and begin dragging me from the room. The last thing I see is Xavier picking up the bronze statue I used earlier and throwing it across the room, shattering some of his father's belongings.

Chapter 9

"I WARNED YOU THAT your lies would come back to haunt you. At least you only hurt yourself with your lies, unlike your mother."

I lean my head back against the bars and continue ignoring Seraphine. Since the guards deposited me in my cell she has come to visit me several times, always with the same gloating tone. She continues talking like I'm not ignoring her.

"Well, I suppose you hurt Xavier, but I am taking care of him. He won't be hurting for much longer," she comments.

I close my eyes and try to tune out the annoying witch. What a mess that this has turned into. How could I have thought that I would win the dangerous game I was playing. I should have known that sooner or later Xavier would find out I was lying about my feelings for him. I hurt him and it bothers me that I did. My feelings for him are much more complicated than I am comfortable with. If I learned one thing from the crazy experience with the spell it is that I still have some feelings for Xavier. He was my first love and those feelings will probably never go away. I will always care for him, no matter how toxic his love may be to me. The fact that I hurt him pains me, and the fact that his father is lying to him infuriates me. He is a pawn in all this as much as I am. A much more willing pawn, but a pawn nonetheless.

I sigh as Seraphine continues on her ramble. She is enjoying this entirely too much. It makes me wonder how much of all this is playing into whatever plan she has. She can't possibly want Rolland to have the Prakera.

The door to the prison cells opens and heavy footsteps approach us.

"Seraphine, I would like a moment alone with Cara." My eyes snap open at Xavier's deep voice.

"Do you think that is wise? Why don't I stay and make sure she behaves?" she says sweetly. It makes me want to puke, this sweet-sounding Seraphine sounds wrong. She's up to something.

"I can handle her. Go." His voice is as sharp as a blade.

"Fine. I'll wait for you outside." She exits the prison cells and I feel Xavier's stern gaze descend on me.

"Look at me," he says softly, a completely different voice than the one he just used with Seraphine.

"I'd rather not."

The key turns in the lock and the door to the cell swings open. Xavier enters and squats in front of me, gripping my chin to meet his gaze. He stares at me in a mixture of anger and deep longing.

"So, you love the baker." He states it like a fact, not a question. His deathly calm tone is a little frightening. I was expecting his anger, not this cool temperament. "How long?"

"Does it matter?"

"Answer the question and no more lies."

"Since I saved him from that monstrous arachpid in the Mystic City. He almost died and it made me realize I couldn't live without him."

Pain flashes across his face and he turns away from me to hide it.

"I was going to tell you that night, after the celebration in the Mystic City, but then," I shrug, "well, you know what happened."

"So you lied all this time to protect him? You played me like a fool, for him."

"You were going to kill him."

"I *am* going to kill him."

"No, Xavier, please. You can't."

"Give me one reason why I shouldn't."

"I know deep down you love me, Xavier. I know that you don't want to hurt me."

His arm shoots out and grabs my braid, pulling my face to his, his eyes wild. "You are *mine!* And once he is gone and no longer a distraction, you will learn to love me again. There will be no more obstacles to us being together."

"You will destroy whatever love I have left for you if you kill him."

He releases me, once again back to his calm demeanor. "Possibly, but that's a risk I'm willing to take."

"Xavier, there is something I need to tell you. There is something your father is keeping from you. He is planning to take my powers away from me. He—"

"He told me this already." His sharp voice interrupts me.

"He did? And you're okay with that?"

"Why wouldn't I be? He gets what he wants and I get what I want."

"What are you talking about? If he takes my powers, I die."

Xavier snorts. "Nice try, my love. When he takes your powers, you will become human and we will be together."

"No, Xavier, they are lying to you."

"And why should I believe you?" he bitterly asks and when I give him no answer, he shakes his head in disgust. "That's what I thought."

He stands to his feet and lets himself out of the cell, locking it behind him. "Tomorrow, Jordan will die, and, in a few days, Father will take your powers and we will finally be together."

I face him, gripping the bars tightly; my knuckles white. "Please, Xavier, I'm begging you. Don't do this. I'll do anything you ask."

"It's too late for that. You should have thought of that before you decided to deceive me."

The door opens behind him and guards clamber in carrying an unconscious Jordan. They dump his body in the cell next to mine and leave. Xavier eyes us with disgust as I scramble over to his side of my cell. My once-beautiful ruby dress is covered in dirt and ripped in more places than I'd like to admit, but I don't care. I strain through the bars for him, but he is just out of reach.

"As a token of my love, I am allowing you this final goodbye," Xavier comments. "I know that you will hate me for this now, but I hope that with time you will come to realize that I am doing this for us."

"Xavier, please." But my words fall on deaf ears as Xavier slams the door on my pleas.

Jordan groans softly and I lift my head off the dirt-packed floor of the cell. I've watched him for what feels like hours as he lay unconscious, memorizing every line of his face. He groans again and his eyes flutter a bit before finally settling on me.

"Cara? What is going on?" He slowly crawls his way over to me, lying next to me, the only thing separating us is the metal bars. He grabs my hand and kisses it. "What happened? One second I was retrieving something for that awful woman and the next I was getting beaten up."

Tears fill my eyes and fall uselessly to the ground. "He found out. Xavier knows that I was deceiving him, pretending to love him to protect you. He's going to kill you."

"I'm not afraid to die."

"Jordan, I can't do this without you."

Jordan lifts his arm and runs his knuckles along my cheek. "Oh, Buttercup, you are stronger than you realize. You can handle anything they will ever throw at you."

"I don't have my powers right now, Jordan."

"I'm not talking about your powers. I'm talking about you as a person. I have faith in you, it's time you had faith in yourself."

A sob escapes my lips, "I'm not strong enough to survive losing you."

"Shh." He wipes away my tears, gently. "It's going to be alright. I promise, you will survive this and you will go on to be the strongest Aurora. You have the power to save them all."

"How can you be so sure?"

"Because I know you. I know you better than you know yourself. Where you see weakness, I see strength. Where you see flaws, I see beauty."

"I'm so sorry that I got you into this mess. This is—"

"Not your fault," he finishes, with his finger over my lips. "I told you, all of this was in motion when you were just a babe."

We fall into silence, as I refuse to accept his words and he waits patiently. I watch his face as he watches mine, our hands interlocked. Why did it take me so long to realize how much he means to me?

"How long do we have?" he asks some time later.

"Until morning. I'm not sure how much time has passed."

"Guess he doesn't want to waste any time."

"I told him, if he does this, he will be killing whatever love I had left for him. I thought that it would sway him."

"Promise me something."

"I would promise you anything."

"Don't let this destroy you. Use it to strengthen your resolve."

"Can we talk about something else?" I ask, my heart breaking at his words.

He smiles at me indulgently but with a promise to revisit the conversation later. "Of course, what would you like to talk about?"

"So, Seraphine? How'd that happen?"

He rolls his eyes, completely out of character and says, "That woman is crazy. Please be careful around her. There is more to her than meets the eye. She is hiding something."

"Did she say something around you?" I run my thumb over the calluses on his hands. I never want to let him go.

"No, she made sure of that. My time spent with her was split between her taunting me about you and her ordering me to do ridiculous things. I think she just relishes in seeing people suffer."

"I noticed. I agree that she is hiding something. There is more to her. Why take out all her revenge on me when Rolland was the one that killed most of her people. There has to be more to her plan."

"Maybe when she shows her true colors it can be an opening for you to escape. You must always be prepared to escape, never waste a single opportunity."

"I won't."

He smiles, then closes his eyes and begins humming a random tune.

"How can you be so calm right now?" I ask.

He grabs my hand and kisses it, then holds it to his chest, all while holding his tune. He doesn't reply for a few minutes and I almost doze off listening to him hum. "Because of you. You've always been my calming presence. Remember when I was trying to convince the head baker to let me become the pastry chef? I was so nervous that for several weeks I couldn't bake a single thing unless you were sitting in the kitchen with me."

"I can't take credit for that. Your wonderful baking got you your job."

He shakes his head. "No, it was you. I could tell you dozens of times that your presence calmed me. Honestly, I probably would have strangled Xavier if it were not for you." He smirks. "You know what, you're right, this is your fault."

I laugh at his expression but it feels bittersweet and my tears start anew. When he sees my face he kisses me.

"Hey, no more tears. It's going to be alright, I promise."

"You can't promise that, Jordan."

He plants kisses over my face the best he can with the bars between us. "I can. I'm just that amazing."

I give him a small smile. "I love you."

"Good, then I can die a happy man."

I shake my head at his joking tone and then freeze when I hear movement outside the prison door. I watch it fearfully, not ready to say goodbye. Jordan turns my head back to him and his beautiful cerulean blue eyes stare back at me.

"Hey, look at me. It's going to be okay. Remember what I said, don't let this destroy you, use it." There is a renewed urgency in his voice, he must have heard the noise too. "Cara, promise me."

"I promise." My suspicions are confirmed when the door to the prison cells swings open, revealing Xavier and a team of guards.

He kisses me again and this time it is desperate and raw. I feel his love, his anger, his pain, even his fear. He continues to kiss me even as Xavier and his guards enter the room. He doesn't stop even as the door to his cell opens and the guards enter. I cry out as the guards pull him to his feet and away from me, separating our connection. I reach out for him but they drag him out of my reach.

Unbridled tears fall as I watch him being taken further away from me. Our eyes lock and I see all the love I feel for him reflected back at me. Xavier is standing just outside my cell, watching the exchange with barely restrained fury.

"Xavier, please, don't do this." I beg.

He turns his back to me, ignoring my pleas. I reach through the bars and grip his forearm. He stops but does not turn around. "Please, I'll do anything."

"It's too late for that." He shakes off my hand and motions for the guards.

"No! Stop, please! Jordan!" The door to the prison cells slams on my cries as they echo off the vacant walls. I crumble to the floor in a broken heap. Sobs rack my body and I pull at the Red Star bracelet at my wrist. Blood runs down my fingers from where the stones have dug into the delicate skin. No matter how hard I try, it stays put, effectively doing its job. Adding the extra stars has completely cut me off from my powers. No Prakera comes to melt the bars away. Jordan is gone and there is nothing I can do about it.

He is wrong; I am weak. I'm not the person he thinks I am. I cannot hold up my promise. With those thoughts, I curl up into myself and I cry until I have no tears left to shed, and only then do I fall into a fitful sleep.

Chapter 10

I DREAM OF JORDAN every time I close my eyes. He tells me to be brave and remember my promise, and every time I wake up it's with deep feelings of despair. I am a shell of myself and drowning in endless sorrow. Jordan is gone and all I have left of him are my dreams, so I sleep. On the fourth day of him being gone Alexia brings my food instead of the usual guard. Xavier has yet to show his face, the coward. She opens my cell and places the new plate of food next to the untouched one from the day before.

She frowns, "You need to eat, miss." She grabs a piece of bread off the plate and offers it to me. I stare off into the distance, not acknowledging her presence. She sighs and sits down on the dirt-packed floor and pulls my head into her lap. She gently wipes my tear-stained face with her apron, taking away the crustiness. I barely feel it; my whole body is numb.

She rambles on as she cleans, "The Prince has been in a horrible mood for days. Everyone has been steering clear of him. The only people who dare to be in his presence are the King and Seraphine. I heard that he put a hole in his wall with his fist."

Once she is done with my face she undoes my mangled braid and runs her fingers through my hair, working out the knots. It hasn't been washed since the banquet; it is an oily, filthy mess but she doesn't seem to mind.

"I don't know what you did to end up in here, but I'm sure if you apologize the Prince will come around," she comments.

A small sliver of anger slips through my haze of grief. "What are you doing here?" my voice cracks, rusty from misuse. Alexia hands me a glass of water but I ignore her offering.

"One of the guards asked me to do it. We began working here around the same time and help each other out every once in a while. His name is Ben and he seems pretty concerned about your wellbeing."

The small sliver of anger grows and I sit up sharply, startling her. "You tell him I want nothing to do with his concern."

She attempts to hand me the cup of water again. "He also wanted me to tell you that you need to have faith in the Mitera, that she is always watching. What is a Mitera?"

"Ask your friend." I grab the bread off the plate and munch on it absently. It falls heavily to the bottom of my stomach. I take only a few bites and push it away. Alexia hands me the water and this time I take it. I drink it slowly and watch her as she fiddles nervously with the hem of her apron, now stained with whatever gunk was all over my face.

"Thank you."

She shrugs, "I was worried. I hadn't been called to your room in days and the Prince was in such a rage I didn't dare ask him where you were. I thought something had happened to you. I was worried I was going to be executed for treason like the maids before me. I went to Ben and he told me you were in here. He was able to work it out so I could bring you your food and I agreed." She grabs my hand. "Are you alright, miss? I don't understand what is going on."

"My friend," I choke up a little, "the one you asked me about, is there a reason you asked? Did someone put you up to that?"

"No, miss. I honestly overheard the conversation. I'm sorry if I upset you with my questioning."

"No, it's alright. And to answer your question truthfully, yes I do love Jordan." Tears fill my eyes. "Well, I did."

"I don't understand."

"Xavier killed him four days ago. He found out I was deceiving him, pretending to love him to keep Jordan safe. That's why I'm in here."

"Oh, miss, I am so sorry. I knew there was an execution but I chose to not attend it, after the Queen's I just couldn't bear another one."

I take another sip of water and consider the maid in front of me; the beginnings of a plan developing in my mind. "They are planning to kill me too."

Alexia's eyes widen. "Why? That doesn't make any sense."

"The King and Seraphine are planning to take away my Mystic abilities, which will kill me. Please, Alexia, will you help me escape?"

She pulls her hand out of my grasp and rises to her feet. She paces nervously above me. "Miss, I don't know. I-I want to help, I do, but I have a family. What if they hurt them because I help you?" She casts nervous eyes to the door and chews on her bottom lip. She begins muttering more to herself than to me. "What kind of person does that make me if I don't help you? I can't just let you die. I don't know what to do."

She paces for several minutes going back and forth on whether or not she should help me. I sip my water silently, trying not to focus on the grief that is trying to crush me. I already miss the numbness of the last few days. But I know deep down that I have to uphold my promise to Jordan, I have to use his death to strengthen my resolve. Once this is all over, then I will allow the grief to swallow me whole.

"Alexia, I won't make you do something you are not comfortable with," I murmur.

She heaves a massive sigh, seeming to make a decision. "No, I will help you. It's the right thing to do."

"Are you sure?"

"Yes." She grabs my hand and helps me to my feet. "I know a way out of the palace where we shouldn't run into anyone."

"I want you to be sure. This could be dangerous."

"I'm sure." She unlocks the door to my cell but she stops me before opening the outside door. "Let me check to make sure the coast is clear."

She slips out and returns a few seconds later, motioning for me to follow. She leads me down the hall and through a series of doors to an area I've never been in before. The area is cluttered with several small armchairs and tables, littered with games and papers. The little space is quaint and looks like it is used often.

"Where are we?" I whisper.

"Servants common area. This is where we congregate when we have some time off."

"Where is everyone?"

"It's the middle of the day so most everyone is pretty busy." She pushes through another door and I toy nervously with the bracelet on my wrist. A memory attempts to surface but it stays just out of reach.

"We are going to take this corridor until it ends just before the front entry. Then it's just a matter of getting past the guards."

I nod in understanding and follow quietly behind her until she stops before another door. She pushes it open just a crack and murmurs, "That's weird."

"What?"

"There are no guards at the front entry."

"Has that ever happened before?"

Alexia shakes her head, looking unsure, "I don't know, I don't come this way that often. They are probably just changing shifts. This could be our chance though, so let's not waste it."

She pushes the door open fully and I follow her out, heading straight for the entryway. We reach the door in a matter of seconds, I can almost taste the freedom.

A loud crack splits the air and Alexia drops to the ground next to me with a cry of pain. To my horror, blood begins pooling around her, coming from the gunshot wound in her chest. I drop to my knees and gather her in my arms, propping her up against me. I push my ruined dress frantically down on the gushing wound, hoping to stop its progress, but it is too late. I can see it in her eyes as she gives my hand a little squeeze and then it falls lifelessly to the ground.

"Going somewhere, my love?"

Xavier stands just a few yards away with his gun raised and a triumphant expression.

"You honestly didn't think I would leave you unguarded, did you? I knew your maid was bringing your food and I knew you would use your venomous tongue to sway her into helping you."

I close Alexia's eyes with blood-stained hands, guilt swirling inside me. He's right, I did convince her to help me. She would have been safe if I hadn't talked her into helping me escape. I rise slowly to my feet, my dress and arms covered in Alexia's blood.

"If you knew this then why you let us get this far?"

"So, you could see the consequences of your actions and to show you that I will never let you leave me." He steps closer and grabs my chin, forcing my gaze onto him. "Anyone who tries to help you escape me will die. You are mine."

"Xavier, this is insane. Please, just let me go. If you truly love me like you say you do, let me go."

"I will never let you go. We are meant to be together and someday you will accept that."

"And if I don't?"

"Well, for your sake and those you care about, let's hope it never gets to that."

My anger flares and I push him away, leaving bloody handprints on his white shirt. "Those I care about?! And who's that, Xavier? You've taken everyone from me. There's no one left." A sob escapes but I'm not done. "You are a monster! You have taken everything from me! Any love I had left for you died with Jordan and that will never change."

"It's a shame that you feel that way. Maybe a little time under Seraphine's spell will change your mind. It will give you some time to think being trapped inside your own mind."

"They already tried that and it didn't work."

"With a token of mine, yes. But I believe there is a special locket that is always on you that will serve as a token from him. Where is it?"

My heart races in alarm until I realize that I no longer have the locket. Ben took it. Now I understand why, he somehow knew that it could be used against me. He took it as a precaution. "I lost it."

He grabs my arm with a vice-like grip, pulling me towards him. "I believe I told you I wanted no more lies."

"I swear, I haven't seen it since our agreement. I hid it so it wouldn't upset you and I haven't been able to find it since. I'm telling the truth."

He shoves me away from him in disgust just as Seraphine enters the entryway. She tsks as she takes in the pool of blood that is spreading around my dead maid and the furious prince.

"My, what do we have here?"

"This doesn't involve you, Seraphine," Xavier snaps.

The witch smiles as she takes in my disheveled, bloody appearance. "Oh, how far you have fallen, princess."

"Do not talk to her," Xavier snarls.

Seraphine raises an eyebrow. "Someone is in a mood."

He runs his hand through his shaggy blonde hair. "You have no idea."

"You are not bleeding, are you?" she asks Xavier and again a memory stirs but stays just out of reach.

"No, this is all the maid's blood."

"Her name was Alexia," I grind out.

They both ignore me and turn their backs to me, having a private conversation. I'm left staring at the lifeless body of Alexia, her blood slowly drying on my hands and dress. Again, I question how I never saw this side of Xavier, how I was so easily deceived? I inch towards the door in a final desperate attempt to escape while they are seemingly distracted, but my progress is halted by an invisible barrier.

"You have to admire her determination," Seraphine remarks, smirking as I ram my fist against her spell.

"I don't," Xavier mutters as he approaches me once more. I have nowhere to go as he inches closer to me. My back hits the door behind me as he places a hand on either side of my head, gaining my full attention.

"I want to make something very clear, my love." His voice is menacingly low and the way he said 'my love' sends dangerous shivers down my spine. "You will never escape me. But keep this in mind if you ever manage to, however unlikely—I will hunt you down and kill anyone that helps you. Nothing will stop me from returning you to my side. So, save us both the trouble and heartache and stop testing my patience. You are mine and you will always remain mine."

"Why are you doing this? You could have anyone, why me?"

He runs his lips along my ear and whispers, "You are the air I breathe, you are the only person I want." He pulls away from me and yells for guards, "Take her back to her cell and find out who gave her maid permission to bring her food."

The guards grab my arms and start dragging me away, but Xavier's voice follows after us. "I will find your locket, my love, and when I do you will have plenty of time to think about the consequences of your actions."

The sound of the prison door opening wakes me out of a dead sleep. I sit up as Seraphine enters and stands in front of my cell.

I rub my eyes and mutter, "What do you want?"

"It's time, little mystic."

Suddenly, I'm instantly awake and jump to my feet. The guards open the doors and advance on my corner of the cell. I fight them off, pushing and clawing like a caged animal but they quickly overpower me, dragging me out of the cell.

"Don't do this, Seraphine, don't give him this power."

"Nothing you say will stop this."

"He is insane, imagine the people he will hurt! Imagine the families he will tear apart. Please, Seraphine, listen to reason. Don't let him hurt others as he has hurt your people."

Seraphine whips around and smacks me. My head snaps back but I do not fall, thanks to the guards holding me upright. Before I can recover, her hand wraps in my hair and she jerks my head to face her. Her eyes burn with intensified anger.

"Don't ever try to use my people's tragedy against me. You know nothing." She pulls my head back and it feels like all my hair is going to come out of my skull. "I cannot wait to watch you die, you spoiled little brat."

We continue our journey to wherever they are taking me for my end. I become dead weight as the guards drag me, no use in making it easy for them. We enter the same room that I manifested the Prakera in, with the only inhabitants in the room being Rolland and Myka. The guards drag me over to an empty chair and force me to sit down, tying down my hands and feet. I pull against the bonds, but they do not budge.

Rolland approaches and smiles maliciously down at me. "I am not sorry it has to be this way, girl, so I won't apologize. You are a means to an end and that time has come."

"Xavier will never forgive you for this."

"My son is no longer your concern and he will be fine. Once you are gone he will move on and find a proper future queen for himself."

"I think you underestimate his feelings for me."

"And I think you overestimate your importance. I look forward to not having to deal with you any longer." He pats me on the cheek and walks away with a satisfied smile.

"So, you are sure we will not be disturbed by my son?" Rolland asks.

Seraphine nods as she pours a green liquid into two cups. "I gave him a sleeping draught that should have him out until morning and a guard posted at his door. He is not going anywhere."

"Good."

Seraphine hands him one of the cups and instructs him to drink it. He does so and then she moves on to me, putting the cup to my lips. I tighten my lips and stare back at her defiantly.

She laughs, mirthlessly, "Oh, little mystic, you are only delaying the inevitable." She shoves her fingers into my cheeks, prying my jaw open. My eyes widen as she pours the green liquid between my lips. I attempt to spit it out but she covers my mouth with her hand and I'm forced to swallow it. It burns down my throat and leaves a trail of agony behind it. I scream out in pain, withering in my chair.

"What did you do to me?" I pant.

"Just preparing you for the transfer of power."

I let out another cry of pain as heat spreads throughout my body. My entire body feels like it is on fire.

"The potion brings all her powers to the surface, that's what is causing her so much pain." I hear Seraphine explaining before Rolland drops to the ground. "And now your body is preparing to accept it."

Rolland's grunts of pain join my cries as Seraphine busies herself with gathering her items for her spell. She watches the scene in front of her with a smile of satisfaction.

"Did I forget to mention how painful this process was?" she asks as Rolland's grunts turn into cries of pain. She walks over to him and digs her heeled shoe into his cheek. "You do realize it's what you deserve, don't you?"

"What have you done?" he spits out between gritted teeth.

"I'm just giving you what you want, Rolland darling. You will have Cara's powers, but what I failed to mention is that they will kill you. Your body is not meant to hold such power. It is not worthy."

"And I take it yours is?" I ask.

"Why, yes, you are correct. The Prakera will be mine and then no one will be able to hurt me or my people again."

"Why not." I cringe as a wave of fire ripples under the skin. "Why not just take it from me? Why give it to Rolland first?"

"It's old magic, but effective." Seraphine smiles down at Rolland and steps out of the range of his arm as he lashes out at her. "Long ago a spell was cast on the descendants of the original mystics. Any being that took a mystic's power from them directly would be cursed. They would have the power of the mystics but their very existence would be cursed. By taking it from Rolland, I get my revenge and save myself from the curse."

"You don't need my power. You are powerful enough on your own."

"As an ordinary mystic, you would be correct. I was originally going to do this, let both of you die and that would be the end of it. But then you showed your true worth; the legendary Prakera." Madness shines in her eyes. "I will be the most powerful being that ever lived."

Seraphine looks down at the spell book in front of her and begins chanting. As soon as the first words leave her mouth the pain I was feeling intensifies to a whole new level. My body begins to glow and Rolland withers on the ground next to me, his mouth open in violent screams. The glow surrounding my body begins to lift slowly from my skin like a fine mist and drifts towards Rolland's body. The separation is agony, like ripping off a layer of skin.

Seraphine's chanting mixes in with our cries of pain. With every passing second, the pain intensifies and I feel my body draining. I watch the glowing mist, almost in a daze, my meek attempts to loosen my bonds have stopped completely. The mist is slowly engulfing Rolland's body and he convulses on the ground.

Suddenly the doors to the room swing open and Xavier comes rushing in with Ben and a squad of royal guards closely behind. Their abrupt appearance startles Seraphine and she momentarily stops chanting as the mist settles again on my body.

"What is the meaning of this, Seraphine? Why was I not informed about this?" Xavier comes to my side and touches my cheek. I lean into his touch, grasping for any type of comfort.

Seraphine has the gall to look innocent. "I had no choice. Your father threatened to separate me from our ancient artifact, taking my powers away if I didn't perform the transfer of power tonight. I couldn't risk it."

"Then why not inform me?"

"It was killing me, Xavier." My voice is raspy and my throat raw.

Xavier looks sharply at Seraphine, his voice deadly. "Is this true?"

"Yes," she replies hesitantly.

In a blink of an eye, Xavier pulls out his sword and stabs his father in the heart, killing him immediately. His eyes drift closed and he sighs in what almost sounds like relief. Seraphine lets out a scream sending everyone but me flying backwards.

"No!" Her eyes blaze dangerously.

Xavier gets to his feet and faces the enraged witch. Blood trickles down the side of his face from a small gash on his forehead. Debris from Seraphine's explosion of power litters the floor around us.

"I told him that if he ever hurt her, I would kill him." He walks to my side and begins undoing my bonds. I watch the trail of blood make its way down his cheek and finally the memory that has been nagging at the corners of my consciousness bursts to the forefront of my mind.

"You said my blood was the only thing that would remove the bracelet and give her back her powers." Xavier's voice replays in my head from when I was barely conscious after the Prakera manifested. His blood deactivates the Red Stars!

"Xavier, she planned this. She was trying to kill us both. She wants the Prakera. She was manipulating your father."

"Don't listen to her lies, Xavier." Seraphine's voice has once again returned to its silky, musical quality. "She will tell you anything to save herself."

Xavier stops untying my hands and looks at her with uncertainty. "Why would she lie about this?"

"Because she is a liar, Xavier. She's only ever cared about herself and the wellbeing of that boy. All she's ever done is lie to you and all you've ever done is love her. She uses your love against you because she knows it blinds you." As Seraphine talks, I twist my wrist, attempting to loosen the ropes that Xavier had begun untying. "She doesn't deserve your love, Xavier. She is a manipulative viper that will continue to hurt you."

"And why should I believe you, were you not just trying to kill her?"

"Have I not proven my loyalty to you and your family? I was only doing as your father commanded. He threatened to take my powers away from me. He—"

"I don't care about your stupid magic. She is mine! No one will ever take her from me!"

Seraphine looks at me as my wrist finally slips free of the bonds. "Does that include her?"

Xavier swings his possessive gaze to me and he stalks over to my chair. He gets within inches of my face, sliding his hand menacingly close to my neck, and grinds out, "You will never get away from me."

Tears fill my eyes in both pain and regret, I am about to prove every word that Seraphine uttered true. If this works, and I get away, he will hunt me for the rest of my life.

"I'm sorry, Xavier," I whisper as I rest my hand on his cheek.

He looks at me quizzically until realization dawns when my bracelet slides against the blood on his cheek. A blast of power blows out from the bracelet sending Xavier and Seraphine soaring into a nearby wall. Rapidly, I feel my powers coming back to me like an old friend. My body welcomes them willingly, unlike the painful process of having them ripped away. The Red Stars scatter across the floor but I pay them no mind; if I never see one of them for the rest of my life it will be too soon.

Ben suddenly appears at my side as Xavier and Seraphine begin to rise to their feet. "Princess, I think it would be a good time to leave."

"Cara, if you know what's good for you, you will stay where you are," Xavier demands.

Seraphine sneers, "So, you're the snake that has been slithering around the castle causing problems. I was wondering when you would show your face."

"I will not allow you to hurt the Aurora," Ben states.

"Then we have a problem, because I plan to do much worse than that." She calls for Myka and he comes to her side. "I added a bit of my blood to Myka's ring just in case something ever happened to Rolland, so now he belongs to me. Myka, attack."

"No!" I throw my hands up to push Myka back with the wind element but nothing happens. No gust of wind pushes him back, not even a gentle breeze. I look down at my hands in trepidation. Did the Red Stars permanently damage me? No, that can't be right, I felt them return, they are there.

The sound of flesh hitting flesh breaks me out of my thoughts as Ben's fist connects with Myka's face. Myka reels back but he is quick to recover as he barrels Ben to the ground. The two of them are a jumble of limbs as they wrestle for control.

"Myka, please, stop this. I know you are in there," I cry out.

"Oh, it's too late for that, little mystic. He lost that fight and he is fully under my control. The only way to stop him now is to kill him," Seraphine explains.

"Or I could kill you."

"I'd like to see you try." Seraphine gets into a fighting stance.

Just as I'm about to lunge for Seraphine, the doors to the room burst open once again and a flood of unfamiliar armed soldiers descend on us. They surround us and Seraphine watches them with open disdain, until her eyes settle on a figure cutting through the crowd. Her gaze soon turns to shock and disbelief.

"Mother?"

Melinda stands before her daughter, very much alive. She is dressed like a fierce warrior; a complete contrast to her daughter, who is dressed in finery. Like Seraphine, Melinda's hair is red, but with grey streaks cropped close to her head.

"Seraphine, you need to stop this. This is not how it has to be," Melinda says, and it's safe to say that Seraphine got her silky, musical voice from her mother.

Seraphine snaps out of her shock and sneers at her mother, "So, this is where you've been all these years? Leading a little band of rebels. You left your own people for this?"

"I left to make sure that our people had a future. Your madness was spreading and it was only a matter of time before you made a rash decision, as you have."

"I am guaranteeing our future!"

"No, Seraphine, you're not. You're guaranteeing our destruction."

"You lost any say in what I do when you abandoned us." Darkness surrounds Seraphine as she begins murmuring a spell.

Melinda's eyes widen. "What are you doing? You can't."

Seraphine pupils glow red. "You should have studied the ancient books more, like I did, Mother."

Shadows spew out of Seraphine's hands, morphing into humanoid beings with glowing red eyes. They attack the surrounding soldiers and cries of terror and pain fill the small space. The smell of blood, metallic and raw, consumes the air.

"Mitera, what should we do?" a soldier asks just before he is tackled to the ground by a shadow creature and impaled by its razor-sharp claws. His lifeless eyes stare back up at me as Melinda calls for her men to retreat.

Melinda turns her sparkling green eyes to me as she pulls out her sword to fend off an approaching shadow creature. "Maia, you must get out of here. Go with Ben, he will show you the way. I will be right behind you."

Ben materializes next to me and tries to lead me out of the chaos. It's then that I realize that there is blood on the sword that he using, something that could not have happened with the shadow creatures. I pull out of his grasp.

"What did you do?"

"Princess, this is not the time. We have to get out of here. Those creatures will overwhelm us."

"Where is Myka?"

"I had no choice." His defeated tone tells me everything I need to know.

"No!" I pull away from him and charge back into the fight, looking for my fallen friend. I find him among the chaos, his forgotten body lying alone.

Tears cloud my vision as I drop to my knees next to him. His empty eyes are once again their natural color and not the depthless black that had recently consumed them. "I'm so sorry, Myka. I'm so sorry I failed you."

A terrible cry, filled with my deepest regret and sorrow, rips from my lips. All of my feelings of losing Jordan, and now Myka, rise to the surface. Pain like nothing I've ever felt before shatters whatever control I have left. My hands begin to glow and I send a blast of energy into an approaching shadow creature. It disintegrates without a sound. The room settles into silence as all eyes turn to me. A slow clapping fills the air and I swing my gaze to Seraphine.

"Very good, little mystic." Her mocking tone incites my anger. "But you are no match for me." Another wave of shadows comes flowing out of her arms. "Do not let them get away."

I pick off as many of the creatures as I can, sending energy blasts in every direction, but there are too many of them. Melinda fights her way to my side and instructs me to retreat and we slowly start backing away to the door. Some of her men are still fighting inside but there are too many shadow creatures between us and them. They will have to be left behind.

Before I make it out of the room I hear Xavier's voice above the chaos. "I will find you, Cara. There is nowhere you can hide from me."

His quiet threat sends shivers down my spine, inciting more fear than the shadow creatures in front of me. He will stop at nothing to have me. How many more people will be hurt before he gets to me? And what will happen if he gets me? I have finally proven every word that Seraphine has uttered about me. I once again used his love for me against him. Melinda slams the door on the room, trapping Seraphine and Xavier inside with their shadow army. Their claws scratch against the steel door and their cries bleed through the cracks.

"Find something to jam the door with," Melinda commands to her followers.

They look around but there is nothing in the bare hallway. I touch my hand to the ground, hoping upon hope that my powers work this time, and call upon the earth. Giant gnarled tree roots come up through the tiled floor and wrap themselves around the door frame and handle. Melinda nods in satisfaction.

"It won't hold them long, but it should be enough for us to get away," she says as she grabs my hand and pulls me along behind her to freedom.

Chapter 11

"HERE, DRINK THIS." MELINDA hands me a cup and I sniff at it, a little leery of its green appearance, but it smells divine and I take a sip. Melinda smiles. "It's just tea, dear, made from the valusian flower. It will help relax you after our ordeal. I may not have my powers but I can still brew a fine tea that magically heals all sorrows."

I continue to sip at the tea as I glance around Melinda's space. It's bare, with only the chair I sit on, a desk, and a small cot that looks like it is not comfortable at all to sleep on. And from what I can tell it has not been slept on in some time either. My observations turn to the woman in front of me. She has heavy bags under her eyes and she sits as though she has the world upon her shoulders, but her laugh lines run deep and her gaze is always sparkling.

"I don't understand any of this," I comment. After escaping the palace, Melinda and her men had led me deep into the surrounding city to an underground network of tunnels. Once we had locked Seraphine and her shadow army in the room it was a relatively easy escape out of the palace. Since arriving, Melinda had ushered me into her room and informed her soldiers to ensure we were not disturbed. She also provided me with a change of clothes, but shedding the blood-stained dress does not take away the memory of Alexia's death. I pull the blanket tighter around my shoulders, a chill running through me. Her poor family will never know about her sacrifice.

"I will answer any questions you may have," She says as she sips something that is probably a lot stronger than tea.

"You're Melinda, my mother's childhood friend?"

"Yes. Alera and I were very close, the best of friends. She was like a sister to me." She smiles fondly.

"Seraphine said that my mother took advantage of that friendship."

Melinda sighs sadly, her smile disappearing at my words. "Yes, that is my daughter's favorite story. And that is what it is, dear—just a story. Alera and I were the best of friends and we helped each other out in any situation. I would have died for her, just as she would have died for me. She actually saved me from a fate worse than death. Seraphine tends to forget that."

"What was it?"

"When I was brought to live with Alera's parents after my parents' death, I had an arranged marriage. It was not something I was looking forward to, but I knew as a future queen I had a commitment to my people. I was engaged to be married to Rolland. It would have solidified the peace between the witches and the humans.

The first time we met I was in my early teens and he was very charming. He gave me flowers and kissed my hand, made me feel wanted. I fell for him very quickly. But it wasn't long before he started becoming very disrespectful to me and tried to pressure me into doing things I did not want to do. He would try to manipulate me into using my powers to get his way. As he grew older, he got worse. He was cruel and demeaning, and never saw me as his equal. I was almost like a prize to him and he treated me as such. But to everyone else he was a gentleman and a saint; a true future king. He was extremely manipulative.

I kept a lot of this from Alera and her parents because I did not want them to think I was trying to get out of my arranged marriage like a spoiled child. I was afraid they would not believe me and think that I was ungrateful for all that they had provided me.

Just before our sixteenth birthdays, we were attending a ball at the palace. Rolland was being his typical self, he had pulled me into a room and was yelling at me for some imagined indiscretion. Alera had come looking for me and had walked into the room just in time to see Rolland slap me. She reacted by charging him but he just laughed and pushed her away. He left then, confident in his position. I begged Alera not to tell anyone as she looked over the bruise developing on my cheek. She kept her promise but the next day she went directly to her parents and convinced them to cancel my engagement to Rolland. I don't know what she told them or how she convinced them, but I will be forever grateful. I never had to see Rolland after that day."

"I'm so sorry that happened to you, Melinda. You didn't deserve that."

She waves off my empathy. "It's in the past, dear, nothing to concern ourselves with now."

"Well his son is not much different. I learned that the hard way."

"Yes, I have noticed. Though Xavier seems to have an obsessive quality about him that Rolland never had. Rolland loved nothing but himself. I think that Xavier truly believes he loves you and that his toxic version is true love."

"Why would my parents side with Myridia during the war, if my mother knew all this about Rolland?"

"Because that was a political decision, not a personal one. Your mother and father were very good at keeping personal feelings out of their decisions. I did not begrudge them for siding with him. When Rolland first became king he was actually a very good ruler. Your mother more than likely believed he had changed. He took care of his people and was fair and just. The kingdom flourished under his rule until the war began and Mystics began disappearing. He and Gaven became very close. I think he fell for his charm just as I did when I was young. He has a way of drawing his victims into his web of lies."

I sip my tea thoughtfully, digesting all that Melinda has revealed. So much history that I did not know about and so many questions I still need answered.

"How does Seraphine fit into all of this?"

Sadness flickers across her face. "My daughter is very sick. You see a witch is not supposed to be without their powers. It is an unnatural thing. We are born with it in our blood, and even though our bodies are not ready for it until we turn thirteen we feel its presence, even in infancy. It is a part of us. When the time is right the power of the ancient artifact activates the magic in our blood and allows us to fully feel its power. When Rolland separated us from the artifact and destroyed our home, Seraphine was our youngest survivor. She has lived the longest without her powers and she has paid the price for it. It has since driven her mad.

Her madness started at a very young age and it drove her to find anything that would once again link her to the magic that lay dormant in her blood. It's how she knows so much—she has studied and restudied every spell book and history book she could get her hands on. At first, I thought her passion admirable, she wanted to find some way to save our people or at least never let something like that happen to us again. I was very wrong. By the time I realized how wrong I was, it was already too late.

I walked in on her and some of our more zealous witches developing a plan to infiltrate Myridia to retrieve our ancient artifact and kill the King. I punished them for putting our people in danger and forbid anyone from leaving our lands. We had a simple life in the forgotten lands, but we were safe and I knew that if they tried to attack Rolland it would end in our complete destruction. This went on for many years; she would bring more and more easily influenced witches into her group and her madness spread. She had developed quite a following and everything I did to slow it down did nothing.

It wasn't long before an attempt was made on my life. One of her followers took it upon themselves to rid her of her opposition. I killed the witch in question and then slipped away in the dead of the night. I knew that the only chance I had of saving my people from themselves was to leave. If I remained, more attempts would be made on my life and I would be no good to my people. I abandoned them to save them."

"You did what you had to do."

"Yes."

"I don't—"

A commotion at the door interrupts me from my next statement. The sounds of a scuffle and shouts filtered through the wooden door until it finally swings open. Melinda and I both rise to our feet in alarm but the person that walks through the door is not an enemy. Standing in front of me, sweaty, panting, and bruised is Jordan. Tears flood my eyes as I drop to my knees in shock.

Our eyes lock and I see a flood of emotion crashing in his gaze. He drops to his knees in front of me as well and takes my face gently in his hands. The calluses from years of working in the kitchen graze against my cheek and nothing has ever made me happier.

"Jordan? Is it really you?"

"Yes, Buttercup, it's really me." His voice sends my heart soaring. I never thought I'd hear that sound again. I vaguely hear Melinda leaving the room, saying something about giving us privacy, but I barely register her words. All of my focus is on the beautiful boy in front of me.

"How is this possible? How are you here? I don't understand." I touch his face, reverently. This has to be a dream, there is no way possible that he is in front of me. Yet the face that I touch is warm and scruffy. His facial hair is coming in and it grazes against my palm.

"The rebels saved me. The Mitera was able to orchestrate a rescue. As Xavier and his guards were leading me to my execution they were ambushed and the rebels took me to safety. They didn't know what hit them, Xavier was livid."

"He made me believe you were dead."

"Of course, he did." He pulls me into his arms and tightens his arms around me. "There was no way that he would have told you that I was still alive. It would have given you hope that he didn't want you to have."

My tears soak into his shirt as he holds me. "I can't believe you are alive and here. It seems too good to be true."

Jordan kisses the top of my head. "I know, Buttercup. But it's all true. We're both alive, we're both safe and we're together."

"I wouldn't exactly say we are safe," I mumble.

I feel his laugh against my cheek. "Well, you're not wrong. But at least in this moment we are both safe."

"Alright, I'll give you that." I pull away from his embrace and stare at him for a second, still in complete disbelief that he is alive and in front of me. Overcome by emotion, I pull his face into mine and he meets me gladly as we slip into a paradise that is just for us.

After a time that is much too short, he pulls away. He leans his forehead against mine. "We should probably let Melinda have her room back. And she probably has a lot more to talk to you about since I rudely interrupted."

"I'm glad you interrupted."

"I would have gotten here sooner, but they failed to tell me you were here. I had no idea they had planned your rescue for tonight."

"They probably had to make a last-second decision because Seraphine and Rolland were attempting to take my powers and kill me."

Jordan's eyes blaze with anger. "When I get my hands on that witch, I am going to kill her."

I kiss his cheek." As much as I appreciate that. I will handle Seraphine."

"At least give me Rolland then."

"He's already dead. Xavier killed him because he thought Rolland was trying to kill me, but it was Seraphine. She is behind everything. She wants the Prakera and she was manipulating Rolland to get it and she will do the same to Xavier. She will turn him against me."

"Hey," he brings my gaze to his, "he was already against you. He was never on your side."

I shake my head. "I know you'll never understand this, but a part of me will always love him. It is nothing compared to my feelings for you but there is no denying that some sort of feelings are still there. And I know that deep down there is still good in him. He is misguided, not evil."

"You're right, I don't understand." He shakes his head and his shaggy hair flops wildly, in serious need of a haircut. "How can you defend him after everything he has done?"

"I'm not defending him. I'm just saying that deep down there is something good, I've seen it."

He kisses me again. "I love that you can see the good in people. I wish I could say the same. I love you."

My eyes fill with tears once again. "I never thought I'd ever hear that again. Say it again."

Jordan kisses my cheek and says it again, then he gives my other cheek the same treatment. He kisses every inch of my face as he declares his undying love and I melt completely. He hovers over my lips, the last place left untouched on my face, and whispers the three words again. We stare into each other's eyes and I know that every word he said is true. Every feeling that I have for him is reflected back in his eyes and I make a promise to myself then and there that I will do everything in my power to give Jordan the future he deserves.

"I love you, Cara."

"Maia. I want to go by my real name. I want to leave that name in the past where it belongs, it died with Rolland."

He looks at me like he has never been more proud. "Very well, Maia." The name brings a smile to both our lips and it's a very long time before we give Melinda back her room.

After vacating Melinda's room, Jordan leads me down the darkened hallways to a mess hall. Hundreds of people are clamoring in the tiny space, but that all stops when we step into the room. All eyes turn to us with mixed reactions, some are adoring and disbelieving, while others are distrusting. An arm in the back of the hall shoots up and I quickly see Ben's smiling face. We make our way over to him where Jordan deposits me and tells me he is going to get us food. He disappears into the crowd, which has thankfully turned back to their own conversations.

"I am glad to see you are doing alright, Princess," Ben states. He reaches into his pocket and pulls out a tiny box, dropping it in my hand. "I kept it safe."

I open the box and gasp silently at the contents, inside is my locket. I grab his hand from across the table. "Thank you for keeping it safe, Ben, as well as for thinking ahead by taking it. And thank you for keeping your promise and making sure that Jordan was safe."

He pats my hand. "You're welcome, Princess. It was my honor."

"I will never be able to thank you enough for saving Jordan. I truly thought I had lost him."

"I'm sorry that I was not able to inform you that he was still alive."

"I understand why you couldn't. I am just thankful that he is safe." I find Jordan in the crowd, laughing as a tall blonde girl says something to him. A sliver of jealousy races down my spine but I quickly quash it, after the words we exchanged earlier I know Jordan would never hurt me. I turn back to Ben.

"So, this is the Kamora?"

He nods as he stuffs a roll into this mouth. He smiles ruefully while I wait for him to elaborate. "I know we don't look like much in here but there are thousands of us throughout the city, in different levels of the King's guard."

"Was Alexia a part of the Kamora?"

Regret and sadness fill Ben's expression. "No, she was completely innocent. I feel awful about what happened to her. If I had known that she would have been in any danger I wouldn't have asked her to bring you your food."

"No, the fault is mine. I convinced her to help me escape. It's my fault that she is dead and I'm going to make sure that her family gets taken care of. She was sending them money."

Ben nods. "Yes, her family was very important to her. They are the only reason she took the job. She has five brothers and sisters. Her father was killed in an unfortunate accident with a horse and her mother is unable to walk. She and one of her sisters were the family's only providers."

"Do you know where they live?"

"No, but I'm sure I can find out."

I pull off the engagement ring that Xavier gave me and hand it to Ben. "Will you give this to them if you find them? I know it cannot replace her but at least it will help."

He smiles and slips the ring in his pocket. "I will do my best."

Jordan returns and places a tray of food in front of me, sliding down on the wooden bench next to me. He kisses my check. "Everything okay?"

I give him a reassuring smile and nod, which he accepts and turns to Ben.

"Hey, Ben, how are you doing today?" Jordan asks in between bites.

I pick at my food while the boys converse, not really in the mood to eat. I know I should; it's been a while since I've had a good meal, but I just can't bring myself to do it. Guilt over what happened to Alexia still eats at me and uncertainty about what to do next fills my mind. How am I going to be able to go up against Seraphine when she has a shadow army behind her? I have the Prakera yes, but I can barely control it. She's an all-powerful witch that seems to have an unlimited amount of power. How do I go up against that? I'm only one person.

"Buttercup?"

I snap myself out of my thoughts and focus on the concerned face of Jordan. "Yes?"

"There you are. I called you a couple of times. You okay?"

I give him another reassuring smile. "I'm sorry, just lost in thought. Where did Ben go?" I feel bad that I didn't see him leave.

"He said he had some things to take care of and he would catch up with us later. So, what has you so lost in thought? Anything I can help with? Also, you need to eat." He glances pointedly at my food.

I push the food around my plate and avoid his gaze. "I'm just not hungry."

"When was the last time you ate?" I shrug and Jordan sighs. "Maia, you need to eat, please."

I stuff a roll in my mouth just to please him but it tastes like dust.

"So, what's on your mind?" he asks again.

"A lot. I'm feeling guilty over what happened with Alexia. The poor girl was killed because of me. I convinced her to help me escape and Xavier killed her for it." Jordan grabs my hand reassuringly as frustrated tears cloud my vision. "And how am I supposed to defeat Seraphine? How am I supposed to go up against her when she has all this power? I'm only one person."

Jordan kisses my hand. "You are the Aurora. You were born to do this. I know things seem bleak right now but I have faith that we will figure all this out in the end."

"I wish I had your optimism."

"Hey, we can't all be awesome like me."

I laugh and swat at his shoulder. He smiles and my insides turn to mush, I don't think I'll ever get used to seeing that smile again. I will never take it for granted.

I take another bite of my roll before I embarrass us both. He strokes my hand idly with his thumb as he finishes off his own plate. Out of the corner of my eye I notice a table staring at us and I nod my head towards them. "Is this normal?"

Jordan notices the gawkers too and laughs. "Sorry, Buttercup, but you are kind of famous here. Everyone here knows about you. Since Melinda started this underground resistance they have been preparing for your powers to manifest. They have all heard the stories of the Aurora."

I groan. "Great. I hate being the center of attention."

He kisses away my blush. "I think you are going to have to get used to it." He eyes my still mostly untouched plate of food and raises an eyebrow. "So that's all you're going to eat?"

"I'm sorry, I'm just not hungry."

"Alright, fine. Promise me you will let me know if you get hungry later, okay?" When I promise, he grabs my tray and removes it from the table. He returns and reaches for my hand. "Want a tour of this place?"

I grab his hand and he leads me out of the mess hall, among the stares and whispers, which I do my best to ignore. The hallways we pass through are narrow and made of packed dirt. We pass several closed doors and a few people, but for the most part we are alone.

"This area we are in is the living area. The mess hall is here, as well as many of the sleeping quarters." Jordan explains.

I touch the walls of dirt. "How is this possible?"

"Believe it or not, your parents. Alera and Gaven, with their council, made this place. It was shortly before the war, when tensions were rising between Estera and Myridia. They wanted a safe place that was closer than the Mystic City for Mystics to go in the event war broke out. Your people hid here for some time until the Mystic City was properly protected."

"Melinda told you this?"

"Yes."

"I'm assuming my parents told her this was here, as well?"

"Yes, from what she says, she was the only person outside of the Mystics that knew this was here. So, it was an ideal location for the Kamora. She's been right under the King's nose and he's never had any idea."

"How long have they been here?"

"I will let her tell you the rest. It's not my story to tell."

I nod in understanding. Jordan continues our progress through the narrow halls. He points out a few empty cavernous rooms that he tells me are for trainings and meetings.

"How many people are here?"

"Depends on the time of day. People are always coming and going. They are implanted throughout the city, in different levels of power. I believe this place can hold about a thousand people comfortably if they don't mind sleeping on the floors. There are only a few dozen rooms; most people do not stay here long."

Some shouting up ahead grows louder as we near another cavernous room. There are perhaps twenty people standing around two fighters as they exchange blows. Cheers ring out as one of the fighters lands a hit to their opponent's midsection. I send Jordan a questioning glance, who shrugs as we approach the circle. My jaw almost hits the ground as I recognize the small figure in the middle of the circle. Melinda has her opponent in a headlock and is waiting patiently for the man to submit. He finally taps her arm and she releases him with a smile.

"Maybe next time, Oren."

Oren groans and wipes his face with a small towel that was tossed to him. "I don't know how you move that fast for someone…"

"My age?" Melinda finishes for him.

Oren eyes widen. "You know that's not what I meant."

Melinda laughs. "How about this, once you beat me in a match then you can mock my age. Until then, just try and keep up." She exits the ring and approaches Jordan and me, greeting us with a warm smile. "I see you two have finally vacated my room."

I feel the blush creep up my neck as I stammer out an apology. She waves off my words. "Trust me, nothing to apologize for. I should have informed your young man here that you had arrived right away, but I chose to wait. I am glad that the two of you are reunited."

"There are not enough words to thank you for saving him."

"You remind me so much of your mother." Melinda begins to walk out of the room, ignoring my thanks. "Walk with me?"

Jordan and I follow her into the hallway as another match begins behind us. "Do you often spar with the men?" I ask.

"Yes, I find that it gains me their respect and allows me to bond with them. Most of the people who have joined the Kamora are lost, abandoned, or broken. I give them a purpose and a home; I give them direction. We become a family. They know that I would die for them, just as I know they would die for me."

"How did you manage to amass so many people to your cause?" I ask.

Melinda doesn't answer right away as a little girl with blonde pigtails comes running up to her. She attaches herself to Melinda's leg, who laughs and attempts to dislodge the tiny human.

"Mitera, where were you? You missed our lesson, I was worried."

"I'm sorry to worry you, little one. I am safe. Does your mother know that you have left your room?"

The little girl puffs out her chest. "I'm brave, Mitera, like you."

Melinda gets down in front of the little girl. "I know you are brave, but that doesn't mean you get to run off without someone knowing where you are. Your mother could be worried."

The little girl looks uncertain. "I guess you're right."

"Have I ever steered you wrong before?"

The little girl bites her lip and glances at Jordan and me. "I guess not."

Melinda grabs her little hand. "Why don't I walk you back to your mother and I will stop by later for our lessons? Does that work for you, little one?"

Just then an exasperated woman rounds the corner and stops in front of us. "Morgan, what have I told you about wandering off?"

Little Morgan crosses her arms, defiantly. "I was worried about the Mitera, Momma. I needed to know she was okay."

The woman sighs. "Morgan, the Mitera is very busy. Why don't we go get something to eat? I hear there are sweets in the mess hall."

Morgan's face lights up and she takes off down the hall in the opposite direction. Her mother follows behind her with another exasperated look.

Melinda gets to her feet with a chuckle. "That little girl is a handful."

"She's adorable and seems to really admire you."

"Yes, that she does. Out of all the children here, for some reason she has attached to me the most."

"How many children are here?"

"Too many, if you ask me. Some are orphans, others were abandoned. We have tried to save as many as we can." She continues her trek down the hall. "Forgive me, dear, what was it that you asked me?"

"How did you manage to amass so many people to your cause?"

"When I left my people, this was the only place I knew of where I could hide out for a while. Your parents showed it to me when they had built it and offered it to my people if the need arose. I checked in on you a few times because I promised your parents I would if anything ever happened to them. From what I could tell you were happy and well taken care of. But you were not the person I was most concerned about.

On my journey to the capital city I found poverty and grief-stricken towns. The fifteen years that I had been banished in the forgotten lands were hard but it seemed life here was even harder. The kingdom that I had left behind was gone. Everything had changed. It was no longer the flourishing land from before the war. It appeared that Rolland had finally showed his true nature. So, I began slow; I started bringing in people I found on the streets. They were poor and had nothing; I gave them a home. Ben was actually one of the first I brought in. I found him in the streets, barely alive. He had been beaten by some palace guards for helping a young boy to steal food for his starving family."

"That's awful," I comment as we step around a group of children who all wave excitedly at Melinda. She waves back and they continue on their way.

"It was, but it is also why Ben is one of my most trusted soldiers. He is very committed to the cause and wants to see his home flourish once again. He and so many of the others I have found to help us are fighting for that dream. We all want mystics, humans, and witches to live in peace once more. We want Rolland's line of tyranny to end."

"Rolland is dead."

"Yes, but his son still lives and now it seems my daughter is planning to take control of the kingdom, which will send us further into darkness. Now that Seraphine has access to her witch powers she will be near impossible to stop. She is the first of her kind and she is the strongest of us all."

"First of her kind? Do you mean that she is half Mystic and half witch?"

Melinda glances back at me in surprise. "So, she told you?"

"More showed me than told me, but yeah."

"Interesting. She tends to keep that a secret. She is ashamed of it. She hates the Mystic part of her."

"She controls wind and what else?"

"Fire."

"Who is her father?"

Melinda doesn't answer at first and I begin to think she isn't going to until she stops and turns towards us, her face twisted in conflicting emotions. "Seraphine's father is dead. That's all you need to know about him."

"So, what is the plan now that we are here?"

"I have been in talks with the king of Estera. He wishes to help our cause but he has been reluctant to get involved. I am hoping that soon we will be able to come to an agreement."

Jordan clears his throat and some of the color drains from his face. "Estera, are you sure that is wise?"

I squeeze his hand and send him a questioning look but he is too focused on Melinda to notice.

"Yes, I have many soldiers here but they are not enough to form a proper army. Especially now that Seraphine has all of her power. We cannot defeat her with the Kamora, we need more men. King Erik can provide that."

"We have the Aurora, we don't need more men," Jordan argues.

I place my hand on his chest, directing his attention to me. "You didn't see her power, Jordan, I'm not strong enough to defeat her alone. I need help."

"Then we will look for the remaining Mystics. We have no reason to involve Estera."

"The remaining Mystics are in Estera." Melinda comments.

"What?" My tone is much sharper than I intended.

"King Erik informed me that the remaining Mystics had sought refuge in his kingdom. He is allowing them to stay for the time being, but in his last letter he encouraged us to finally come to him after we had extracted you from King Rolland."

"For what purpose?"

"He did not say. My thoughts are so that we can begin strategizing our plan of attack. With you here now, he may be finally taking our cause seriously."

"I highly doubt that," Jordan scoffs.

I look at Jordan quizzically, unsure of what exactly has gotten into him.

Melinda stops in front of the door to her room, completely unfazed by the moody baker. "It's getting late. Why don't you two get some rest and we can talk about this more in the morning."

Jordan pushes open a door and gestures me in. I slip past him into a quaint little room with barely enough space for the two beds that line the walls and the small table that sits between them. He lights a small lantern next to the bed.

"I hope you don't mind sharing a room. Like I said, there isn't a lot of space and honestly I never want to leave your side again." It could be just me but I swear I see him blush a little.

"This is perfect. I feel safer with you anyway." I follow Jordan as he drops down on one of the beds and snuggle up next to him. "What got into you in the hallway?"

"It was nothing."

"It didn't sound like nothing."

"I just don't think we should be trusting Estera so easily. I don't feel that they were completely blameless in the war."

I lace my fingers with his and throw my leg over his, trapping him in my embrace. "No one is completely blameless. Plus, the war was a long time ago and it seems like the King wants to help. There is no harm in at least traveling there and hearing him out."

He kisses the top of my head. "I suppose you are right."

"I still can't believe you are here, that you are alive. I thought I had lost you forever."

He rubs my back comfortingly. "I know, Buttercup. I hardly believe it too. I was a wreck when they brought me here and I knew that you were still in Xavier's clutches."

"I'm sorry that you have been involved in any of this. You don't deserve this."

"I would do it all over again if it meant me getting to this moment with you."

"I love you, Jordan."

"I love you too, always have and always will." He sighs heavily and his next words are reluctant. "There are some things that we need to talk about."

I let out a loud yawn and Jordan chuckles. "I'm sorry, can it wait until tomorrow? Now that I'm lying down I'm sleepy."

"Of course." He attempts to disentangle himself from me but I wrap my arms and legs around him tighter.

"Please, stay with me until I fall asleep," I murmur sleepily into his chest.

He kisses my head again. "As you wish, Buttercup. Now get some sleep."

Comforted by the strong arm encircling my waist and the steady heartbeat that assures me he's alive, it isn't long before I drift off to sleep.

Chapter 12

THE NEXT MORNING, WE meet Ben in the mess hall for breakfast. He greets us with a warm smile as we join him at the same table and Jordan ventures off to get us food. "Did you sleep well, Princess?" Ben asks.

"Please, Ben, call me Maia, and yes I did sleep well."

"Good, I know we do not have much here but it is enough for us." Ben frowns and reaches across the table to grab my hand. "I should have said this yesterday, but I'm sorry about your friend Myka."

Sadness fills me. "I know you had no other choice."

"He was going to kill me. It was either me or him. If I had any other choice I wouldn't have done it."

I pat his hand. "I know, and I appreciate that. I just don't know how I am going to tell his family."

"I will tell them, or at least be there when you do. They deserve to see the face of his killer."

"You are not a killer, Ben, we talked about this," Melinda states and sits down next to me with a stern look directed at Ben. "You did what you had to do. You would have died if you hadn't done what you did."

Ben doesn't look convinced but he replies with a, "Yes, Mitera," and then excuses himself from our table.

We watch him leave and Melinda sighs. "He will carry that guilt for a long time."

I nod and we slip into silence until Jordan returns with a tray of food for us. He nods to Melinda and says good morning.

"Did you both sleep alright?" she asks.

Jordan nods as he shoves food into his mouth. "Though my new roommate snores in her sleep," he comments as he smirks.

I smack him in the arm which just sends him into a fit of laughter.

"You two remind me so much of Alera and Gaven. He was always giving her a hard time and they were so in love, just like you two," Melinda comments fondly.

"You must miss them very much. I wish I could have had the chance to know them."

"Me too, my dear. Your parents were amazing people and were truly great leaders. They would be proud of the woman that you have become. They only wanted the best for you and your brother."

"Melinda, did King Erik tell you if my brother was among the surviving Mystics?"

"No, he did not say. He just informed me that he was housing the refugees and once I had secured your safety we were to come to him."

"So, when do we leave?"

"We haven't decided yet if we are going," Jordan states.

I turn to face him. "Um, yes we have. We are going."

"I don't think we should make any rash decisions," Jordan reasons.

"We aren't, there is nothing to think about. My people are in Estera, we have a potential ally in the King and a safe place to hide out away from Seraphine and Xavier. There is no reason not to go."

"I just think—"

"No. I am tired of people making decisions for me. I am making this one for myself. We are going and that is the end of it." I turn to Melinda, ignoring Jordan's sullen expression. "Now, when are we leaving?"

"I just have to make sure the people I am leaving in charge while I am gone understand their instructions. So maybe a day or two. I will send a messenger ahead of us to ensure that the King knows we are on our way."

"And who will be making the journey with us?"

"I think we should keep our party small. We are going to have to sneak out of the city, Seraphine cannot know where we are going. I think it would be best if it were the three of us and perhaps two of my soldiers."

"Okay. I will be ready when the time comes to leave. Is there a place that I can train?"

"Yes, you are welcome to any of the training rooms, just be careful using the earth element. We can't have you bringing the roof down." She laughs and pats me on the shoulder, rising to her feet. "I will leave you to the rest of your breakfast. I will let you know when my preparations are complete."

"Thank you, Melinda."

"I'm not Xavier, you know."

I cringe at the hurt tone in Jordan's voice. I give him my full attention and grab his hand.

"I know you are not Xavier."

"Do you? 'Cause the way you just talked to me says differently. I'm not trying to make decisions for you, Maia, I just want you to make sure that you have considered all the options. That's more than Xavier ever did for you."

"I'm sorry. I guess I'm so used to the way that Xavier treated me that I think that everyone treats me that way."

Jordan moves fast and pulls my face to his. He kisses me passionately and hard, it is possessive and demanding but feels nothing like Xavier's did. Instead of feeling consumed by his kiss I feel cherished and protected. A whistle off to our side makes us break apart and I feel the blush creeping up my neck, so I start to pull away. Jordan is not done though, and pulls me back, leaning his forehead against mine, his beautiful blue eyes consuming me.

"I will never treat you like he did. You will never be treated like that again by anyone, I guarantee it. You deserve to be revered and loved. For the rest of my days I will prove that to you. You are my everything and I will support you in everything you do. You are a strong, independent person and I will never take that away from you."

Tears prick my eyes but I blink them away. "I don't deserve you, or your love."

He kisses my nose. "Just take the compliment, Buttercup." He rises to his feet. "I believe you said something about training? Why don't we go and do that?"

I shove one last bite in my mouth and we carry our trays to the trash through the staring crowd. When we exit the mess hall, I sigh. "Do you think they will ever stop staring at me?"

"You are the Aurora, the most powerful Mystic, people are going to look up to you. Plus, right now you have an adorable little blush going on from my awesome kiss."

I shake my head at him and laugh. He responds with the sweetest smile and I can't help but kiss it, which I do.

"I thought we were going to training," He says against my lips, amusement coloring his tone.

"Couldn't help myself." I feel my blush getting deeper as I grab his hand and start walking towards the many training rooms we saw. The first one we come upon is, thankfully, empty and we enter it.

"So, what would you like to train?" Jordan asks.

"I need to test my elements. Right after Seraphine tried to give my powers to Rolland I tried to use wind and it didn't work, but I was able to use earth. I want to make sure that all my powers are okay. I also want to see if I can manifest the Prakera without having to be in distress."

"The Prakera? Is that the power you used to save me?"

"Yes, according to Seraphine it hasn't been seen since the ancient times. It's not the fifth element that normally appears."

"So, what is it?"

I touch my hand to the ground and slowly bring up a small wall of dirt, conscious of the earthy structure. It comes up with ease and with barely any effort on my part. Satisfied, I answer Jordan's question, "It's pure energy."

Jordan looks impressed. "Wow, that could do a lot of damage."

"Yep, hence Seraphine wants it. She would be unstoppable if she had the Prakera." I concentrate on a lantern that illuminates the room, hanging on one of the walls. I pull the flame to me and send it circling around us. It flows easily through the air and then returns safely to the lantern.

"Two for two. Going well so far." I place my hand on the earth again and concentrate on the particles of water that reside within. I extract the water from the soil and I send it splashing at Jordan. He ducks at the last second, narrowly avoiding a puddle to the face. I laugh at his sour expression but it isn't long before his face breaks into a smile as well.

I stretch out my arm to pull him towards me with wind and nothing happens. I try again and Jordan remains in the same spot. Dread fills my stomach. What happened in the palace wasn't just a fluke, my wind element is gone.

"Jordan, it's gone. My wind element is gone." I try to pull him towards me again but he comes to my side by the power of his own legs. "I tried to use it when we were escaping but nothing happened. I thought maybe it was a fluke, that it just needed time to reboot. I don't feel anything, it's gone."

"Okay, don't panic. I'm sure there is a logical explanation for this. It was your strongest element, maybe it takes longer to come back to you."

I shake my head frantically. "No, I don't feel it at all, Jordan. It's gone. They took it from me."

I feel my body warm up and Jordan backs up as my hands start to glow. Panic and dread are swirling around in my gut.

Jordan puts out a calming hand, just out of my reach. "Buttercup, take a few deep breaths. You are starting to glow."

"I'm going to kill her, Jordan."

"Look at me, Maia." His soothing voice draws my eyes to him and instantly I feel the warmth slowly recede. He takes my face in his hands, confident that whatever is left of the glow will not hurt him. "It's going to be alright. You are powerful enough without the wind element. You don't need it."

"Like you said, it was my strongest. It was the most useful, the first I ever manifested. It was as easy as breathing."

"I know, Buttercup, I know. But it's going to be alright. I promise, you don't need it."

"I don't understand why it's gone."

"You said that they had already started the process before Xavier and Ben interrupted, right?" I nod and he continues, "Then it probably was in Rolland's body when he died. It was your first element, it must have been the first to go."

I clench my fist in anger and pull away, pacing the floor. He watches me patiently, allowing me my space. Anger swirls inside me but I am in control. I can feel the Prakera just under the surface, waiting to be released, fueled by my emotions. I need to let it out, I need something to release my tumultuous feelings.

As if reading my thoughts, Jordan drags over a large target and places it several meters away from me. I send an energy blast at its center and it disintegrates the entire target. Jordan eyes the pile of dust it left behind with wide eyes but says nothing as he drags over a new target. We continue this until there is one target left and Jordan stops me.

"Okay, so you have proven that you are powerful. You've taken out ten targets easily. But can you aim?" he asks.

"I'll try."

Jordan throws the target away from him and I admit I am momentarily distracted by the bulging of his shoulder muscles and completely miss the target. It crashes loudly against the far wall and Jordan eyes me knowingly, but says nothing as my cheeks flame. He sets up the target again and throws it, but this time I purposely don't look his way. I send an energy blast at the target, confident that I will hit it this time, but I don't. The target crashes against the wall again. I scowl at the offending target like it is its fault I missed.

Jordan picks up the target and instructs me to try again. After what seems like hours, I finally hit the target and it joins the others in a pile of dust. I drop to the ground in exhaustion and stare up at the ceiling. Jordan smiling face enters my vision.

"You ok?"

"I'm tired. That took a lot out of me."

Jordan joins me on the ground and intertwines his fingers into mine. "It certainly taught us something."

"What's that?"

"That you can't aim."

I elbow him in the ribs and he grunts between his poorly restrained laughter. He's still smiling as he rubs his sore ribs absently. "But in all seriousness, it did teach us that it's more powerful than your other elements. It drains you faster, so I think you should use it sparingly."

"Maybe I just need to use it more so my body adjusts. When I first started using the elements they exhausted me but now I can use them and be completely fine."

"True, but this seems different to me. With the elements you are just moving what is around you, you don't actually create it. But the Prakera, it seems like it is coming from inside you. You are creating that pure energy and I'm afraid of what will happen if you use too much."

I squeeze his hand, reassuringly. "I promise to be careful."

"Want to call it quits for the day? We can pick back up tomorrow morning."

My stomach growls before he even finishes his sentence and we both laugh. He gets to his feet and reaches his hand down to help me up. "Come on, let's get some food in you."

"Amazing shot, Buttercup!"

My chest swells with pride at Jordan's words. We woke up early this morning, grabbed a quick breakfast and have been in the training room ever since. Thankfully, he was able to acquire us some more targets, which I have finally been able to hit on a consistent basis.

"Now that you can aim, I want to try something else."

"Can't I just enjoy this victory before having to move on to something else?" I ask, taking a quick gulp of water.

He playfully plucks my cup of water out of my hand and drains it with a wink. "Sorry, love, no time."

I sigh dramatically. "Fine, what do you want to try?"

"I'm curious about your control. You are very good at destroying things completely." He nods towards the growing pile of dust. "But what about controlling it so that you don't destroy what you're aiming at. I can't imagine you throwing an energy blast at a person and watching them disintegrate. If you are able to maybe focus the energy, then you could use it to injure someone instead of kill them. And it could also help you use less, which means your energy drains slower."

I nod. "Makes sense. Definitely worth trying."

He sets up a target again, this time immobile. He smartly backs away from it and gives it a wide berth. I concentrate on the center of the target, paying close attention to the Prakera that lies dangerously close to the surface. I draw a small amount to my hand and form an energy ball in my palm. It flies to the target and disintegrates it.

"Well, that didn't work," I grumble.

"You can't expect to be perfect the first time. Try again." His tone is infinitely patient as he sets up a new target.

I try for a smaller energy ball this time, no bigger than my finger nail. A bead of sweat rolls down my brow, my concentration completely focused on keeping my small ball of energy contained. I send it soaring towards the target and it hits the far corner but it doesn't completely destroy it.

Jordan nears the target and eyes the damaged corner. He smiles over at me, proudly. "Your aim's a little off, but you did it. You didn't destroy the entire thing."

I wipe the sweat off my brow. "Yea, but the amount of time and energy it took to concentrate on a small ball would be the same if I sent off multiple large ones."

"It will get easier. I have faith in you and I know you don't want to destroy everything you throw an energy blast at."

"Fair enough."

He instructs me to try again and I do. This time it is just a bit easier and faster, but I definitely feel the difference. I hit the target again successfully around the same place as my last toss. I'm just about to celebrate when a cry sounds from the hallway. Jordan and I rush out to investigate and find Melinda on the ground. We both rush to her side; her eyes are closed and she is lying immobile on the ground.

"Melinda?" I rest a hand on her forehead. "She's burning up. What do you think happened?"

Jordan looks just as perplexed as I do and jumps in alarm when Melinda suddenly sits up from her place on the ground. She drops her head in her hands and takes several deep breaths.

"Melinda?" I tentatively lay a hand on her shoulder.

She takes another breath and then lies her hand on mine. "I'm fine, dear, I didn't mean to worry you."

"What happened? We heard a scream and then we found you on the ground."

"A complication."

Unease fills my gut and one look at Jordan reveals that he is feeling the same. "What type of complication?"

"My powers returned."

"That's great!" I feel some of my unease lessening until Melinda starts shaking her head and her next words send my unease soaring.

"This means that Seraphine gained access to the ancient artifact and activated it. She gave all witches back their powers, which means all her followers that she left back in the Forgotten Lands will be coming here to join her. She'll have an army."

Chapter 13

"I DON'T UNDERSTAND HOW the ancient artifact works," I ask Melinda as she throws clothing into a pack. After the return of her powers, she informed us that we would be leaving tonight under the cover of darkness. Now I'm helping her pack while Jordan and Ben gather food and supplies for our journey.

"The ancient artifact is the connection to our power. When Seraphine activated it, it reopened the link to our powers. Most of the witches will not have much knowledge of their powers, but they will learn quickly. We will be lucky, though, that none will be as powerful as Seraphine. No one studied the books like she did."

I hand her a shirt that is lying on her bed. "But how was Rolland able to cut all of you off from your powers, and how was Seraphine able to get hers back while they rest of you didn't?"

"One thing you must learn about this world, dear, is that where there is power, there is a way to take away that power. The Red Stars are your weakness, the blood of a dragua is ours."

"What is a dragua?"

"Thankfully not a creature that you will see anytime soon. Its blood can be deadly to witches. In small doses it cuts us off from our powers but in large doses it can kill us. The dragua were almost killed off several hundred years ago by our ancestors in order to protect ourselves. As far as I know, only a few still remain. It was how Rolland was able to defeat us so easily when he invaded our homes. His soldiers were armed with dragua blood."

I touch her arm in quiet sympathy and she nods her thanks, returning to her packing. "How is it that Rolland knew about the dragua blood but not the Red Stars."

Melinda gives me a bitter smile. "I guess the Mystics are better at keeping their secrets."

"So, the dragua blood is how he blocked the power from the ancient artifact?"

"I believe so. I can't know for sure, of course, because I have not seen it since that day. But it is the only explanation I have. He must have covered the artifact in dragua blood and when Seraphine came to him, allowed her to remove some of it and touch it, giving her back her powers. By removing the blood, she gave us all back our powers. The rest of her followers will be here soon and that is why we must leave now. This place is no longer safe for us and we must put as much distance between us and them as we can."

"What about the rest of the Kamora? We can't leave them behind."

"The base is being evacuated. The Kamora will disperse and make their way to Estera in small groups. The woman and children will be evacuated first and then the soldiers will follow."

"Then we must stay and assist with the evacuation."

"No."

"But—"

"You have the stubbornness of your mother," Melinda grumbles.

"You can't abandon them."

Melinda turns to me and I finally notice that her eyes are brimmed with tears. "You think I want to leave them, that I want to risk their safety? One day you will understand that as a leader you must make hard choices, and this is a choice I have to make. If we want any hope of defeating Seraphine I need to keep you safe. You are the only one with the power to defeat her. So, I am getting you out of here tonight and we are going to Estera. The rest will follow. Now go finish packing."

She turns her back to me and I realize I have been effectively dismissed. I frown at her back but she says nothing else and I leave the small room. Jordan is waiting for me outside.

"I thought you were gathering food and supplies with Ben?" I ask as he matches my stride.

"I was, and we're done. All ready to go. Plus, Ben wanted to spend some time with his lady friend before we left."

"Lady friend?" I laugh when he waggles his eyebrows. "Am I your lady friend?"

He grabs me around the waist, stopping my progress and pulls me against him. He kisses me like no one could come across us at any minute. He ends the kiss with two feather kisses to the corners of my mouth. "Buttercup, you are more than my lady friend. You are the woman I'm going to marry someday."

Momentarily I forget to breathe and he chuckles, kissing me again, which does nothing for my breathing. I put some distance between our mouths and pull in a lungful of air.

"Is this you asking me?"

"No, when I ask you for real, you'll know. I'm just making sure you know my intention."

"Well, thanks for making that clear." I kiss his cheek and smile at him over my shoulder as I continue down the hall. He follows with a smirk of his own.

We enter our quaint little room and I start gathering what little belongings that we have. I toss our blankets into a bag and a few changes of clothes. A knock on the door draws Jordan's attention and he greets Oren, the boy who was fighting with Melinda before, who hands him a stack of black clothing. Jordan nods as Oren gives him a few instructions and then closes the door. He hands me some of the clothes.

"Oren provided us with some dark clothing. He said it will be helpful when we are sneaking through the streets tonight." He hands me a long-sleeved black shirt and long black pants. I slip them on quickly and the material fits snuggly but not uncomfortably.

"You should wear black more often." Jordan's gaze is smoldering as he looks me up and down.

His gaze warms my insides and I legitimately giggle, not sure what exactly has gotten into me. He really knows how to get under my skin. I watch him rummage through his own bag, taking things out or adding as he goes along. I stare at him for probably more than necessary, my heart filled with love for the baker in front of me. How I was so blind for so long is beyond me. How I ever thought what I felt with Xavier was love is also a mystery. The love that Jordan and I feel for one another is pure and special, and he's right—we will marry one day. I don't want to be with anyone else. When this is all over, I want to be with him.

"Are you done packing?" His deep voice breaks into my consciousness.

"Huh?" I question, completely and blissfully lost in my own thoughts.

"Are you done packing?" he repeats. "Because you have been staring at me for a good five minutes and as much as that helps my ego, we're short on time."

My cheeks flame at being caught in my daze. "I wasn't staring; I was lost in thought."

He wraps his arms around my waist and I tuck my head under his chin. We fit together so perfectly. He is at least a head taller than me and his arms, that have seen years in the kitchens, engulf me in a safe cocoon. Here, with him, in his arms, is one of the safest places for me.

"Anything I can help with?" he asks, concern evident in his tone. He rests his cheek on my head and squeezes me for good measure.

"No, I'm alright, I promise." I answer, but it is pretty muffled by my cheek being mushed against his chest. He seems to get the idea though because he kisses my head and then releases me with a pat on the butt.

"Well then get to it, Buttercup. Can't have you standing around looking pretty all day."

I return to my packing but the smile on my face never leaves. Even in this time of crisis and turmoil, I know that I can depend on him to keep me smiling.

Our small travel group gathers in the hallway near the entrance of the underground safe house. There are five of us in total so far, as we wait for Melinda to arrive—myself, Jordan, Ben, and two soldiers I have never met. One is short and stocky, carrying a pretty deadly looking axe. While the other is long and lanky, with at least a dozen weapons strapped to his long appendages. They look funny standing next to each other, such complete opposites but they don't seem to notice.

"This is Enyo," Ben motions to the short soldier, "and that is Fin," he says pointing to the taller man.

"Nice to meet you both," I reply and Jordan nods his greeting.

Enyo grunts in acknowledgment of my greeting and as Fin laughs I catch a glimpse of several missing teeth. He sticks out his hand to shake mine. "Don't mind him, he's just a little grumpy. He hates traveling at night. Don't let him fool you either, he's a softy at heart."

"Fin and Enyo are some of the best soldiers we have. We thought it best that they accompany us to Estera in case we run into anything along the way, as well as to ensure your safety while in Estera," Ben explains.

"Are we expecting a lot of issues on the journey or while in Estera?" I ask with an eyebrow raise.

"On the way there, probably not. Once we are out of the city, it should be an easy journey. Seraphine does not know that we plan to head there so that definitely is in our favor. It's in Estera that I have the most concern."

"Why?"

"Honestly, I don't trust the King," Ben states plainly. The corners of Jordan's lip go up in smug smile, satisfied that he is not the only one that feels that way.

"What is it that you don't trust?" I ask, not bothering to address Jordan's smirk.

Ben eyes the end of the hallway, looking for Melinda. "I trust the Mitera's judgment, but he could have helped us at any time. The Kamora has been making a difference for a few years now. We have infiltrated the King's guard and implanted ourselves in important positions in a very short time. He could easily have joined with us before now and made a difference in this kingdom. But, now that we have the Aurora with us, he's suddenly interested. I just don't trust his intentions. My gut is telling me to be prepared and that's why I picked Enyo and Fin to accompany us. They are the best and will act as your personal guard."

"You do realize I don't need a personal guard? As you said, I am the Aurora."

"I know, Princess, but it will make me sleep better at night."

"Alright," I acquiesce. "I will be on my guard as well. Thank you for being honest with me about your concerns about dealing with Estera. I will keep them in mind."

Ben nods but says nothing as Melinda finally joins our group.

"Sorry for my lateness. I was leaving some last-minute instructions," she states. She is dressed similarly to the rest of us, in all black, with a bag strapped to her shoulders. We are traveling light so that we can travel fast.

"According to our spies inside the palace, Seraphine and Xavier are attending a meeting with the former King's council, which is why we are leaving tonight. Seraphine is working on getting them over to her side now that the King is gone. She wants to name herself Queen. The general public still does not know that the King is dead," Ben explains.

"You still have spies within the palace?" Jordan asks.

Ben nods. "Yes, there are many, but they are well hidden. It will be very hard for Seraphine to root out all of them."

"Did they say how Xavier is?" I ask in a small voice, equally afraid and hopeful of the answer. I feel Jordan's gaze on my face but I don't look his away. I am too scared of what I will see in his expression, be it accusation or pity.

I do get a very blatant look of pity from Ben though, but he at least answers me. "The reports say he spends most of his time in his room, which has been mostly destroyed."

"Destroyed?"

"He has destroyed it. That and your room. When he is seen out of his room, with Seraphine usually, his fury is clearly evident. Most of the servants and guards steer clear of him. But one thing is sure, his single purpose and goal is to get you back. It appears that you leaving sent him into an ever-deeper well of insanity and obsession."

"He wants what he can't have," Jordan comments.

Ben nods. "Exactly."

"I don't understand why he is working with Seraphine. Why he would allow her to take his crown from him." I say, almost to myself.

Jordan grabs my hand and this time I do see the sympathy in his eyes. "Don't waste time trying to figure out the reasoning of a madman."

Before I can reply, Melinda steps to the middle of the group, drawing all of our attentions. "I'm sorry, but we need to go. This conversation will have to wait until we are out of the city. The council meeting will be starting soon, we must move." Melinda addresses me, "Maia, do not use your powers unless absolutely necessary. We don't want Seraphine alerted that we have left the city and you using your powers will draw her attention. The guards will handle any concerns we come across."

"I understand, only when necessary."

"Good. Everyone stay close to the walls, stay out of sight, and keep quiet."

Ben and Fin lead the way out the door, and I'm followed by Jordan and Melinda. Enyo with his giant axe brings up the rear. Jordan gives my hand a quick squeeze in reassurance and then releases it, filling both his hands with short daggers. I notice that he also has a bow and arrows strapped on his back under his bag. The sight of them reminds me of my near death experience with the rhifter on our journey to the Mystic City. I really hope we don't meet another one of those on the way to Estera.

The streets of the capital city are empty; most of the people probably asleep in their beds. Ben halts our progress on one intersection to let a loud group of men by who are clearly enjoying their evening. They pass without incident and we continue our journey. Tension ripples off of all of us. If Seraphine were to discover us, we would have no chance against her shadow army. I am not ready t]o face her; I need more time, more training. Ben halts suddenly and our group skids to a stop. I barely brake in time and almost barrel into Jordan's back. Ben's body stiffens and he sucks in a quiet breath. He motions Melinda up to the front of the line and she has the same reaction. I send her a questioning gaze and she puts a finger to her lips, signaling my silence. She motions the group to follow her and we do so quietly through a few different alleys. She slips into a plain-looking door and we all file into a small area that looks like a storage room. Ben stands guard at the door, leaning against it for extra effect.

"We should be safe here for now," Melinda whispers.

"What did you see, Mitera?" Fin asks, calm and respectful of his leader.

"It appears that Seraphine was right and I should have read the ancient books as she did. This is magic I do not know." Melinda sounds so unsure of herself that it makes me feel uneasy.

"What did you see?" I repeat Fin's question.

Melinda does not answer so Ben does. "Her shadow creatures, but they were different. They were not the creatures that we saw before. These looked like men." Ben pauses and looks down at the ground, clearly unsettled. "They looked like our men."

"What?" I say a lot louder than I should and it earns me a hand clamped over my mouth. I send Jordan an annoyed look but he returns it with a stern one of his own. When his hand is gone I ask, "How is that possible?"

"I don't know. The only thing I can think of is that her creatures possessed the bodies of the dead men we left behind. But I've never heard of such a thing and I always thought the shadow creatures had to stay near their master." Melinda's eyes search the floor as if it holds the answers to her questions.

The three soldiers seem unsettled by their leader's unease and the fact that their comrades may be possessed by some shadow creature. I glance at Jordan but he offers no assistance, clearly as unsure as I am. The only thing I know is that we have to get out of this city and we have to go now.

Taking charge of the situation, I draw the attention of our little group. "Look, I know this is unsettling and I know that it may seem like the odds are against us, but it changes nothing. We still must get out of the city and we still must get to Estera. So, I know it's hard but we have to put our fear behind us and move forward. We will face this crisis once we are safely out of here."

Melinda eyes me in shock before her face splits into a proud smile. "The Princess is right. We must move forward. But we need a new plan. With those things patrolling the city it may be harder to move with six people. I think we need to split up into groups of three."

"Are you sure that is wise, Mitera?" Ben questions.

"Yes, we will rendezvous at the ruins that are about five miles outside the city limits. You remember where they are?" Ben nods and Melinda continues, "Good, you go with Maia and Jordan and I will stay with Enyo and Fin. We will meet at the ruins by dawn. If a group doesn't show up by then, then we continue on without them."

"If we run into one of these things, how do we kill them?" Fin asks.

"We can't run into them. If we do, Seraphine will be alerted. They are linked to her. We must avoid them at all costs. Do not let them see you," Melinda explains.

"But what if they cannot be avoided?" Fin inquires again.

"The Prakera is the only thing that can destroy them completely. Fire keeps them at bay and will hurt them, but they are quick to recover."

"I want to go with the blonde," Enyo grumbles but we all ignore him.

Melinda starts for the door but turns back, catching Ben's eye. "Remember, leave by dawn if we are not there. That is an order, the Aurora is priority."

"I understand, Mitera."

"Good." With her final words she slips out the door with the two guards in tow and I can't help the feeling of dread that engulfs me.

Ben turns to us, his face blank, hiding whatever feelings that may be troubling him. "You two ready?"

We both nod and he nods back in acknowledgement. He commands us to follow his lead and we creep out in the same direction as the Mitera's group. It could just be me, but the night now feels darker and more ominous. It is eerily quiet; the only sound I hear is the racing of my own heart. Those creatures lurk in the night and I can taste my fear on each breath.

Ben leads our trio with Jordan taking up the rear. I am safely sandwiched between them. It isn't lost on me that I am the only person who can defeat these things, yet they still feel the need to protect me. It simultaneously annoys me and warms my heart. Ben winds us through different alleyways, clearly familiar with the many passages of the capital city.

Ben rounds a corner and stops short, backing up quickly. I run into his back but he stays upright.

"What is it?" I whisper.

"Two of the creatures." He raises an eyebrow. "On horseback."

I shoot him a disbelieving look as I scoot around him and attempt to look around the corner. My eyes widen in alarm and realization that Ben is definitely not exaggerating. At the end of the next alley are two of the creatures atop brown mares.

The creatures' backs are to us so I am allowed a few seconds to take in their ghostly appearance. They are shrouded in darkness, every part of them inky black and void of light. Their bodies are the shape of men, just as Ben reported, but their posture is stiff and controlled. One of the creatures turns its face and I'm able to see it more clearly. My heart sinks and my breath catches in my throat. It's Myka, but it's not him. The face that I knew so well is the same but his once pale skin is now the inky black like the rest of him. His lips pull back in a sneer and even from a distance I can see the rows of sharp teeth that now line his jaw.

He lifts his face to the sky, as if he is sniffing something and then his face whips to mine. His glowing red eyes bear into mine until he lets out an inhuman scream. It sends goosebumps down my arms and I turn to my companions, urging them to run. They obey immediately, Ben taking the lead once again. The sounds of scratching and the cries of the shadow creatures urges us to quicken our steps. With silence no longer needed, Ben barrels through stores and through market stands while Jordan works on blocking alleyways and hopefully slowing down our pursuers.

The inhuman scream rips through the night and my sense of dread increases. The creatures are hunting and we are the prey.

A crash behind us makes me jump and I chance a glance behind our group and immediately wish I hadn't. A half-dozen creatures are in pursuit and they are fighting each other to get to us. I can feel the Prakera under my skin, ready for me to use, but Jordan grabs my wrist and shakes his head, like he can read my mind. I nod in understanding but I keep the feeling of the Prakera close.

Ben takes a sharp left and then another quick right and skids to a stop, ripping open a metal grate on the ground. He instructs us to get in and we quickly obey, crawling on our hands and knees into a dark tunnel. The space is tight and I feel my breath coming in short, sharp spurts. Jordan's hand on my ankle has a calming effect and I continue my crawl in the dark. I can hear the distant sounds of the creatures and it urges me to crawl faster, even though I can feel the skin on my knees fraying. My hand touches something slimy and I grit my teeth against the cry that wants to come out.

Up ahead I see a small amount of light and scramble faster, eager to reach it. The sound of the metal grate scraping against the ground makes me jump and the eerie scream of the creature filters into the tunnel. The light grows brighter and the sound of flowing water meets my ear. The tunnel ends and I drop down onto a thin walkway, next to a river of dirty water. I cover my face in disgust as Ben and Jordan drop down next to me.

"We have to hurry, one got into the tunnel behind us. It seems they are tracking us by our scent." Ben whispers and his expression turns contrite. "I'm sorry, Princess, but you're going to have to get in the water."

"What?" I grind out, eyeing the water in distaste.

"It will give us a place to hide now. It will also mask our smell and will give us a chance to get away. This is the sewer system that sends all the waste away from the city." The scratching and cries in the tunnel are growing closer and I eye the tunnel with wide eyes.

Jordan grabs my hand. "Come on, Buttercup, together." He slips into the churning water slowly and reaches his hand out to me. I grab it and he pulls us in deeper and it isn't long before we are treading water.

Ben is next to us and his face shows he's just as unhappy as I am about our situation. "Stay under until I signal the all-clear. Hopefully it will pass quickly."

We both nod, slipping under the water. Jordan grabs my face and pulls our lips together, keeping us connected through the entire ordeal. I don't dare open my eyes or attempt to move; Jordan's weight keeps us below the water's surface, his arms and his lips the only thing I am focusing on. The cries of the creature are muffled and distant, and I pull Jordan a little closer. My lungs are beginning to burn but I don't dare go to the surface. Spots fill my vision and I'm just about to take a lung full of water when Ben's hands land on our shoulders, pulling us up.

We both take in large amounts of air and the spots in my vision begin to recede. The three of us pull ourselves out of the water and sit on the edge, our feet still hanging in the murky depths.

"We can't stay here for long. It will be back," Ben whispers when he recovers.

"Where did it go?" I ask.

He points in the direction of the flowing water. "It followed the water south, thankfully. But I have a feeling it will figure out we didn't go that way and may double back. But at least it can't track us now by smell."

Ben's statement couldn't be more true. Our trio is now covered in dirt and too many other things I don't dare to think about. Ben helps us to our feet and we walk single file along the narrow walkway that lines the water. The terrible stench that was once overwhelming has now at least become bearable but I can feel whatever is on me getting dry and crusty and it grosses me out. There are lighted lanterns every couple of meters, so it is pretty dark and we use the wall as a guide.

"How do you know where to go?" I whisper to Ben.

"I used to hide down here when I was a boy, before I joined the Kamora. The guards were never too keen to look here for thieves. It was a safe place for me to regroup," he explains quietly.

The tunnel dead-ends and Ben instructs us to climb up a ladder in front of us. Jordan goes first and assures that the coast is clear before Ben and I follow. We exit the vile sewer and I take in a breath of fresh air. The cries of the creatures can still be heard in the distance but they seem far away and I can only hope that they are not in pursuit of our companions.

"Where are we now?" I ask.

"Almost to the city limits. I don't know why I didn't think of the sewer earlier, it would probably have saved us a lot of trouble." His voice is laced with regret.

I lay a comforting hand on his filthy shoulder. "It's okay, Ben. We made it now, let's just make it to the ruins."

He nods and then sets off in the direction of the ruins, with Jordan and I following closely behind.

Chapter 14

"I T'S ALMOST DAWN." BEN says from his perch on the crumbled building. The sky is slowly brightening and is painting the horizon a hazy red and orange, making the way to a beautiful dawn.

"They will be here. We just need to give them more time." I watch the desolate landscape that surrounds the city ruins. I never knew of this place and it seems as though no one has been here in quite some time. When we arrived several hours ago we set up camp in one of the many abandoned buildings. We didn't dare light a fire for warmth. Jordan made quick work of unpacking all our bags, salvaging what he could and tossing away what was ruined by the sewage water. Now all of our belongings lie scattered across our camp, drying out.

I had asked what the ruins used to be and Ben had frowned, not immediately answering my question.

"Did they never let you leave the palace growing up or teach you about the outside world?" he had asked.

"No."

"I'm sorry, Princess, that there is so much you don't know." His eyes are sad and full of pity, until they swing to the ruins. "This was the home to the witches before Rolland took everything from them. Welcome to Odeca."

"We cannot wait for them much longer. My orders are to leave at dawn." Ben's voice breaks me out of my thoughts. "You are the priority."

"We never should have split up."

"I agree, but it is not my place to disagree with the Mitera."

I take a seat next to him, keeping an eye on Jordan, who is fitfully sleeping not too far away. "You seem very close to her."

"She saved me. She saved a lot of us. The Kamora would be nothing without her, and a lot of us would be dead. She gave us a purpose and a plan, she gave us meaning." Ben fiddles with a chain around his neck, completely bare but for a small ring.

"Is that for your lady friend?" I nod towards the ring.

Ben laughs. "I see Jordan gave away my secret. Yes, I plan to ask her to marry me once this is all over and I can provide her with a real home."

"I'm sure if she feels the same about you as you do for her, it won't matter where the home is."

"I know, but she deserves a proper home, not the dirt walls and crowded spaces of the home base."

"What is her name?"

"I call her Hope. We found her a few years ago, wandering the streets of the capital city. She had no recollection of who she was or where she came from, and still doesn't. I knew I loved her from the moment I met her and it gave me hope for the future, so I started calling her that and it stuck."

"That's beautiful."

Ben shrugs and eyes the horizon with melancholy. He is quiet for some time until he says, "I don't want to leave her either, Maia, but her orders were clear."

I nod reluctantly. "You keep watch. Jordan and I will pack our bags."

I jump down from our perch and walk over to Jordan's sleeping figure. I crouch down next to him and touch his shoulder to rouse him. His eyes flutter open and I'm once again taken aback by the beauty of his blue eyes. Said eyes that are beginning to focus on me now, staring at him like a fool.

"It's almost dawn. Ben wants to leave," I blurt out, trying to cover up my embarrassing ogle.

Jordan sits up and stretches and my eyes follow his shirt line as it rises up, exposing his six-pack abs underneath. Being a baker sure did not hurt his physique; it only seemed to help it. I swallow and draw my eyes up to his face, where his smoldering blue eyes pierce mine. My face flames but he just smiles, completely aware of what he is doing.

"You were saying, Buttercup?"

"Ben wants to leave, we should start packing what we can into our bags."

He gets to his feet and we take in everything that we have lying out. He picks up a white shirt, now dyed brown, and wrinkles his nose. "Well, most everything is salvageable, just can't guarantee we won't all smell."

"Too late for that. What I would do for a warm bath."

"We'll make it a priority as soon as we get to Estera."

I laugh. "I have a feeling the King will want to meet with us right away."

He shakes his head. "Nope, my girl needs a bath. Priorities."

I kiss him, careful to only get his lips and not the disgusting mystery gunk on his face. I really hope we at least find a stream or a river on our way so that we can wash off.

"You two ready?" Ben appears next to us, looking very conflicted and I can completely understand why.

"No sign of them?" I ask, shouldering one of the bags.

"No, and we can't wait any longer. She'd kill me if she knew I waited as long as this," He replies, accepting the last bag from Jordan. He tests its weight. "This is incredibly light."

Jordan gestures to the discarded items on the ground. "Because of our stint in the sewer I had to discard a lot. Mostly the food and a few clothing items that were beyond saving. We're going to have to hunt for some food if we want to make it to Estera without starving."

"How long of a journey is it, again?" I ask, really not looking forward to another long journey.

"No more than a week, depending on how many stops we have to make."

"Good, at least it isn't as long as our journey was to the Mystic City," I comment and Jordan nods in agreement.

"What was it like?" Ben asks as we start heading north.

"The Mystic City? It was beautiful, everything that the Mystics ever needed was taken care of. Melinda made sure that they were safe and provided for. I'll never thank her enough for ensuring their safety."

"She takes care of those she loves for sure." He replies sadly, glancing back behind us.

I touch his arm, sympathetically. "She's alright, Ben. They probably had to lie low for a while." He nods and gestures for me to continue. "The city was run by magic, the streets glowed when it was day and dimmed at night. The water never ran out and food was provided by the nature that surrounded the city. It was truly a remarkable place."

"I heard it was protected by some pretty gruesome creatures."

I see Jordan shudder from the corner of my eye, probably remembering his near-death experience with the arachpids. The day I almost lost him and when I finally came to terms with my feelings for him.

"Yes, the arachpids. They guarded the entrance to the city but when Rolland attacked it, he allowed them in. They aided in the destruction of it."

We slip into a companionable silence and I take the opportunity to look around at our surroundings. The town of Odeca was decently sized, not too small and not too large. We should be out of the ruins soon. Most of the buildings are crumpling and charred, as if they were burned. When Rolland set out to punish the witches, he did so with no mercy. I can't fault Seraphine for her anger and desire for vengeance. I just wish that vengeance wasn't directed at the wrong people.

"Stop." Ben halts our progress, focusing on something in a nearby building. "I heard something."

Jordan and Ben draw their weapons and face whatever threat is looming. I hold my breath in anticipation. Did the shadow creatures follow us? Were they able to track us? To our surprise and elation though Fin steps out from around the building with his hands up informing us it's him.

Ben's face breaks out into a relieved smile. "You stupid fool, I could have sent this dagger right into your heart."

Fin shrugs, good naturedly. "Sorry, needed to make sure it was you. Never know who could be lurking around these ruins." Fin lets out a high-pitched whistle and another answers in the distance. A few minutes later, Melinda and Enyo make their appearance and I rush to Melinda, enveloping her in a hug.

"You smell very bad, dear," she comments as we pull away.

I chuckle at her sour expression. "We had to hide in the sewers to escape one of the creatures."

"I can see that." Her nose wrinkles in amused disgust.

"I'm happy to see you are alive, Mitera." Ben hugs her as well, as I greet Enyo and Fin.

"I'm sorry we were so delayed. Though you should have left hours ago." Melinda sends Ben a sideways glance, which he shrugs away. "I am happy to see you. We took a very roundabout way in order to avoid the creatures. We thankfully didn't encounter any but we did run into some royal guards, who took some time to get away from."

"You aren't hurt, are you?" I give all of them a quick survey and see nothing amiss.

Melinda shakes her head. "No, it was just a small group. We were able to handle them with ease."

"We did learn some things from them though," Fin interjects.

Ben motions for us to continue on our journey, as we talk.

"Those creatures are called the vaekua. As the Mitera mentioned, they normally can't stray far from their master but Seraphine has found a way to put them in the bodies of the dead. This allows them to travel further from her. In that form they are more mobile and intelligent, using the knowledge of their victim. The more people she kills, the larger her army will be," Fin explains.

A shudder runs through my body as the ramifications of what he said settles in. How are we going to be able to stop her?

Sensing my unease, I feel Jordan's hand slip into mine. I look up into his face and see the same uncertainty I am feeling reflected in his gaze. I attempt a reassuring smile but it comes off as a grimace so I give up and just give his hand a quick squeeze.

"We came across one of the vaekua and it looked like Myka. Does it have Myka's memories?" I ask Fin.

He nods. "From what we understand, yes, they have access to the brain and use that to their advantage. The guard that we questioned was all too eager to share information. The guards are uneasy with all the vaekua in the palace, they fear they will be killed so their bodies can be used as vessels for them."

"Myka didn't know where the Mystics were going or where we are heading. Layla and Sage are safe," Jordan comments, once again picking up on my emotions.

I send him a grateful look and ask, "Do you think having King Erik's army will be enough to stop her?"

"To be honest, I don't know, dear. I hope so," Melinda replies. "But first we must convince him to help us, so one problem at a time."

"You think he won't help us? Seraphine is as much a threat to him as she is to us."

"We just have to prepare for anything, dear." Melinda turns to Fin and begins conversing with him. I rub my hands up and down my arms, suddenly chilled. It never occurred to me that Estera would not want to help us. What if they don't help us and we have to face this threat alone? Will we even stand a chance?

Chapter 15

AFTER A WEEK OF traveling, we finally stand on the edge of Estera's capital city, Ester. It was a long week and we all need food, water and baths but, thankfully, we had no issues on the journey and didn't run into any vaekua or palace guards. It seems that, at least for now, Seraphine does not know where we were heading and so we are safe.

"Buttercup, if you don't close your mouth soon, you might swallow a bug." Jordan states and I snap my jaw shut, not even realizing that it was open.

The city of Ester is beautiful and magnificent, nothing like the poor and desolate place that is Myridia. There, the buildings are run-down and poorly maintained. From what I can see of Ester, the buildings and dwellings are strong and well-kept, clean. We step onto a crowded bridge that crosses over a large body of water. The water stretches on as far as the eye can see and seems to twist around the city.

"The city has three entry points by three different bridges. This bridge is the main one, used by traders and workers, the other two are used by the King and the military." Jordan comments. "It is completely protected by the water surrounding it. The body of water is man-made; it was constructed to protect the city in the event of an attack—the bridges can be brought up and the city cannot be reached."

"Smart." I watch several people walk by us, noticing that, for the most part, everyone seems content and happy. "People here are different. They don't seem so sad and hopeless."

"The war between Estera and Myridia took more of a toll on Myridia. They never truly recovered while Estera continued to flourish. King Erik also tends to take better care of his people than Rolland ever did," Jordan explains.

"How do you know so much?"

Jordan stops walking and faces me, halting our group's progress. He grabs my hand and his face is filled with what looks like regret. "Buttercup, there is something—"

"Mitera!" A young boy, probably in his late teens, picks his way through the crowded bridge and runs to our group, bowing before us. "I'm so glad you finally made it. King Erik has been worried."

Melinda ruffles the boy's hair. "I'm glad to see that you got here safely. You had no troubles along the way?"

The boy shakes his shaggy head. "No, Mitera, I arrived two days ago with your message for the King and we have been anxiously awaiting your arrival."

"Then let us not keep the King waiting, shall we?"

Melinda and the guards begin to the follow the boy but when I take a step to follow, Jordan's hand on my arm stops me. "Maia."

I cover his hand with mine and kiss his cheek. "We can talk later, Jordan, I promise. We don't want to keep the King waiting."

I run to catch up with the group and trust that Jordan will follow. It isn't long before I feel his warm presence next to me and I send him a grateful glance. He doesn't see it though because his eyes are focused on the doorway that we are now entering. The entrance to Ester is breathtaking. An imposing archway with doors that must be twenty-five feet tall greet us. I run my hands along the door and feel the solid wood within. As a Mystic, I could rip this door straight off its hinges but if their enemy was a human they would be safely protected.

Another difference that I immediately note between Myridia and Estera is that the streets here are made of cobblestone, which seems to be why the town is so clean. From my gilded cage that I called a home I could see that the streets of Myridia were made of packed dirt, which probably didn't help the filthiness of the city. The buildings along the street tower above us, like nothing I've ever seen. Merchants and traders line the wide streets, but instead of feeling overwhelming the chaos is a comfort. I almost feel safe being lost in the anonymity.

Our young guide chatters rapidly to Melinda and she accepts it all good naturedly, nodding as he points out structures and landmarks. Fin chuckles besides me.

"It's his first mission. I think he's pretty excited," He states.

"Another orphan?"

"Yep. The youngest among our soldiers but he wouldn't take no for an answer so the Mitera has been training him. He's been itching to get in on the action, so sending him as a messenger felt like a safe mission."

"That's a good idea on Melinda's part," I remark as we go deeper into the heart of Ester.

We round a corner and I let out a gasp of surprise. Looming in front of us is a magnificent castle that dwarfs the palace that I lived in all my life. Its columns and turrets reach to the sky as if in a desperate attempt to touch the clouds. The effect is beautiful and I can only imagine the time and energy it took to build such a place. No gates protect the castle grounds or any barrier whatsoever; the palace grounds lie open and people can be seen coming in and out as they please.

I nod towards a pair of maids as they make their way past us. "They are allowed to leave the castle like that?"

Jordan is suspiciously quiet and I glance at him in question but once again he is too focused on something else. He eyes the castle with an expression I cannot read and it makes me feel uneasy. Maybe I should have stopped and let him tell me what he needed to say. But what could be so important that it couldn't wait? Is there something that he has been hiding from me? I shake my head to clear it, no, Jordan would never hide something from me. I trust him more than anyone and he would never hurt me that way after everything I've gone through with Xavier. I trust him; it's probably nothing.

The courtyard of the castle is magnificent and is filled with hundreds of people milling about. There are even carts selling their wares just feet from the palace. Maids and guards make their way through the crowd, collecting items and returning to the palace. Our group passes through the open door of the palace into an entry hall, and Jordan's steps slow. I glance back at him but he doesn't seem to notice that he is falling behind. I grab his hand and his eyes find mine, coming back to reality.

"You okay?" I ask.

He gives me a reassuring smile. "Yes, Buttercup. I'm sorry, just a little lost in thought, that's all."

I think he can tell that I don't believe him because he kisses my hand and tells me he loves me. I return his affirmation, but once again can't shake the feeling that something is wrong. I tell myself that as soon as we get this meeting over with I can give him all the time in the world to tell me what is bothering him.

"Maia!"

My head snaps up at the sound of my name and my heart beats rapidly in my chest, recognizing that voice. My eyes frantically search the source of the voice until they land on the familiar face of my brother.

"Kaden! You're alive!" I break away from the group and throw myself into the waiting arms of the only family I have left. Tears leak out of my eyes and into his shirt but he doesn't seem to care because I feel the wetness on my scalp where his head is resting.

"I've been so worried about you," he whispers.

I chuckle. "You've been worried about me? I thought you were dead!"

"Fine, you win." He kisses the top of my head. "I'm so glad you are safe, Maia. I'm so sorry that I wasn't able to protect you from those monsters."

I pull out of his grasp, shaking my head. "No, I'm the one who should be sorry. I led Xavier and Rolland straight to the Mystic City. It's my fault that it was destroyed."

"As Father's letter said, it wasn't meant to be our permanent home. Now we all have something to fight for."

"What's that?"

The smile he gives me is warm and filled with hope. "A new home."

I wrap my arms around him once more and allow the warmth of his embrace to calm my racing heart. My family is not all gone and, at least for today, that is enough.

A throat clears behind us and I'm reminded that there are others with me. I reluctantly detach myself from my brother but I don't let go, instead looping my arm through his, and lead him over to Melinda.

"Melinda, this is Kaden, my brother."

Melinda stares at Kaden as if she's seen a ghost, the color completely draining from her face. She reaches a hand out tentatively, lightly touching his cheek. Kaden raises an eyebrow in question and her cheeks redden and she drops her hand. "I apologize, you just look so much like Gaven. I cannot believe it."

"You knew my father?"

I pat Kaden's hand. "I have a lot to fill you in on, Kaden."

"As I do for you."

"Are Layla and Sage—" I can't seem to say what I want to ask, too afraid of the answer.

Understanding what I am asking, Kaden nods. "They are safe, little sister. They are with the others. King Erik has been most gracious and has given us a temporary home as we figure out our plan of action. I have come here every day since the King informed me you were coming, awaiting your arrival."

Our guide touches Melinda's arm. "Mitera, the King awaits."

She nods and sends me an apologetic look. "I'm sorry to cut your reunion short, but he is right. We should not keep the King waiting."

"Of course," I agree, still not willing to relinquish the hold on my brother. He chuckles but allows me to hold on to his arm as we follow our guide to the throne room.

Two guards stand at attention and nod at the young boy in greeting as they open the door for us. Our little group files into the massive throne room. The ceiling is made entirely of glass and allows the sunlight to stream in, creating a beautiful bright atmosphere. All of the walls are white and seem to shine in the sunlight, causing the light to bounce in all directions. As with Rolland's throne room, there is a red carpet that leads to a raised dais, where four thrones sit, each of them occupied.

Our long walk to the thrones allows me a moment to take in the four occupants. Upon the largest throne is who I can only assume is King Erik. He is smiling welcomingly at us as we enter and is talking softly to the woman next to him. His hair is blonde and cut close to his face, and his figure is large and bulky, filling in the throne he sits on.

The woman next to him is petite and elegant. She is dressed in a formal blue gown that sparkles in the sunlight and has a small tiara atop her head. She smiles up at the King demurely and laughs softly at whatever it is that he is saying. She reminds me of Queen Evelyn, the once regal queen of Myridia, and a sliver of sadness shoots through me.

I move my observations down the row to the next two thrones, each occupied by young men. The first of the pair has dark raven hair that almost looks blue in the sun. He eyes our approaching group with curiosity and I notice that his stare lingers on me before his mouth up turns into a smirk. His gaze moves to mine and I almost stop in my tracks due to his brilliant blue eyes, which sparkle when they catch the light. They are stunning and remind me of the cerulean blue eyes of Jordan.

Unsettled by his gaze, I break our connection and observe his companion, another young man. He has brown hair and blue eyes, but his are not nearly as striking as the raven-haired man. My eyes drift back to him and to my surprise he is still watching me with an amused smirk.

The King stands as we approach his throne, his face breaking into a giant grin. "Welcome, my friends, to Estera."

Melinda bows. "Your Majesty, thank you for allowing us refuge in your kingdom and for allowing us an audience."

He waves off Melinda's thanks as he descends the stairs from his throne. He stops in front of me and takes my hand, kissing it in greeting.

"Princess Maia, it is a pleasure to finally meet you. You are even more beautiful than your people described."

I can't help myself as hysterical laughter slips past my lips. There is no way that he believes I look beautiful in this moment.

My usual blonde hair is matted and full of grease and dirt, looking as though it's almost brown. I smell like horse's manure and my clothes haven't been washed in a week. The quick dip in the river we found two days ago did barely anything when it came to washing away the filth of the long journey.

King Erik's smile does not drop at my rude laughter but a muscle does tick in his cheek. I gather my composure and bow my head in respect.

"I apologize for my rudeness, it was a very long journey and I feel less than beautiful at this moment."

"On the contrary." The raven-haired man's sultry voice floats over to us. He stands and makes his way to the King's side. "Even through the filth, your beauty is apparent. I look forward to seeing what lies beneath the dirt, Princess Maia."

King Erik smiles at him and slaps a hand on his back. "Such a way with words. Allow me to introduce my son, the Crown Prince Colieus."

The beautiful blue eyes of Prince Colieus capture mine and he follows his father's example, kissing my hand in greeting. His stare never breaks mine and I feel trapped in its intensity. He smirks as if he knows what he is doing.

"Nice to meet you, Prince Colieus." I manage to squeak out.

"Please, my friend's call me Cole and the pleasure is all mine."

"It's nice to meet you, Cole." Sounding like I've run a mile. What has gotten into me? And when did it get so warm?

The skin around Cole's eyes crinkle a little as his smile widens at my discomfort. He is clearly adept at this game and I am a new piece on the playing field. He holds my hand for a moment longer before almost reluctantly letting it drop. His gaze still captures mine and I can't bring myself to look away,

I'm so enraptured by their—

"You must forgive my rudeness as well, Princess." The King's voice breaks whatever was going on between his son and me and I pull my eyes away from his in relief, unsettled by what passed between us. Annoyance flashes across Cole's face but it's gone so fast that I question even seeing it. "I was so eager to meet your acquaintance that I did not consider that you would require some rest after your long journey. Please allow my servants to show you to your rooms and we can get better acquainted tonight at dinner."

He motions for servants to come forth but I make no move to follow them. "And my companions?"

"Have no worries, Princess, they are all to be assigned to rooms in the same wing as yours. You shall not be far from your friends. Please trust me when I say you are safe here; no harm will come to your or friends while you are in my castle."

"Thank you, King Erik. I will take you up on your offer. My companions and I are in dire need of rest and a bath."

We turn to follow the servants out of the throne room when Erik's voice stops us.

"Were you going to leave without saying hello, Son?" His voice is calm but I sense a dangerous undertone that I can't place.

I turn back to him and notice that his smile is gone and his eyes are trained on someone behind me. I follow his gaze and when I find their target the floor drops out from underneath me. I shake my head in denial, my heart not allowing my brain to accept what it is I'm seeing and what I heard. The King is staring at Jordan and he is staring, unflinchingly, back at the King.

"Jordan?" I look back and forth between the two men.

The King finally breaks the stare down between Jordan and himself and his smile returns, but it does not reach his eyes.

"My apologies again, Princess, I thought you knew my son traveled with you. It appears I am not the only one he has kept secrets from."

I do not miss Jordan's cringe at his father's words or the look of pain that flashes in his eyes as he meets my gaze. "Jordan?" I say again, not recognizing the raw emotion in my tone or the faint desperation for him to deny the King's claim. This can't be happening. He would not lie to me like this. He would never keep something like this from me.

With his next words he shatters my reality and I physically feel the blow to my gut, without a single person near me.

"What he says is true. I am his son."

Chapter 16

I PUSH OPEN THE balcony doors and take in several deep breaths. After my weeks of imprisonment with Xavier, feeling the fresh air against my skin still feels like freedom. The journey to Estera was long and tiring but I enjoyed every moment we spent outdoors.

I jump on the balcony railing and lean back against the palace wall, allowing one leg to dangle over the edge. I run my hands through my damp hair, working my way through the knots. After the longest and best bath of my life I finally feel clean and a little bit more like myself.

As I braid my hair I finally allow my thoughts to drift to Jordan. While I bathed I didn't allow myself to think about his betrayal and the lie that he kept from me, keeping busy with scrubbing off week-old disgustingness. But now that I am outside, with nothing else to think about, everything floods back. He's King Erik's son. All this time, he could have told me, but he didn't. What does this mean for us? For him? Has he been reporting to his father all this time?

"I was right."

I jump, almost losing my balance on the balcony at the silky voice in my ear. Strong hands steady me and I settle back on the railing glaring at the raven-haired prince.

"About what?" I snap, annoyed at being startled.

"You are even more beautiful than I imagined under that dirt." He leans against the railing in front of me, inches from my feet, and flashes me a devastating smile.

I pull my legs closer and rest my chin on my knees, suddenly very tired. "What are you doing here?"

"I wanted to make sure you were okay. I saw your face when father exposed my brother; it was quite the surprise to you."

"Do you always make sure your guests are okay?"

He gives me a genuine smile, flashing his white teeth. "Only the ones I like."

I chuckle. "You're quite the charmer, Prince Cole."

"Only when it matters."

"And I matter?"

He leans in, close enough that I can smell the soap he uses and see the specks of green in his sparkling blue eyes. "More than you know."

"What's that supposed to mean?"

He leans back, giving me some space, and shrugs. I eye him suspiciously but it's clear that he is not going to elaborate on his statement.

"Thank you for coming to check on me."

"You are most certainly welcome." He winks. "And don't worry, lying does not run in the family."

I can't help myself, I laugh. "I'll keep that in mind."

"In an effort to prove my trustworthiness, would you like to have a little fun?"

I raise an eyebrow. "What did you have in mind?"

"On my way to your room, I happened to come across a rather grumpy-looking brother on his way to speak with my father. I happen to know of a place that we could overhear their conversation."

"You would do that for me? Why?"

His eyes turn soft. "Because you deserve to know the truth."

"I'm sorry but I don't trust you. I don't know you." It's really hard to trust people when I keep being betrayed.

"I wouldn't expect you to." He holds out his hand. "But give me a chance to prove that you can."

I eye his hand and contemplate my options. I want to know what is going on with Jordan but I also don't know if I can trust the charming prince in front of me. I trusted a prince before and look where it got me. In the end, though, I need to know if I can still trust Jordan. I need to know what he is hiding from me. I slip my hand into Cole's and his face breaks into a relieved smile.

He tightens his grip on my hand and drags me behind him out of the room and I'm suddenly very happy that I'm already dressed for dinner. Two maids had stopped by while I was bathing and dropped off a dress for me to wear. It is the deepest blue, almost black like the hair of the prince that is currently dragging me behind him. It has a beautiful sweetheart neckline and it fits snuggly along my body to the floor.

Cole stops next to a tapestry, depicting a golden knight upon a white steed and pulls it aside. He pushes against the wall and it opens with a hiss. With a quick tug, he pulls me inside the passageway and closes the door behind us. I stumble a bit from the abrupt motion and fall into him. He wraps his arms around me to hold me up but I pull away quickly, a blush creeping up my neck. His face is lit up by the lantern above his head and I see the small smirk that graces his lips.

I follow his figure down the passageway and it occurs to me that I am alone with a person I just met, but I made my decision so now I have to deal with the consequences if this goes wrong. Muffled shouting up ahead causes us to quicken our steps and Cole puts a finger to his lips as he nears a small panel. He slides it open and we can easily see Jordan and King Erik in what appears to be the King's study, through a small grate in the wall.

Jordan is on his feet and he is pacing along the floor in front of his father, who is watching him calmly with his fingers steepled in front of him.

"Are you done shouting at me and prepared to talk to me in a calm manner?" Erik asks. "I would have thought you had time to calm down by now."

"You had no right." Jordan sticks his finger in his father's direction.

"No right?" Erik raises an eyebrow. "I had no right to welcome my son back into his home?"

"You know what you did, Father, don't be coy. You knew exactly what you were doing. You could have waited, you didn't have to do it in front of her."

"You love her." Erik states it as a fact, not a question and Jordan does nothing to confirm or deny it. "Well, now I know why you left her out of your reports."

"That has nothing to do with it."

Erik slams his fist down on his desk. "Don't lie to me, boy, you are lucky I don't have you arrested for treason."

Jordan lets out a bitter laugh. "Treason, really? And here I thought we were having a civilized conversation."

Disbelief sends my jaw to the ground. I cannot believe that the person I am seeing is the same one that I fell in love with. He is acting nothing like I know him to be. I am watching a stranger; what else has he hidden from me.

"So why hide her? You were sent there to spy on the King and be our inside man and yet you left out a rather important piece of information. Just imagine my surprise when I found out all this time there was a mystic inside Rolland's castle." Erik levels his son with a deadly glare. "You are very lucky you were out of my grasp when I became privy to that information or you would already be dead. I don't take kindly to traitors and you know this."

"I did not betray you, Father."

"Then what else do you call it, Son." The word 'son' is sharp as a knife.

"Strategy. Imagine what would have happened if you had known she was there. You would have tried to extract her, stolen her from the only home she ever knew. You would have turned yourself into a villain in her eyes and she would have turned against you. Now she is coming to you for aid, in need of your help. You have all the power now."

Bile rises in my throat and I turn away from the strangers in the room. I cannot believe what I am hearing, there is no way that is my Jordan. The boy who held me and comforted me for most of my life. The boy who, just days ago, told me that he plans to marry me someday.

I take off running down the passageway, hoping to dispel whatever it is that I just witnessed, but the words follow me. My stomach roils and I begin to dry heave and Cole lays a comforting hand on my back as the contents of my stomach empty into a nearby drain. Tears mix with snot and I must appear to be a horrible mess but Cole pulls me to his chest and rubs my back.

"I'm sorry, Princess," he whispers. "If I had known…"

I shake my head against his chest. "No, I needed to hear it. I appreciate your honesty."

"You will only ever get honesty from me."

I pull away from him and take in his handsome face. He passes me a handkerchief and I wipe my mouth and nose. "Why are you being so nice to me?"

"Because I know what it's like to be a pawn in someone's game. And you are no one's pawn, you are the Queen."

Cole's words stay with me as we walk silently to the dining hall. All evidence of my breakdown in the passageway is gone, our secret safe in its tunnels. Have I allowed myself to be pawn in other people's game? Is it time for me to stop being pushed around and start acting as a queen, a leader, the Aurora?

Cole's hand is on my lower back, guiding me gently towards our destination. My dress dips low in the back and I can feel his fingers lightly touching my bare skin. I glance up at him and contemplate his motives. As much as I appreciate him allowing me to see the conversation between Jordan and Erik, something holds me back from completely trusting his motives. Why would he want me to hear that conversation, what does he have to gain? Have I been hurt too many times by people that I thought loved me that I am now questioning everyone's motives?

"You look like you are questioning your whole world," Cole quietly comments.

"Maybe I am."

He chuckles darkly. "I suppose I shouldn't blame you." Cole slows his pace. "Maia, I would like to get to know you more. Will you join me after dinner in the gardens?"

I consider his request, unsure of his motives and also wanting to learn more about him, it seems like a good idea to spend more time with him. I nod and he rewards me with one of his charming smiles.

"Wonderful."

We pass into the dining hall and find that all of my companions have already arrived and are awaiting us. All that is missing is the presence of the King and Queen. Cole guides me to my chair and I spare a glance at Jordan and notice that his eyes are zeroed in on the hand that is on my lower back. When Cole pulls out my chair and sits beside me, Jordan's eyes promise murder but he says nothing. I promptly ignore him, which only seems to make his glare more murderous.

A hand on my arm draws my attention to my right and I turn to address Melinda.

"I went to your room to retrieve you for dinner, but you were already gone. Is everything alright, dear?"

"Yes, I was just taking a walk, exploring and then I ran into Prince Cole. He was showing me around and we lost track of time." The lie slips easily past my lips.

"How very noble of him." Jordan mumbles under his breath from across the table.

I continue to ignore him and glance around the table. Next to Melinda is Ben, and Fin, who waves at me and I wave back, with a wide grin. Across from him are Enyo and Jordan, who is still glaring at Cole. I turn back to Melinda.

"Where is Kaden?"

"He mentioned something about meeting with his council. He wanted to inform them that you had arrived. He said he would catch up with you tomorrow morning after you'd had a chance to settle in." Guilt trickles in at her words. Here I am planning to spend time with Estera's Prince tonight and my brother is taking care of our people. I must show it on my face because she pats my hand. "He also said to not feel guilty that you haven't come by to see them yet. He knows you had a long journey and wants you to rest. You can visit them tomorrow."

I let out a reluctant laugh. "Am I really that predictable?"

"Only when it comes to the people you care about."

The doors at the far end of the dining hall open revealing the King and Queen, effectively ending all conversation. As they make their way to the table we all stand out of respect and the King immediately motions for us to sit.

He smiles warmly and says, "Please, we are all friends here. No need to stand on such formality."

As we take our seats, he pulls out the Queen's seat and she takes her place. He is quick to join her and motions to the servants to begin serving dinner. The servants bring out the first course and conversation resumes among the table's inhabitants.

"Forgive me, Princess Maia, I failed to introduce the Queen earlier. It appears in my happiness in your safe arrival I lost my manners. Please allow me to introduce to you my lovely wife, Queen Enora," King Erik states, drawing my attention to him and his wife.

"It's a pleasure to meet you, Maia. I have heard so much about you." Queen Enora's voice is soft and lyrical. It reminds me of a gentle breeze.

"It's a pleasure to meet you as well, Your Majesty."

Her face breaks into a smile and I immediately see the family resemblance between she and Cole. He has his mother's smile as well as her hair. Her raven-black hair is long and runs down her back in cascading waves. It's beautiful and I am almost envious as I self-consciously touch my hastily-put-together braid.

"Please, call me Enora." She turns to Cole and the look she gives him shows the admiration and love that she holds for her first-born son. "Cole, honey, were you able to stop by the orphanage this morning?"

"I was. I delivered the new shoes as you asked. They were very appreciative."

"So, Maia, what was it like growing up in Myridia." Erik's booming voice quickly overshadows the conversations taking place between mother and son.

"It was…" I bite my lip in indecision, not sure how much I want to reveal.

"She was a prisoner," Jordan plainly states.

My irritation flares and I snap, "I can speak for myself."

Hurt flickers across Jordan's face but it quickly disappears behind the new mask he wears, one I have never seen in all my years with him.

"Forgive me, Princess." His tone is cold and I try to not let it affect me, but hurt feelings invade me. I feel a soft hand sliding over mine under the table and it takes me a second to realize that it is Cole's. His hands are so different than his brother's. Jordan's are rough and calloused from his years in the kitchen, while Cole's are soft and smooth. I send him a grateful smile and he gives my hand a squeeze in response.

"I was raised by the King and Queen as their adopted daughter. They kept my identity as a Mystic secret to protect me. Only the King, Queen, Xavier, and the King's council knew of what I was."

"And my son," Erik states, matter a fact.

"Yes." I glance over at said son and he seems to be staring intently at our second course, finding whatever is on his plate very interesting. "I told him once we became friends."

"And when exactly did you and my son become friends?"

"Father." Cole warns under his breath.

"What?" Erik sends his oldest son an innocent look. "I am just trying to get to know our guest."

"Jordan and I met when I was ten years old." I absently toy with the locket around my neck. "We have been friends ever since."

"I see," Erik comments. "And what dramatic story did the King conjure up about your parents and the reason you were being raised in his kingdom?"

"They told me that my parents were killed protecting Rolland in the war. They told me that they were killed by the Esterians."

"And how did you manage to learn the truth?"

"Father, really? We're having a nice dinner; must you interrogate her?" Cole snaps and I'm starting to realize why Jordan was so nervous about coming to Estera. Something is off about King Erik, but I can't put my finger on it.

"My apologies, Princess. I don't mean for this to be an interrogation. I am just curious." He smiles lightly but it doesn't reach his eyes.

"Why didn't my parents side with your kingdom in the war?" My question takes him off guard and his smile slips a little but remains mostly intact.

A tense silence descends on the dining room and several of the inhabitants are staring at me with wide eyes. But they shift to the King as he begins chuckling softly.

"You are quite the amusing creature, Princess Maia. I can see why Prince Xavier was so reluctant to give you up. And you are right to question your parents reasoning." Cole looks at his father in disbelief at that statement. "Those were very dark times. The war was brutal and it was soon forgotten why the war even began. I think if you had asked Rolland, he would not have been able to tell you why either. But it very quickly became ugly. My father, King Bane, was not a nice man, and he and Rolland hated each other. They had a rivalry and a hatred that dated back centuries.

I will not lie to you, my father was just as bad as Rolland. He was killing Mystics. Mystics in both kingdoms were disappearing every day and my father and Rolland were to blame for their deaths. They both craved power and both wanted to rule the other's kingdom. So, when the Mystics sided with

199

Rolland my father knew the game was up. He may have been a rough and angry man, but he was a fair and just king. He only wanted what was best for his people, so he surrendered."

"And Rolland killed him at the peace treaty gathering," I state.

"Yes, and I became king soon after." Erik grabs his wife's hand. "It has not been easy, but the past eighteen years, we have worked to reverse the damage that the war caused. Most of the mystics had fled to the Mystic City but the few who remained in our kingdom were honored and protected. I refuse to make the same mistakes as my father. It is why we never sought revenge for the King's betrayal. The war ended with King Bane's death. We live in peace and harmony in our kingdom."

"And witches?" Melinda speaks up for the first time.

"As you know, the witches kept to themselves in their town of Odeca. There were not many witches outside of there when Rolland attacked it. If they are in our city, they are here under the guise that they are human."

"If you wish for peace between the people, why have you not helped the Kamora until now?" I ask, secretly proud of myself for all my hard questions.

Enora lays a hand on her husband's arm before he answers. "Erik, darling. Why don't we save the rest of this discussion for another time? We should be enjoying our dinner, not talking politics."

Erik smiles at his wife and nods, visibly relaxing. "Of course, my wife is correct. The dinner table is no place for politics."

An awkward silence once again descends on the table as we all pick at our food. Slowly little bits of conversations pick up between the King and Queen and Melinda. Enyo says something to Fin that has them laughing loudly and obnoxiously.

Cole leans over and whispers in my ear, his breath tickles

and sends shivers down my spine. Jordan's sharp gaze sees it all and he glares daggers at his brother. Cole pulls away and is staring at me expectantly and I suddenly realize that I didn't hear a word he said.

I blush. "I'm sorry, what did you say?"

Cole chuckles and leans his elbow on the table, blocking his parents from my view. "It was nothing. How are you enjoying your dinner? Our chef is the best."

"I don't know, our chef at the palace in Myridia was amazing. He made this delicious roast that made my mouth water every time." I can't help the dreamy look I make when thinking about that roast.

I watch Cole's eyes drop to my lips and the next thing I know, he's running a finger across my lower lip. A growl sounds from across the table and there is a thump that makes me jump.

Cole smirks. "I think your chef may have some competition because you were drooling." He lifts his damp finger for my inspection.

Not sure how I feel about him touching me like that, but not willing to make a big deal about it, I shrug. "Only because I was thinking about that roast."

He throws his hands up in surrender. "Fair enough." He leans back in his chair and throws his arm on the back of mine, the perfect picture of nonchalance. He answers Jordan's glare with a look of confidence and something passes between them that has Cole smirking.

I ignore them both and turn to the Queen. "So, where are you from, Enora?"

Her face brightens. "I am from Aquia. It is a beautiful island off the coast."

My brows come down in confusion. "I have never heard of Aquia."

"And you probably never will again. Erik has made sure to keep the island off any map."

Now I'm even more confused. "Is it dangerous?"

Enora shakes her head. "No, but it is my home and the last thing I have of my people."

"Mother is a nymph." Cole clarifies next to me.

"A nymph?" I really wish these people would stop confusing me.

"We are elemental, like you, but we can only control water."

"I've never heard of a nymph before."

The Queen's eyes turn sad and the King is quick to offer comfort. She sends him a grateful look and then turns back to me. "I am the last of the nymphs. They were all slaughtered when I was a babe. I only survived because my mother hid me when the humans came to destroy us."

"That's terrible. Why would the humans destroy the nymphs?"

"Nymphs have another ability that humans found threatening. They eliminated us so that we could never use it against them again."

"What is it?"

"I have the ability to influence emotions in a way. My presence calms people and I am able to coax a person into a calm state, like luring them into a false sense of security."

"Why would the humans find that threatening?" I'm quickly realizing I know nothing about this world.

"Let's just say one of the nymphs attempted to help the wrong person."

I reach across Cole and cover the Queen's hand with my own. "I'm sorry for your loss, Enora."

She smiles, but it is sad. "It's the past and there is nothing to do about it now. I have a wonderful life here surrounded by my sons and husband."

"So, if you are a nymph, does that make Cole and Jordan half nymphs?"

Cole and Jordan share identical snorts and the King sends them both warning glares and they quiet.

"You are correct that Cole is half nymph, but Jordan is not. He is not Enora's son," Erik explains.

"Who—"

Erik stands quickly, interrupting my question. "I'm sorry, Princess Maia, but my wife and I have grown tired. We can meet again tomorrow and discuss all of your questions. I am sure you will want to meet with your people in the morning, so shall we say midday?"

Taken aback by his sudden change of attitude, I only have the ability to nod at his request. He and Enora make their way out of the dining hall and leave the rest of us in stunned silence.

"Forgive my Father, Maia, he is a little sensitive when it comes to Jordan's mother," Cole comments quietly.

Jordan glares at his brother for a moment and then his gaze slips to mine, softening. I see everything that I had been wanting to see since I found out about his lie—love, regret, longing. I see my Jordan in his eyes. But he shutters his eyes from me and the next thing I know, he's also rising to his feet and slamming the dining hall door behind him.

"Well, that was interesting," Fin states and Enyo nods his head in agreement.

"I think, perhaps, it is time for us to retire as well. It has been a long day and a good night's rest will do us good." Melinda rises from her chair and the men rise with her. She glances down at me. "Are you coming, Maia?"

I shake my head. "No, you go on ahead. I'll be alright."

"As you wish. Don't stay up too late, dear." A strange look passes across her face but she says nothing as she and the three guards exit the dining hall, leaving Cole and I alone.

"I promise our family dinners are not normally like this." Cole stands and offers me his arm.

"I didn't mean to upset anyone with my questions." I accept his arm and he guides me out of the dining hall, most of our dinners untouched.

"Like I said, Father just gets a little sensitive when it comes to Jordan's mother. They were engaged to be married and she became pregnant. She was supposed to be his Queen and he loved her. But there were complications in her pregnancy and she was put on bed rest for most of it, causing them to push back their wedding date. They were to be wed once she was well again but she died giving birth to Jordan. And since they were unmarried when Jordan was born, he has no claim to the throne."

"Wow." Apparently, that is the only reaction that I can come up with.

Cole guides me through a set of double doors and into a quiet garden. It is nothing like the luscious and vast garden that I had back in Myridia, but it is quaint and intimate. A small pond rests in the far corner next to a large wooden swing, big enough for two. A graveled path leads through the small bushes to the pond and swing, and that is where Cole leads us. He waits for me to take my seat and then he joins me, pushing the swing with his long legs.

"I used to sit outside in the garden back at home. It was my sanctuary," I comment quietly as I gaze up at the stars, feeling at peace.

"I've always liked the garden, myself. I had plans to make it larger, but unfortunately time and responsibility got away from me."

"Yes, that's how it was for Xavier. Once he was old enough to start attending meetings and learning about his role, he was always busy shadowing his father. I can't imagine the pressure of being the crown Prince."

"You loved him." I feel Cole's gaze on my face and nod, not willing to look away from the stars just yet. "Do you still?"

I contemplate his question, far longer than I should. I know that I am no longer *in* love with Xavier. My heart belongs to Jordan and, no matter how angry I am at him, I can admit that hasn't changed. But do I still love Xavier? Do I still possess feelings for the boy who loves me to the point of obsession and who has betrayed me time and time again?

"In a way, yes," I reluctantly admit, not even sure why I am opening up to the practical stranger next to me. I blame it on the calm that the garden gives me and the fact that Cole has been nothing but honest to me. I owe him, at least, the same. "He was my first love. We were engaged to be married, I believe a part of me will always love him."

"That seems fair. I know my father will always love Nadia, Jordan's mother, but I also know that he loves my mother. They have a wonderful marriage built on mutual respect and admiration. It was definitely not a marriage built on love, but it works."

"How did they meet?"

"As she said, her island was destroyed and she was the sole survivor. She was discovered by the Forie Kingdom, which was Nadia's kingdom. The Forie are a peaceful people, rich in many ways and they raised Enora as their adopted daughter. The Forie and Estera had an arranged marriage planned for Nadia and

Erik, much to their happiness. They had always been in love. But when Nadia died the Forie offered Enora as a replacement. She satisfied the arranged marriage between the kingdoms and strengthened the alliance."

"That's so sad. He lost his true love and then had to marry someone else. I'm surprised he ever grew affection for Enora."

"You must do what you must for your kingdom, it is the price we pay for being royalty. And my mother made it easy on him, she was patient and did not push him."

"I've never heard of the Forie." I admit, self-consciously.

"Did they not teach you in the palace?" Cole puts his hand on the chair, inches from where mine rests.

I should be insulted by his tone, but I'm not. I'm getting used to the fact that I know nothing, apparently, and that my education growing up was obsolete.

"I had tutors. Xavier and I attended education together, but I guess I wasn't being taught everything."

Cole looks at me in quiet sympathy, the moon reflecting in his dark gaze. His fingers move slowly and lightly touch mine.

I turn my gaze to the stars again. "Deep down I always knew something was off, like I was missing something, but I always ignored it. They lied to me my whole life and I had no idea. No idea of the life I was missing, because I was too blind to see it."

"Sometimes, ignoring something we know is going to hurt us is all we can do. You couldn't have known what they were keeping from you. Plus, with eyes that beautiful you can't possibly be blind." He smiles and it breaks my heart a little because it reminds me so much of Jordan. Cole stands and offers me his hand. "Come, I want to show you something."

"We just got here," I mildly complain.

"I know, but I think you'll like what I have to show you more."

I slip my hand into his and he pulls me to my feet. Instead of releasing my hand he tucks it into the crook of his elbow, guiding me. We stroll leisurely through the halls of the quiet palace and I begin to wonder just how late it is. It doesn't take us long to arrive at our destination and Cole holds the door open to me. He lights a lantern and blankets the room in a soft light and for the first time I see the Prince's room. It's small by royal standards, and simple; it makes me contemplate the prince beside me. The enormous bed and a wardrobe take up most of the room and near the far side of the room, by a giant window is a desk. He leads me over to the desk and sits me in the chair while he pulls up another one for himself.

"Your room is…" I struggle for a word to describe it.

"Small, I know," he finishes for me, with a sad smile. "I prefer it this way. I don't like the echo that comes from a large space. It feels empty and lonely."

I blink at him at a rare loss of words. He doesn't seem to notice as he busies himself with looking for something in the many drawers of his desk. Eventually he finds what he is looking for and pulls out a massive sheet of parchment and places it in front of me with a flourish.

"A map of Katear." He answers my questioning gaze. At his words I take another look at the paper and I realize that he is right. I can see Myridia and a few of the surrounding towns that we ventured through on our journey to the Mystic City. As my gaze moves out there are so many other places that I do not recognize and they fill the entire sheet of parchment.

"It's so big," I murmur breathlessly. Xavier had mentioned Rolland wanting to conquer more than just Estera, but I never in my wildest dreams thought that there was this much out there.

Cole points to Myridia. "So here is where you lived, and as you can see to the West of it is just barren desert for hundreds of miles." His finger slides along the map until he hits the word, Mergo. "Mergo is a small sea kingdom. They have adapted to living in the desert by living right on the sea. They generally trade with us and New Port, though they prefer us over New Port. They only ever travel by sea; the desert is a treacherous place." His finger slides along the water's edge, southeast, where it shrinks into a river. I see the words Dun River along the lines. "Here's New Port. Myridia's seaport, it was once ruled by a brute of a man, the Governor, but he has since been replaced by a much more reasonable man."

"I met him, he was disgusting. I was there when Xavier killed him."

"I'm sorry you had to meet him but I am glad that Xavier did at least one thing right. He was a deplorable person, I only met him once. We had traveled there in hopes of convincing him to betray Rolland, but he had other plans that did not involve working with us."

His finger travels to a cluster of giant triangles and I jump at the chance at knowing something. "The Algarian Mountains."

He nods. "Correct. They stretch on as far as the eye can see and have the highest peaks."

"I know. We climbed them and then flew across the giant canyons that separated them. It was the way to the Mystic City."

Cole's eyes widen. "Impressive."

I slide his finger further east, past the Algarian mountains to a blank part of the map. "This is where the Mystic City was before Rolland and Xavier destroyed it."

"We always suspected it was somewhere in the mountains. It was a perfect place to hide and remain safe, and it would have taken us years to even try and locate it. I'm sorry for your loss, Maia." His gaze softens and he gives my hand a small squeeze until I pull it out of his grasp, clearing my throat.

He resumes his trek along the map, his finger heading north. It passes over the land of the forgotten tribes and I can't help but wonder if any witches still reside there or if they all joined Seraphine in her cause.

"Here is Estera, as you can see. We have a few outlying towns like Myridia, but most of our people enjoy the safety of the city." I nod in acknowledgement and then his finger continues further north and my eyes widen.

"There is so much above Estera." I breathe out in complete disbelief.

"Yes, Myridia makes up the southernmost part of Katear. It is the biggest kingdom, with the most land, but it is primarily made up of dense forests, as you know." His finger points to a little island off the northwest part of the Katear. "This is my mother's home, Aquia, right across the water is Forie."

"Which kingdom massacred the nymphs?"

Cole slides his finger to the far side of the map to the east. "That would be the Drigs. They are not the nicest bunch of people. Where the Forie are the most peaceful, the Drigs are the most violent. Personally, I think they descend from the giants. They are monstrous men who thrive on chaos and violence. We only trade with them because they supply some of the best meat in all of Katear. I don't know what they do to it, but it's perfect." He smirks. "Sorry, I digress. Anyway, the Drigs slaughtered the nymphs out of pure spite because one of them attempted to calm the Drig King when he was in a fit of rage and it had the opposite effect. It infuriated him, sent him into a rampage."

"That's terrible."

"Yes, it is." He directs my attention back to the map and drags his finger along the northern part of the map. "Perg, Tougen and Forie, all make up the Northern part of Katear. Each is strong in their own right, each with their own resources and armies."

I run my fingers along the map. How could I not have known that all these kingdoms existed? What was Rolland's reasoning for keeping their existence secret? I ask as much and Cole contemplates my question.

"It seems that Rolland and his son thrive on control. What little interaction I have had with them, shows that. They like to be in control and they like people to know that they are in control. The less you knew, the more control he had over you. You can't want something you don't know about."

"I guess that makes sense." I look at that raven-haired prince, so different, yet so similar to Jordan. "Why do you think your brother kept this from me?"

"I don't know what my brother's reasons were."

I shrug, knowing when I asked that he probably wouldn't know, and turn back to the map. "So, you get along with all these kingdoms?"

"For the most part, yes. We have a strong alliance with the Forie, due to my father's marriage to Enora. My younger brother, Ean, is engaged to the Princess of the Tougen, so that is another alliance that is pretty strong. Because of their close proximity, Perg and Drig tend to stick together and our alliances with them are shaky at best. We always seem to be on the brink of war with them but something always smoothes over and we move into peace talks. It's a rather up-and-down relationship with them."

"Do the Algarian mountains go all the way up to Drig and Perg?" I ask pointing at the large cluster of mountains.

"Yes, they are gigantic. One could easily get lost inside them and never find their way out. You are lucky that you were able to find the Mystic City so easily."

"It was not easy, trust me."

"Forgive me, I did not mean to offend you."

I flash him a reassuring smile. "You didn't, it's okay. Thank you for showing me this."

He folds up the map and returns it to his desk. "It was my pleasure, Maia, I'm glad I was able to open your eyes to this world. If there is anything else you want to learn, I am here to help you."

"Thank you, I appreciate it." I let out a yawn and Cole smiles. "I guess I should probably get some sleep. It has been a long day."

"Of course. Please allow me to escort you back to your room."

"You don't have to."

"Please, I insist. It will allow me to sleep better, knowing you made it safely." He tucks my hand in the crook of his elbow again and leads me into the hall.

"How many siblings do you have?" I ask, curious about the crown Prince. He seems so calm and collected but his room and his reasoning for wanting it small makes me wonder what complexities lie beneath.

"I have four, well five if you include Jordan. Ean is the next oldest at sixteen, followed by the triplets, who are only six. They are a handful but we love them." His eyes sparkle when he talks about his brothers and it warms my heart a little.

"No sisters?"

He shakes his head. "No, mother wanted a girl but, after the triplets I don't think they will be trying anymore. I hope to give her a granddaughter someday so she can at least have that."

"Are you engaged to be married as well?"

"Yes, as crown Prince it is my duty to marry to strengthen our nation."

"I see. Who are you engaged to? Do you at least know her?"

He smiles. "Yes, do not worry for my well being. I happen to like her and am perfectly content in our arranged marriage."

"Oh good, I'm glad to hear it." Our steps slow as we approach my bedroom door.

"I enjoyed your company this evening, Maia. I hope that we can do it again. And please do not hesitate if you have any more questions." He kisses my hand, wishing me good night and then turns back in the direction that we came.

I slip into my room, exhausted from the long day. There were too many ups and downs and I'm hoping that tomorrow will bring with it more clarity. Soft light fills the room and I make a mental note to thank the maids for lighting it so I didn't walk into a dark room.

"Have a good evening with my brother?"

I startle at the familiar voice and turn back to the door. Jordan is leaning against the wall, looking intimidating in the limited light. His usual shaggy mane of dark hair is tamed and appears to have been cut. He's dressed in simple finery, a silky off-white shirt and black slacks. He looks nothing like the baker I knew him to be and everything like the King's son. When I don't reply to him right away he crosses his arms across his chest and raises his eyebrow, which incites my anger.

"And what if I did?" I snap. I raise my hand and pull the fire from the one lantern and send it over to the remaining lanterns on the walls, filling the room with more light.

Jordan pushes off the wall, making a noise that sounds suspiciously like a snort and takes a seat in one of my armchairs.

"We need to talk." His voice sounds tired and it immediately pulls at my heartstrings, but I fight against it. There is no way I am letting him off easy for what he did and especially with the attitude he is sporting right now, like I did something wrong.

"You're right. We do."

"I tried to tell you."

"You didn't try hard enough."

The room falls silent as I wait for him to start, or apologize, or whatever he came here to do.

The corner of his mouth comes up in a sad smirk. "You're not going to make this easy on me, are you?" I shake my head and he sighs. "I suppose I deserve it."

"You think?" Is it wrong that I feel both guilty and justified about my tone?

He cringes and runs his hands along his leg, nervousness rolling off him. "I'm sorry for never telling you who I was. I never told you growing up to protect myself but as we got older I grew afraid that you would turn against me if you knew the truth. You grew up thinking that Estera killed your parents in the war, how could I tell you I was related to their king?"

"You could have tried. You could have told me the truth about everything, instead of continuing the lie that Rolland wove."

"You wouldn't have believed me. I would have been destroying your entire world. It was just easier to wait until the right time, until you found out for yourself. It kept you safer, longer."

"You don't know that, Jordan. I would have trusted you. But, we'll never know, because you made the decision for me."

"Buttercup—"

"Don't Buttercup me, you knew the truth about me, about my family, my entire life and you kept that from me!" My voice rises with each word and tears gather in my eyes, but I refuse to let them fall.

"Everything I did was to protect you. I've loved you since the day I met you and everything I've ever done has been to keep you safe."

"You sound like Xavier." I regret the words as soon as they leave my lips. Jordan's face drops and hurt fills his gaze.

"I'm sorry you feel that way, but trust me when I say I am nothing like that monster."

Silence descends on us again, both of us lost in our hurt feelings. I sink down into the armchair that sits opposite of Jordan, completely drained and unable to stay on my feet any longer. I close my eyes and lean my head back, hoping to gain some composure.

"I never meant to hurt you," Jordan says softly.

"Well, you did."

Jordan lets out a miserable sigh and I hear him murmur a broken, "I know."

"Why were you even sent there?" I change the subject, no longer having the energy to fight with him, or deal with the complex emotions that are rattling around inside me.

He looks almost relieved at the change of subject.

"I was trained since I could walk on how to be a fighter. I couldn't be the future leader of our kingdom but I could be useful in other ways."

"That explains how you know how to use a bow and arrow," I comment off-handedly.

"Yes, among other things. As you've probably already guessed, my father and I do not have the best of relationships. I remind him of my mother and of the life he could have had. He looks in my face and sees her, and it kills him. Growing up he was never overly cruel to me, but he wasn't entirely nice either. He treated me more as a soldier than his son." Jordan runs a hand through his hair, lost in his memories. "When I was ten I was already skilled in most areas of combat; I had a lot of anger built up and it helped fuel me. I was angry at the world for taking my mother, angry at my father for rejecting me, and angry at my mother for leaving me. I was forced to grow up young and I was wise beyond my years.

Father had been talking for years about sending a spy into the Myridian court, to keep an eye on Rolland. He knew he was up to something, and after the peace treaty massacre he withdrew into his palace, only leaving when absolutely necessary. Father did not trust the story that Rolland fed us about Bane attempting to kill him at the treaty meeting and he wanted to know the truth."

"So, he sent you."

Jordan nods. "It served two purposes. It got a spy in Rolland's court that could stay there for a long time without raising suspicion and it got me out of my father's face. He no longer had to look upon the thing that took his beloved away from him. I integrated myself into Rolland's palace, implanted myself in the kitchens, rose up the ranks. I sent my father updates when I could, keeping him abreast of all that went on in Rolland's court. It was during this time that we learned the truth of what really happened at the peace treaty signing."

"You kept me out of your updates, why?"

"By the time you told me that you were a Mystic, I had already grown to care about you, to love you. I couldn't bring myself to tell my father about you. So, I protected you. If he knew you were there and that you were the reason Rolland slaughtered his father, he would have made me extract you. He wouldn't have cared about having a spy in the palace anymore, and would have wanted the ultimate prize—you."

"So, you kept me as a secret to stop him from turning himself into a villain. You waited for me to come to him for aid, in need of his help. Giving him the power." I throw Jordan's words back at him, the very words he spoke to his father.

His eyes widen. "Where did you hear those words?"

"From your mouth."

"How?"

"It doesn't matter. All that matters is that you said them. So, whose side are you really on, Jordan?"

Jordan stands abruptly, his eyes wild. He shoves his hand into his hair again, sending it in all directions, as he paces the floor. "You don't understand, Maia. It is a complicated situation."

"Then explain it to me."

"There is something you have to know about my father. He is not a man that views weakness kindly. That part of him died with my mother. Most of him died with her."

"He seems fine to me."

"You don't know him like I do!" He snaps and I'm completely taken aback. He has never raised his voice at me like that before. He takes several deep calming breaths and faces me again. "I'm sorry. My father has a way of bringing out the worst in me. The way he appears is all due to Enora. Her presence calms him, which is why you will always find them together in a public setting. Away from her he is unstable and quick to anger. No matter what you hear, he never fully recovered from my mother's death."

"So why return here? Why bring us here?"

"Because he is the best chance you have at defeating Seraphine. He is the lesser of two evils. He has the greatest army in Katear and he can rally the other kingdoms to come to his aid. We need him; the Kamora is not strong enough to take on Seraphine and Xavier alone."

"Was there a chance he could have killed you?"

Jordan hesitates but nods a moment later. "Yes. He does not take betrayal well and what I did was a betrayal in his eyes."

"You brought us here, knowing that it may have meant your death." I say it as a statement, not a question, but Jordan nods anyway. I rise to my feet and do something I never thought I'd ever do to Jordan. I slap him. "My life is not worth more than yours."

He stares at me for several seconds, clearly in shock and then lifts a hand to the growing red spot on his cheek. "You slapped me."

"You deserved it."

His lips curves in a small smirk. "I suppose I did."

He stares intently into my eyes and emotions swirl wildly. He slides his palm on my cheek, barely touching my skin. His eyes slide down to my lips and he whispers my name almost like a plea.

He leans in to kiss me but I put my hand up to stop him. "No, I need time."

"Maia." Pain deepens his voice and fills his gaze. "You have to believe me, I never meant to hurt you."

"I know you think that, but the reality is that you did hurt me and I need time to process it."

"I love you." He sounds defeated as he speaks.

His words fill me with a network of complex emotions. They choke me in their intensity. I yearn to accept his apology, forgive him everything and melt into his arms, but I hold back because along with that yearning to forgive is the festering wound of his betrayal. I can feel it as though it were a physical wound, bubbling and decaying in my chest. It hurts more than Xavier's betrayal ever did and I guess that goes to show how deep my feelings are for the boy standing in front of me. It breaks my heart that it took something like this to really show the depth of my emotions and it scares me that I can't figure out a way back from this. How do we recover what we once had? Will we be able to be whole again? That final thought begins to crack the fragile control that I have left and I turn away from him as tears fill my eyes. How can we be together if I can't trust him?

"I think you should go." My voice cracks a little and I pray that he didn't notice.

"Maia."

"Please, go." My voice is barely above a whisper but I know he hears me because he sighs. My control is barely holding on and is slipping rapidly. I need him to leave, I can't let him see how conflicted I am and how much I still want to be with him, even after everything that he has done.

"When you are ready to talk, come and find me. Until then, I will give you space." With those final words, I hear his steps retreat and then the quiet click of the door as it closes. Only when I am sure I am alone do I allow the tears to fall. Broken sobs fill the quiet space and I realize that Cole was right; the echoes of the large space do make you feel empty and alone.

Chapter 17

"YOU LOOK TERRIBLE," KADEN says to me the next morning when he arrives to escort me from my room.

"Thanks," I mumble in reply because I know he's right. I saw myself in the mirror this morning, eyes bloodshot and swollen from crying, and my hair a knotted mess. I cried most of the night, until I had no more tears to shed and, even then, I couldn't fall asleep. I stared at the ceiling until finally I gave up and just sat outside on the balcony, hoping to find peace in the outdoors. When Kaden arrived I hastily put my hair into a messy ponytail and threw on a simple black dress that I found in the room's closet.

"You okay?"

"I'm fine."

"You don't look fine."

I sigh and run a hand down my face in exasperation. "Kaden."

"Is this about Jordan?"

"I don't want to talk about it." Why did I think having a brother was such a great thing I think grumpily and then mentally kick myself for the thought. I should be grateful that he is caring enough to ask, no one but Jordan really ever pushed past my initial reply of fine. The thought sends a fresh wave of sorrow through me.

Kaden lays a sympathetic hand on my shoulder. "Maybe it's for the best." He says quietly.

"Why would you say that?"

He smiles but it seems off and shrugs. "Just trying to show brotherly support. Sorry I'm still pretty new at this."

I decide to cut him a break and give him a small smile. He returns it and we walk the rest of the way in silence. We exit the palace and Kaden leads me into the mostly deserted streets of Ester. It is still early morning and the town is just waking up. The cobblestones crunch softly beneath my feet and a gentle breeze glides across my cheek. It's peaceful, and I allow that peace to settle in me. I have to face the council today. They may be my people, but I barely know them. I can't allow them to see me like this, a mess, over a spat with a boy. I take several deep calming breaths and allow the breeze to fill my lungs, drawing strength from the air. I feel better after a few minutes, at least strong enough to do what I need to do. I can break down again later once I am alone.

"Cara!" A high-pitched excited cry breaks the quiet of the empty streets. Before I understand what is happening, arms encircle my waist and a mop of bright blond hair is tucked just under my chin.

"Layla?"

She disentangles herself from me and snaps, "Who else would it be?"

I laugh, oh how I've missed her snarky attitude. I pull her into a hug again and squeeze her tight until she struggles against me, and I release her. She puts some space between us, eyeing me suspiciously like I might make her hug me again.

"I'm so happy to see you, Layla, and to know that you are alright. I've been so worried about you."

Her eyes soften, and I suddenly realize that she looks so much older than when I last saw her. She looks wiser, almost, like she's seen things that a girl her age should never see. "I'm glad to see that you are safe as well, Cara."

"I'm going by Maia now."

She gives me a single nod. "Good, I like Maia much better."

"Glad I meet your approval." She smiles at my words. At Kaden's beckon we continue following him.

"I had to see you before you got stuck listening to the council drone on for hours. They really like to hear themselves talk. If I hadn't snuck out of the house and found you, I probably wouldn't have seen you until next week." Her words remind me of Silas, the Mystic historian who died during the destruction of the Mystic City. It makes me wonder if his body still lies among the rubble of the city or if someone retrieved it.

"I'm glad you came to see me. I was hoping that I would run into you. I've missed you."

"I missed you too," she mumbles, and I notice that her cheeks are flushed. "This place is pretty cool, we have a lot of space. The King gave us our own sector of the city."

"That's great. I'm happy to hear that you have all been taken care of. I was so worried about all of you."

"Have you met Cole?"

The change in conversation is giving me whiplash but it also warms the cold in my heart because it feels so normal. I never thought I would be having a conversation with Layla again and it makes me happy.

"Yes, I have met Cole."

"Dreamy, right? I mean, wow. Much better than that jerk, Xavier." Her eyes widen. "Whoops, sorry, I wasn't supposed to mention him."

"Why aren't you supposed to mention him?"

Kaden clears his throat, drawing both our gazes to him. He looks mildly exasperated with Layla. "Layla, why don't you catch up with Maia later. I will make sure someone tells you immediately when the meeting is over. Does that work for you?"

She rolls her eyes. "Fine, I know when I'm not wanted." She backs away, giving us a wave. "See you later, Maia."

I raise an eyebrow. "Why was she not allowed to mention Xavier?"

He shrugs. "We just thought it would be best for you to not have the constant reminder of him over your head. Everyone has been instructed to steer clear of the topic of Xavier unless it's official business."

"I see." We pass through a small gateway. "So, what she said is true? The Mystics have been treated well?"

"Yes, we have. King Erik has been a gracious host. As Layla said, he gave us our own sector of the city, it needed a little work but we managed. We were just happy to have a place to lay our heads and be safe."

"How did you all make it here?"

"Once we left the Mystic City we rendezvoused at a safe house that was buried deep in the Algarian Mountains. We could only stay there for a limited time; it was not nearly big enough to house all of us comfortably for any amount of time. After many days of deliberation, the council decided that since Rolland was behind everything, then perhaps the stories about Estera were false as well. We ventured here in hopes that that we may at least find some assistance. We had hoped for maybe supplies or directions to a place that could be safe for us, but Erik welcomed us with open arms."

"Do you trust him?" I can't shake what Jordan said about his father being unstable.

"Honestly?"

"Always. Stays between us."

Kaden looks around to ensure we are alone, when he is satisfied he turns back to me. "No. I'll be honest, he has the council eating out of the palm of his hand. They adore him and everything that he has done for us. Don't get me wrong, I am appreciative of everything he has done, but something just feels off about him. I can't quite put my finger on it."

"Jordan says he is unstable. He says the only reason he appears as calm as he does is because of Enora. She calms him."

Kaden rubs his chin with a thoughtful look. "That would explain why I had never seen him without her." His expression turns guilty. "Maia, there is something you should know."

"There you two are. The council is waiting." Sage appears in the doorway we are standing next to, looking beautiful in her olive-green gown and her curly auburn hair pulled back into a harsh ponytail.

"Sage!" I give her a quick hug and she smiles in return.

She gives my hand a squeeze. "We'll catch up later. The council is getting restless. I want to hear everything."

My stomach drops a little at that because everything involves telling her about Myka and that conversation fills me with dread. I swallow past the lump in my throat and nod back at her, following silently behind her. We file into a large room and the council members stand to greet us. I get bombarded by handshakes and greetings and am quickly overwhelmed. Kaden plays interference and thankfully steps in asking the council members to take their seats so we can get started. I once again marvel at the presence that he commands of the room. He was born to be a king.

"I know we are all very excited that Princess Maia has finally joined us. We have all been anxiously waiting for her arrival, but let's not bombard her and scare her away." A few chuckles ripple through the council. "I know we have a lot to discuss so why don't we get started. Council member Leon?"

Leon steps forward and I immediately recognize him from the council meetings we had back in the Mystic City. He gives me a warm, welcoming smile. He was always kind to me during the meetings and seemed to really care about what was best for the Mystic race. I glance around the room when he begins talking, and I'm happy to see several familiar faces. It seems that most of the council survived the destruction of the city.

"What can you tell us about the witch, Seraphine, Princess Maia? King Erik has informed us Rolland is no longer a concern to us, but that we are now facing an even greater evil," Leon asks, pulling me back into the discussion.

"Yes, Rolland is dead, killed by his son, Xavier. Seraphine was using Rolland to get to me. She wants the powers of the Aurora. She planned for Rolland to take the powers from me and then she would take them from him so she could avoid the curse."

"And what of Xavier? Where is he?"

I hesitate for a moment and then reluctantly admit, "It seems that he is now working with Seraphine."

"How could you have allowed yourself to be fooled by this prince?" a smooth voice says from the back and I cringe. "Were you not his fiancé?"

Council member Zane approaches Leon and me. His black, silver-streaked hair is slicked back and he leers at me like I am beneath him. Where Leon had been accepting and kind, Zane was skeptical of me and the biggest defender for the Mystics remaining in their safe paradise. I'm sure he blames me for its destruction and their removal from the cushy existence.

"I had no idea that Xavier would betray me."

"I find that hard to believe, Princess, given how…" He pauses and his mocking tone grates on my nerves, "intelligent and perceptive you are."

Kaden appears next to me, his expression thick with warning. "Forgive me, Zane, but it sounds to me like you are insinuating that Maia helped Xavier. That she wanted the Mystic City destroyed."

Zane bows his head. "Of course not, Your Majesty, I would never believe that our long-lost Princess, raised by our enemies would ever turn against us. I'm just trying to figure out how she did not see it." The irony of his words are not lost on me or Kaden.

I push Kaden back, ready to face my own battle. "Xavier was, and is, a manipulative human being. I was blind, I will admit. I thought what he felt for me and the way he acted was what love looked like, but I was wrong. His love is dangerous and obsessive. It is not healthy and I know that now. He has hurt me more than you'll ever know. I had no idea what he was capable of. The only thing I can apologize for is not seeing it sooner. But I will not apologize for his actions; those are his and his alone. I had nothing to do with their attack on the Mystic City."

A few claps sound from the council members but they quiet quickly as Zane and I face off. He sneers but stands his ground.

"Then tell me, Princess," again, his tone is mocking, "what have you done since to help our people in their plight."

My face must display the shock that I am feeling because several council members stare at Zane like he is mad.

"What have I done? Are you serious right now?" My voice grows louder with each word. "I was a prisoner. I had my powers stripped away, gone, just like that. I saw my friend killed in cold blood, the woman who raised me executed, and all that time I had nothing with which to defend myself. You have the audacity to ask me what I have done? How dare you!"

Several gasps come from the council members and Kaden softly says my name. Blinding light is streaming through the room and I look for the source, which, unsurprisingly, is me. In my anger I pulled the Prakera to the surface and my fingers and arms are glowing.

"Maia, you have the Prakera?" Kaden exclaims.

I give him a quick angry nod, never taking my eyes off Zane. I get a sick sense of satisfaction when his eyes widen and unease enters them as he stares at my hands.

"The Prakera came to be while I was prisoner. Rolland got out of control and attempted to kill my friend, Jordan. I was able to save him by manifesting the Prakera."

"The Prakera has not been seen in thousands of years," Kaden states.

"Then these are darker times then we imagined," Leon comments.

"You have the Prakera and yet you did not manage to escape?" Zane remarks, his unease has now shifted to disbelief.

My anger snaps and I send a bolt of energy into a far wall. "What is your problem with me?" Everyone jumps except Zane who watches me in mild interest.

"I am concerned about the safety of our people. I watched my friends and family slowly disappear during the war. I will not have what remains of our people killed because some spoiled princess is led by her emotions and allowed herself to be deceived for so long."

"Enough!" Kaden's sharp tone vibrates off the walls of the small room. "Council member Zane, you are talking to the Princess. You should show her the same respect that you show me."

"She is not my princess," Zane snaps. "I will not follow a girl that we do not know, who conveniently led King Rolland to our safe haven resulting in its destruction. We were safe and comfortable there, we had no reason to leave. I will never show this spoiled brat any respect; she is nothing. All she has brought us is pain and suffering."

Silence settles in the room, an eerie reminder that what Zane said is true. These people don't know me, they have no reason to believe me. I have only brought them pain.

"Council member Zane, you are dismissed. You are no longer a part of this council." Kaden's voice is deadly.

"You will regret this, King Kaden. You will regret putting your faith in her. She will be the destruction of our race. She will be the end of the Mystics," Zane cries as he is led out by several other council members. The door slams on his protests and the room once again falls silent. I look around at the remaining council members in the room and I can see the doubt in their eyes. They may not feel the same as Zane, but he has put doubt into their heads. I look at Kaden and I can see by his expression that he sees it too.

"I want nothing more than to make sure that our people are safe. I did not lead Rolland to the Mystic City, and I did not help Xavier. I will do everything in my power to make sure that nothing else happens to the Mystics. I have wanted nothing more than to be a part of a family, my family. You are all my family, I never have, and never will betray you. You must believe me, I am not the person that Zane has accused me of being."

Council member Malachi stands in the back. "I do not share the same views as previous council member Zane, but I do have a few questions. How were you unable to escape when you had the Prakera?"

"When Seraphine began working with Rolland, she

brought with her the Red Stars." A few gasps can be heard throughout the room. "While I was a prisoner in the palace I had a bracelet wrapped around my wrist, restricting my powers. When the Prakera first appeared, they had two Red Star upon my wrist and I was able to break through them, but once they realized my power, they added more and they took the Prakera from me."

"Maia, I had no idea." Kaden rests a comforting hand on my shoulder.

I ignore the pity in his eyes. I face the council, determination straightening my spine and hardening my face. "I am Maia, Princess of the Mystic race, daughter of Alera and Gaven, the beloved King and Queen. They sacrificed their own lives to ensure that I lived to see my full potential. They believed in me and they believed in the power of the Aurora. I will not allow their sacrifice to be in vain. Seraphine and Xavier will never deceive me again, and no one will ever feel the cold press of a Red Star on their skin. I will defeat Seraphine and we will live in peace once more. I will fulfill the destiny that I was put on this earth to do, and I will save us."

The pity in Kaden's eyes has faded and now he looks upon me in pride. We both turn to the council members in trepidation, unsure of how they will react to my passionate speech.

Council member Leon clears his throat. "I think I can safely speak for the group when I say that the council is behind you, Princess Maia, and we do not share the feelings of Zane. Your parents were our beloved King and Queen and you are right, they believed in you and so will we. You have the best intentions in mind when it comes to our people. However," he puts a finger up to stop me when I open my mouth to reply, "as noble as your intentions are, you cannot do them alone."

"That is why we came to Estera. If we are able to ally ourselves with Erik, we will have an army."

"Yes, we need an alliance with Erik and that is why we are here."

Kaden stiffens next to me. "Leon, perhaps we should save this topic for another time. This meeting has not gone as planned."

"With all due respect, King Kaden, this is the perfect time. Zane cannot be the only person out there doubting our Princess. We must silence their doubts and show them that the Princess puts the Mystic people above all else."

"What are you talking about? What will you have me do?" Unease creeps up my spine.

Leon turns to me, giving me his full attention. "You will marry Prince Colieus, solidifying our alliance with the Estera kingdom."

"What?" I am only capable of the single word response. All other speech has failed me.

"When we arrived, the King proposed the alliance and we accepted. As a good faith gesture, he provided us with this sector of the city, giving us a new home and protection. He will provide you your army and will stand against Seraphine and Xavier beside us. The only thing he asks for in return is that when it is over he gets Myridia. He will be king of both kingdoms. And one day when Colieus rises to power, you will stand by his side, as Queen of Myridia and Estera."

I turn to Kaden, finally finding my voice. "You knew about this?" His expression is answer enough and I turn back to the council. "So once again this is about power. Rolland wanted me for my powers and now Erik is doing the same."

"King Erik has done nothing but help us since we have arrived in his city. He is nothing like Rolland and just wants peace for Katear," Leon explains.

"With the added bonus of having the Aurora under his thumb."

"He did not even mention that when he proposed the marriage. His only concern was uniting our two people; creating a strong alliance. Once this is over, he plans to help us rebuild Odeca so that we may live in peace in our own land, in our own city, a kingdom of our own. This will be a strong alliance and the first step in human, mystics, and all beings living in peace."

"And if I refuse?"

"We had hoped that you would not," Leon states, "but if we break this alliance with King Erik, I fear that we will be sent out of the city and you will face Seraphine alone. Surely you must see the benefit in this alliance."

"I do. I just do not appreciate you agreeing to a marriage without me being present."

"This is your duty as our Princess. All of our people will see that you are putting their needs first. There will be no more doubts of your loyalty," Malachi interjects.

I put my hand up to silence him. "I am not saying I am refusing, but I am also not saying I am agreeing either. I need time to process this, can you give me that?"

Leon looks to the other council members and I am met with a sea of nods. "You can have until tomorrow morning, Princess; I hope you will make the decision that is best for our people."

I don't even wait to be excused; I leave the room as fast as my feet can take me. I hear Kaden calling my name behind me but I refuse to turn back. He knew about the marriage and he said nothing. I need to be alone, I need to process all that has been said.

Water runs between my fingers as I send a sphere of liquid into the air and back down. After the council meeting, I escaped to the safety of the garden, losing myself in my abilities. I helped a few trees grow, I pruned and cared for the tiny garden, bringing it to life, under my hands. Once it was to my liking I turned to water, tossing it around and idly playing with the clear substance. It helps to calm my emotions but does nothing to clear my thoughts.

I know that what the council says is true. Marrying Cole would be the best thing for our people. It would solidify an alliance with a strong kingdom, guaranteeing our continued safety. No one would dare hurt the Mystics with the future Queen of Estera being one. But every time I think of marrying Cole, my heart breaks even more than it already is. The future I thought I had ahead of me is slowly slipping out of my grasp. I will never be able to be with Jordan.

Maybe Kaden was right, and it was for the best that Jordan and I are currently fighting. Maybe finding out about his lies was a blessing. I don't know if I could be strong enough to walk away from him if that had never happened. His lies have planted seeds of doubt in my heart and mind when it comes to him, and our being together. But then again, how can I turn my back on him after everything we have been through. I love him, that will never change. I love him with all of my being. Even as my tears fell last night because of his actions, I yearned for his arms to comfort me, for him to wipe away my tears and tell me that is going to be alright.

"Rough morning?"

I drop the ball of water that I was twisting around my wrist with a small splash. It leaves a few splatters of water on my black dress but that is of little concern. I turn to the silken voice behind me, the raven-haired prince, my potential betrothed.

"Did you know?"

He takes a seat next to me on the white swing and pushes us off gently. "I like what you did to the place. It's beautiful. Your powers are truly remarkable."

"You didn't answer my question, Cole." I'm suddenly so tired; tired of fighting, tired of crying, and tired of caring. I never thought I'd miss the days when life was simpler in my oblivious bubble in Rolland's palace.

"Will it change what you think of me?"

I shrug. "Probably not."

He nods. "I did know. Father told me as soon as the council agreed. They thought it was best that the council told you themselves instead of hearing it from one of us."

"So, when you said you knew her and were perfectly content with the arrangement, you were talking about me?" I lean my head against the back of the chair, gazing up at the sky. I watch a few clouds drift slowly by, wishing that I could be free in the sky as they are. How did I end up free from one cage just to end up in another one?

"I was, and I was being honest. I told you that you would only ever get honesty from me."

"Then I'll be honest with you. I love Jordan."

"I know. That was made very clear from your reaction when you learned of his true identity."

"You would marry the woman that your brother loves?"

"My brother and I hold no love for one another. We spent very little time together growing up, and then he was away in Myridia. We have very little attachment to each other. In fact, I barely know him, besides the letters that he wrote back to father. So, yes, I would marry the woman my brother loves. Like I told you before, as a royal, sometimes you must do what is necessary for your kingdom."

"I don't know what to say." My words are barely above a whisper.

"Then I'll speak." He grabs my hand and holds it between his, turning in his seat to face me. "Maia, I know this is not the most ideal situation. I know it is not what either of us ever wanted in our lives. My father has always held any engagements off and I had begun to hope that perhaps he was allowing me the luxury of choosing for myself, but it seems he was just waiting for the right one to come along."

"Not sure how ours is the right one. My people offer him nothing."

"Your people offer him everything he's ever wanted— Myridia, and you."

"It's always about more power." I attempt to pull my hand from his grasp but he tightens his grip.

"Maia, as I told you before, you do not deserve to be a pawn in other people's game, but the reality is that right now, you are. You are a pawn just as I am; that is the life we lead. But if you choose to marry me, one day we will be King and Queen and we will no longer be anyone's pawns. I know I am not who you want and this life is not what you want. Our marriage will not be built on love, and it may never get there. But I swear to you, I will do anything in my power to make sure you are happy. You will want for nothing. I am content in this arrangement, I can see that we will make a good partnership. We will make a strong King and Queen of Estera, that I promise you."

"What will happen to Jordan?"

"I'm not going to lie to you, Maia, he cannot stay here. I will not spend our life and our marriage competing for your affection. When you choose to marry me, you choose me. I will not share you. Once we are married he will have to leave Estera and live elsewhere."

"Would your father really cast us out if I refused to go through with this?"

Cole sighs. "It is, unfortunately, hard to say. My father can be, well, unstable at times. He tries to hide it and my mother helps, but it slips through occasionally. I do not know how he would react if you reneged on the council's agreement."

"So, I have no choice, you are saying."

"No, there is always a choice, Maia. It's just a matter of figuring out which one hurts the fewest people." He stands to his feet after giving my hand a final squeeze. "I will make an excuse for you as to why you are not meeting with Father today. I think you need some time to think."

"Thank you."

He leans down and kisses my cheek. "I can make you happy, Maia, but I will also respect whatever decision you make."

All I can manage is a nod, so lost in the current of emotions swarming me. I barely notice when he leaves and I am alone. He's right; I could be happy with him, it wouldn't be the epic love story that I always dreamed of having but I would be happy and safe. From the little interaction I have had with him, I can see that he is a good man. That thought pauses me—is he? I used to think that Xavier was a good man. For my whole life I thought Rolland and Xavier and Evelyn were all good people. What if Cole is the exact same, what if he is playing me? What if the person he is showing me is hiding a monster underneath?

I drop my head in my hands. These are the days when I miss my mother the most. The days when I wish I had someone to talk to, someone to work through all of these thoughts with. Jordan used to be that person, but, for this, he cannot help. I must make this decision alone, I am the only one who can make this choice. I must decide not only for myself but for my people.

I am a Mystic Princess and I must make the right decision for my people as well as my own heart.

Chapter 18

THE SUN SETS AND the stars blanket the sky before I finally drag myself out of the safe solitude of the garden. No one disturbed me through my dark thoughts and I think I have a certain raven-haired prince to thank for that. Even with all the time I had, I still have not come to a complete decision. My stomach rumbles as I make my way through the strange halls. This could be my home one day, so I guess they won't be so strange soon. A wonderful aroma fills the air and my stomach lets out another rumble in protest of my skipped lunch and dinner. I follow the sweet smell to its origin and thankfully find the palace's massive kitchen. I let myself in, used to the open-door policy of the Myridian kitchen, at least it was an open door policy for me.

The kitchen is dark except for a small corner where a sole person leans over a large bowl, mixing vigorously. Intrigued, I creep closer and to my surprise I find that the person is Jordan.

"You never were very good at sneaking up on people, Buttercup." His soft voice fills the dark kitchen.

"I wasn't trying to sneak up on you. I came for something to eat." I say grumpily, coming out of the darkness and into the light where he works.

"You weren't at dinner." He motions for me to take a seat and then turns to the fridge, pulling out little trays of food. I'm struck by the nostalgia of the moment. How many times have we been here before—him baking in front of me, while I eat whatever is in front of me. It makes me sad and yearn once again for simpler times. He places the food in front of me and then returns to his bowl.

"I'm surprised to find you in here," I mumble in between bites.

"I needed to think and get away. The kitchen has always been a solace for me, just like your garden always was for you. Baking calms me."

I wish I could take away the icy coldness between us. His voice seems so detached, so formal. I want his warm laugh. I want to see the sparkle in his eyes when he looks at me, but since walking in here he has yet to look at me, keeping his gaze shuttered.

"Did I miss anything at dinner?"

He turns away, taking his bowl with him and starts preparing whatever he is making, arranging it to put in the oven. His muscles flex in his shoulders as his arms move and I can't take my eyes off their movements. I want to memorize every part of him, no matter what happens I want his image imprinted in my mind forever.

"Nothing important. Father complained that you had missed both your meeting with him and dinner, but Cole pacified him. He made up some excuse that I can't remember." He slides something in the oven as he pulls something out. Next thing I know there is a small plate of cocoanos sitting in front of me and I can't help but smile at their wonderful aroma, they smell like home. He starts washing his dishes, again with his back to me. "So, where were you?"

I don't answer for a second, my mouth full of the chocolatey goodness. "I needed to think, too."

"I saw Layla today. She was searching for you, said you were supposed to come find her after the council meeting and you didn't. She was pretty worried."

"Oh," I say, guilt filling my gut. I was so focused on myself I forgot about Layla.

"She was asking about Myka. You haven't told them?" It might be my own imagination but I swear I hear accusation in his tone.

"I'm going to, I just, haven't found the right time." I look down at my half eaten cocoano as guilty tears fill my gaze.

"Hey." Jordan's wet hand covers mine and his tone is soft. "You might never find the right time, but they do deserve to know."

He squeezes my hand and then goes back to work and I realize that his accusatory tone was all in my head. He's right, I won't ever find the right time, I will have to tell them eventually. They deserve to know that Myka is dead and now his body is being possessed by a vaekua.

"I'll tell them, I promise."

"I know you will, Buttercup. You always do the right thing." His words cause me to drop my food, my appetite gone. I don't want to do the right thing anymore.

Silence settles in the room and it takes me a moment to realize that he is no longer washing his dishes and he's standing on the other side of the counter, silently watching me.

He reaches across the counter, lacing his clean fingers with my gooey ones. A spark shoots between us as his eyes finally meet mine and they are a storm of emotion. I'm not sure which one of moves first and I know when I look back at this moment it won't matter, but in seconds we are kissing. Kissing like we are starving and the only thing that will satisfy us, is each other. He pulls me out of my chair and hauls me across the counter, sitting me on top of it. He stands between my knees and thrusts his fingers in my hair, controlling its motion. For the first time since last night, I feel whole. I wrap my arms around him and clutch him like he is my lifeline, and maybe he is. He has always been the constant in my life, my saving grace. My anger towards him melts, just as I do in his arms. I love him, I don't care who his father is, I don't care that he hid himself from me. The only thing that matters right now, in this moment, is his lips upon mine and the feelings of love that are coursing through my veins.

He pulls away and rests his forehead on mine, catching his breath. I run my hand along his cheek and he leans into it, his eyes fluttering closed.

"I don't deserve your forgiveness."

"I don't deserve your love."

He opens his eyes and kisses me softly, a complete contrast to what we were just doing. "You deserve the world. You deserve every happiness."

I begin to shake my head but he kisses me to silence my protest. "We'll agree to disagree," He says. He kisses my nose and then gathers me in his arms, tucking my head beneath his chin. I let his warmth seep into my cold and brittle bones, breathing life back into them after the tumultuous day that I had.

"You'll never know how sorry I am for deceiving you, Maia. I should have told you, but I was afraid of how it would affect our relationship." He's running his hands through my hair in a soothing manner and it relaxes me more than anything ever could.

"I understand why, Jordan, I do. I'm just so tired of all the lies and being deceived. My whole life was a lie, and the one thing I thought was a constant was you, and it turned out you were a lie too. That's why I was so upset."

"I never meant to hurt you."

"I know." He plays with my hair in silence and I just enjoy the safety of his arms. I don't want to leave them, I know what waits for me beyond them. "I don't think you're like Xavier."

He chuckles and I feel it along my face. "Well, that's a relief. The only thing I want in common with that jerk, is our affection for you."

"Are you still in trouble with your father?"

His hand stills in my hair for a second and I lift my head to see his face. He smiles down at me reassuringly and his hand continues its motions through my blonde locks.

"For the most part, no. He bought my story of why I left you out of my letters. I provided him with enough good information that it seems to fit. So, I am no longer in danger of being executed for treason, but he is still not entirely happy with me. I've been steering clear of him for the most part, unless he summons me, which he hasn't since that conversation you witnessed."

"Good. I'm glad to know that you are out of danger."

"So, why don't you tell me why you were hiding away all day? What's wrong?"

Instantly the unease and fear of the day returns full force and I pull out of his arms, abruptly. I slide off the counter and begin pacing, gnawing nervously at my bottom lip. This was a mistake, being here, with him. My decision felt easier to make when we were at odds. But now, as I stand here with the taste of his lips on mine, my emotions are in even more turmoil. Now making this choice will be harder than ever.

"Buttercup." The nickname sends flutters to my stomach just as simultaneously pain shoots to my heart. "Tell me."

I hesitate, gnawing so hard on my lip that I taste blood, but he deserves my honesty. What kind of person would I be if I kept this from him after condemning him for his lie. "Before we got here the Mystic council made a deal with your father. His protection in exchange for a marriage alliance."

"Marriage alliance?" Confusion lines his face but I know the second it clicks because his beautiful face collapses in horror. "No."

"They arranged my marriage to Cole." Confirming whatever thoughts he must have been having.

He stares down at the floor, still as a statue. I have to watch his chest to confirm he's breathing, as that's how shallow his breaths are. When he does finally move it is to slam his fist onto the countertop, causing me to jump.

He stalks to me and pulls my face to his, sucking the air from my lungs. This kiss is so different than the one we shared just minutes ago. It is desperate and filled with yearning and pain. It pulls at my heart and I long to pull him closer to soothe his churning emotions but I know I can't because I have nothing to say that will heal his slowly breaking heart. Like me, he is watching the future he thought he had, slipping away.

"Please." His voice is pleading, and I can never recall a time that I heard him plead. "Please tell me, you are not agreeing to this. Tell me that you told the council no."

"Jordan." The one word holds so many feelings. I can't give him the answer that he wants but I also can't give him the other answer either. I stand on a threshold of indecision, both directions a different path of self destruction. Either decision will destroy me—a life without Jordan or a life without a safe home for my people. Either choice will tear something away from me.

Suddenly an explosion rocks the ground beneath our feet. Jordan pulls away from me and his face is sharp in alarm.

"What was that?" I ask.

"I don't know." He grabs a knife off his kitchen counter as

another explosion sounds in the distance. He grabs my hand and pulls me behind him out of the kitchen, knife at the ready. He leads me to a set of large windows that overlook the city. In the distance, smoke billows into the sky from blazing fires that seem to be engulfing parts of the city.

"Well that's not good," he mutters.

"Do you think it is an attack? I thought the city was safe since the bridges are brought up at night."

"It is, but look." He points to the main bridge. "The bridge is down and I can see that the gates are open. Someone has infiltrated the city."

I suck in a sharp breath. "Do you think it's Seraphine?"

He pulls me into his arms for a quick kiss. "I don't know but I will protect you. You will not go back to him."

I don't miss that he says him instead of her and I wonder if he even realizes what he said.

"Maia!" Cole rounds the corner and his eyes immediately drop to notice our joined hands. His steps slow but otherwise he makes no comment. "I've been looking everywhere for you. The city is under attack."

"Do we know who it is?" Jordan asks, his look challenging his brother to say anything about our conjoined hands.

"Father sent soldiers down to find out what is going on and to help those trapped in the fires. We should be hearing back from them soon."

An eerie cry splits the air and the hairs on my arm rise. Jordan and I exchange identical alarmed glances both recognizing the sound—the vaekua have infiltrated the city.

"What was that?" Cole asks, a little bit of color leeches from his face.

"Vaekua, Seraphine's shadow creatures."

"How did they find us?" I ask Jordan.

"I don't know. We made sure we were not followed. Fin and Enyo were constantly doubling back during our journey to ensure that. There is no way that they followed us without us knowing."

I turn to Cole. "Do you think your father could have a traitor in his midst?"

"If there is, they will pay dearly. My father does not take kindly to traitors." Cole eyes Jordan for a split second before motioning for us to follow. "We should move, we should be receiving our report of what is going on at the edge of the city soon."

Jordan and I follow after Cole to the King's study, where we find the King, the Queen, and Melinda. I rush to her side quickly, ensuring her safety. She assures me she is fine.

"Where are Ben, Fin and Enyo?" I ask her.

"Fin and Enyo went down with the King's soldiers to find out what is going on. I have not seen Ben since last night when I went to bed."

"I'm going down there. If there are vaekua down there then I'm the only thing that can destroy them."

Cole blocks my path when I start for the door. "Maia, you should stay put until we know what is going on."

"Cole, I am the one who can destroy the vaekua. The Prakera is their weakness." I summon a bit of energy to my fingers as evidence that I can.

"I'll go with you." Jordan steps up next to me still armed with his rather large kitchen knife.

Cole looks at the glowing orb on my finger in awe and steps aside as if in a daze. I hear Melinda yell at us to be careful before we close the door behind us, but just as soon as it closes it reopens and Cole steps out.

"I'm coming with you," He states, daring us to disagree with him. We don't, and the three of us take off at a run down the winding hallways of the palace. It isn't long before we are in the streets of Estera and heading towards the blazing inferno at the edge of the city. Images of the destruction of the Mystic City flash through my mind. How many times am I going to have to watch a city burn in my lifetime? I pick up my pace, not willing to lose another home to an uncontrollable flame.

To my surprise and relief, I see water rushing over the walls of the city, snuffing out some of flames. I see several Mystics scattered around, working to control the inferno and sending water into its depths. Several buildings have been lost, completely engulfed, and thick smoke chalks the air. My lungs fill with it and I cough, quickly ripping off a piece of my dress and covering my nose and mouth. Jordan and Cole do the same with their shirts.

A soldier runs up to us and bows to the Prince. "What's the status?" Cole asks.

"It appears that the gate was opened from the inside, Your Highness. All the men who were guarding the front gate were slaughtered when we arrived."

"Have you found who was responsible?"

The soldier hesitates, clearly unsure how to answer. Finally, he reluctantly states, "We don't know who let them in, but what was let into the city was not human. They look like men, but they are not."

That eerie scream rips through the night sky again behind us and our group's heads turn slowly to the source of the sound. Two vaekua with blood-red eyes stare at us, snapping their jaws menacingly. One of them is dragging a limp body by its leg behind it. Blood follows in his wake.

"Maia, now would be a good time to—" Jordan's cut off by another scream that comes from behind us and it is answered by several others. A quick glance reveals more vaekua are materializing around us and that we are surrounded. Our group situates ourselves so we are back to back.

"Your weapons won't kill them. It will only slow them down. Only the Prakera can kill them," I say to Cole and the soldier with us. I call the Prakera to my hand and the vaekua around us hiss and snap their jaws but they do not back down.

Before I can take my next breath, the vaekua attack, converging on our location. I send an energy blast at the closest one and it disintegrates as it screams. I can hear the grunts of my companions behind me as they fight off their attackers but I am too focused on the ones in front of me to turn to their aid. A terrified scream comes from my left and I look just in time to see the soldier who met us being dragged into the shadows by a vaekua. His screams end with a sickening sound that sends shivers down my spine. I hurl energy balls in every direction, taking out as many vaekua as I can. I'm losing count of how many are around us. Vaekua after vaekua attack me, a never-ending flow of black death and teeth. Every time I eliminate one, three more appear to take its place. We are in an endless dance of prey and predator. I wish I still had my wind element; I would send Cole and Jordan to safety so that I could take out these creatures without worrying about them. The Prakera is just as dangerous to them as it is to the vaekua.

"Maia!" Cole's cry comes from my right and the split second I take to look for him costs me as a vaekua tackles me to the ground. Its claws dig into my shoulder, leaving a gash, before I am able to destroy it with a touch of my hand. Cole lets out another cry but I can't seem to find him in the ever-growing smoke. Blood is dripping down my left arm but I continue to send blasts of energy out at the approaching vaekua.

A cry of pain quickens my pace, barreling through the smoke, until I practically trip on a vaekua pinning down Cole. I touch the vaekua's shoulder and it vanishes in a flash. Cole's forearms are shredded and bloody, held up in defense of his face. He lowers them slowly, hissing in pain.

"That thing caught me by surprise. It came out of the smoke, before I had a chance to raise my sword." I rip more of my dress off the bottom and start wrapping his arms. As I do that, I inspect him for more injuries but except his arms he seems mostly unscathed.

"I'm glad you've been able to hold your own."

"Jordan and I figured out that if you take off their heads it seriously incapacitates them for several minutes, until it reattaches." He shudders. "It's rather disgusting."

I whip my head around, searching frantically in the smoke. "Where is Jordan?"

"I don't know, we got separated when one of those things dragged Nick away. It came out of nowhere and grabbed him. He stood no chance." He gets to his feet, cringing a bit when he has to brace himself.

"Stay behind me. You are too injured to take on any more vaekua." He thankfully does not argue as I dispatch a few more vaekua that charge us. "Jordan! Jordan, where are you!"

"Can't you use your wind element and push the smoke away?" Cole says from behind me.

"No. I lost my ability to control wind. Jordan!" Panic is seeping in as I continue to look for Jordan. We support each other as we run through the now empty streets of Estera. We frantically look through every alleyway and every door in hopes of finding Jordan.

"Maia!" To my relief, the smoke swirling around us begins to push away and Sage appears next to me. A vaekua is charging up behind her but I dispatch it. Blood loss and the fact that I have used a lot of energy is making me sluggish and it's starting to show. I barely caught the vaekua in the shoulder.

"Sage, what are you doing here?" I ask, scanning our surroundings for any more vaekua.

"I was up on the wall, bringing water in to stop the fires. I saw you fighting off those creatures and came as fast as I could. What are those things?"

"Sssssaaaaaaaaaaaage." Her name sounds wrong coming from the mouth of a vaekua. It's slithery and scratchy and it makes every nerve on my body alert. Two thoughts immediately come to my mind as I search for the vaekua who knows my friend's name. First, when did they gain the ability to talk and second, there is only one vaekua that knows her name, Myka.

I grab her arm. "Sage, you need to go."

"Why? What's wrong?"

A dark figure starts emerging from the shadows and my heart drops to my stomach. It's too late, she's going to find out what happened to Myka. I shouldn't have kept this from her, I shouldn't have been so focused on me. I step in front of her and block her from the nightmarish figure.

"Sage, there is something you need to know."

"Can't it wait, we are kind of in the middle of something," she replies impatiently.

"Sssssaaaaaaaaaaaage."

"What is—" Sage stops mid-sentence as she glances above my head and I know the second her eyes land on the vaekua Myka. Tears fill her eyes and her hand drifts to her mouth. "Myka?"

Myka's blood-red eyes focus on his wife, sharp in intensity and bloodlust. Blood drips from his mouth and his blackened, inky skin seems even darker than before.

"Sage, it's not Myka. It's a vaekua. That is not Myka."

"I don't understand." Her voice shakes.

Cole is watching the exchange between us while also keeping an eye on the approaching vaekua; pain and unease clearly etched into his expression.

"Sage, I'm so sorry." My voice cracks a little with my next words. "I should have told you sooner, but I was ashamed. Myka is dead. That vaekua is possessing his body."

"No." Sage shakes her head in denial.

Myka holds out his hand and beckons to Sage. "Cooooome, ssssssweeeet Sssssage."

"Myka? He calls me sweet Sage. That's Myka, Maia." She starts to move towards the vaekua and I step in front of her again.

"No, Sage, listen. That's not Myka. It has his memories, but it's not him." I push against her as she tries to get around me. Tears fill my eyes as I realize that the only way to keep her safe and convince her that it is not him, is to take him out.

I pull energy to my palm and it flickers uncertainly. I can only hope that he is the last of the vaekua for now. I don't think I can handle any more.

Sage sees the energy and grabs my arm, her eyes wild. "No."

Fresh betrayal stabs me. First, I let her husband die and now I am going to make her watch as I kill what is left of him. "I'm sorry, Sage, I'm so sorry."

I send the energy blast flying with a flick of my finger and it connects solidly with Myka's chest. Its scream of pain as it dissolves blends with the scream of anguish from Sage. She drops to her knees and sobs into her hands.

I rest my hand on her shoulder and hesitantly say her name. She shrugs off my hand and gets to her feet, wiping her tears. "We need to go help the others."

"Sage."

She ignores me and starts towards the still burning inferno on the edge of Ester. Cole grabs my hand in silent support and we follow after her. We both watch for Jordan, checking every dead body we come across. Each time, I hold my breath as Cole or I flip the body over and reveal someone that isn't him.

The fire ahead is sending a cool sweat down my brow and the closer we get the harder it is to breathe. Mystics on the top of the wall are sending water over and into the buildings but the flames continue to climb.

"Sage, can you send me to the top of the wall? I can help."

She raises an eyebrow at my request but does as I ask, sending both Cole and I up and then following behind us. The flames below us lick at our feet and the air is thin but the Mystics upon the wall work tirelessly.

"Has everyone been evacuated from this part of the city?" I ask and several Mystics nod their heads.

I reach out my hand and call to the water beyond the wall. It comes to me in giant waves, larger than anything that the other mystics are gathering. The power of the Aurora flows through me even as I feel how weakened my body is. Cole must sense it, because he wraps his arm around my waist, supporting my weight. I pull the waves up the massive wall protecting the city and send them crashing over the flames, dousing the inferno that was engulfing this part of the city. I sag against Cole, completely and utterly drained.

He kisses the top of my head and whispers, "Thank you. You saved our home."

I don't comment on his use of the word 'our', even though I haven't made my decision yet. The group of Mystics make their way back down to the ground, checking for any remaining vaekua or flames that may have been missed. Sage helps us down but then disappears into the wreckage without a word. I watch her back as she goes, feeling the loss of her friendship and wondering if I'll ever get it back. Cole and I support each other's weight as we continue our search for Jordan.

"Cole, I have a bad feeling," I comment as we check another dead body.

"I do too." We search in silence for several minutes until Cole looks at me again. "So that vaekua was a friend?"

"Yes. His name was Myka. He was killed during my escape from Seraphine. He was under her control and Ben had to kill him or he wouldn't have been able to escape. Those creatures that Seraphine controls possess dead bodies and take on their memories. It knew Sage and was using that against her. I had to kill it; it wasn't Myka." I turn my face away to hide my tears but he turns it back with a finger on my chin.

"You did nothing wrong, Maia. You are right, it wasn't him. You did what you had to do to keep your friend safe."

"She'll never forgive me."

"You didn't kill him."

"No, but it's my fault that he was a prisoner of Rolland and Seraphine. It's my fault he's dead."

"Don't put that pressure on yourself, Maia. It isn't fair."

"It isn't fair that Myka died," I respond miserably.

"I think it's pretty fair. I survived after all," a familiar voice says, emerging from one of the crumbling buildings, with someone in tow behind them.

It takes me a second to realize that it is Ben, and that it's Jordan that he is dragging behind him. His words don't even process as I immediately try to jump to Jordan's aid, but Cole's arm shoots out to stop me. It gives me pause and then Ben's words finally penetrate the panicked haze in my head.

"What are you talking about, Ben? You didn't mean to kill Myka, it was an accident."

Ben drops Jordan unceremoniously on the ground and I cringe when his head bounces off the hard earth. Jordan is clearly unconscious and doesn't respond at all to his manhandling. Ben smiles but it doesn't reach his eyes. The bad feelings I had earlier multiply; something is very, very wrong.

Ben shrugs. "It was either me or him. Pretty sure I'd choose me every time."

"What has gotten into you? You were upset about this the last time we spoke, it was tearing you up and now you are okay with it?"

"Maia." Cole's quiet voice draws my attention to him and he nods to Ben's hand, which is holding a very large knife. I honestly don't know how I missed that. But nothing is making sense. Ben's behavior is so different than the Ben that I knew back at the Kamora base.

Then it all comes together. "Seraphine."

"Very good, little mystic," Ben sneers, his face morphing into something I have never seen before and Seraphine's nickname for me sounding wrong coming from his lips.

"What has she done to you, Ben?"

The laugh that comes out of him is pure Seraphine. "Now that I've had time to really work on my magic, I was able to alter the spell that I used on Myka. Now, not only do I control everything that the person does, but I can also speak through them when needed."

"Let him go, Seraphine."

"You have to be more specific, little mystic. Are you referring to your precious Jordan or your friend Ben?"

I grind my teeth, failing miserably in controlling my anger. "Release them both."

Ben taps his chin. "I don't know, this could be fun. I wonder who you would choose." Ben crouches next to Jordan and lifts his head up by his hair and runs the knife along his throat. He doesn't pierce the skin but I don't breathe again until it's safely away from the delicate area. He rests the blade on Jordan's cheek. "He really is handsome, I suppose I could see the appeal in him. Not my type though." He drops his head again.

"Your type is power."

"Guilty." Ben now runs the knife along his own throat and smirks mockingly. "So, who would you choose, little mystic?"

"I will not choose."

"That's because you know it would be Jordan. It's always Jordan. You would do anything to keep him safe. It's a wonder that Xavier never noticed your attachment to him."

The mention of my previous fiancé sends a sharp pain to my chest. I betrayed him, I did everything that Seraphine ever said that I would do. I used his love against him and used it to help us escape.

"Speaking of Xavier." It takes me a moment to realize that Ben is still talking. "He has been quite the moody prince since you left. He is tracking down anyone that has ever helped you and killing them. He's losing control; it seems that you were the only thing keeping him together. You showing your true colors broke him, it was the best thing that ever happened to him. He will make a fine king."

"What are you talking about?"

Ben twirls the knife between his fingers and cocks his hip. If it wasn't such a serious situation it may have been funny, but it only sends terror through my veins. She is truly in control of my friend.

"So much has changed since you've run away, little mystic. Xavier and I are to be wed and together we will rule Myridia and bring all other kingdoms to heel."

"I will stop you."

Ben laughs. "No, you will be on your knees at our feet, begging for a mercy that will never come. Xavier and I have come to an agreement that you will live. I don't need the Prakera to exact my revenge and rule this pathetic land. You will live with the decisions that you and your parents have made. You will watch Katear burn and there will be nothing that you can do to stop it."

"You will not touch her," Cole snarls and steps in front of me.

Ben quirks an eyebrow. "Oh, who is this? Another man that you will twist around your finger and use? You are just like your conniving mother."

"I am her betrothed and you will not touch a hair on her head." I don't correct him, he knows I have not given him an answer yet.

Ben looks in between the two of us and then bursts out in laughter. "Oh, this is rich." He gasps out between breaths. "You leave Xavier for your precious Jordan and then you move on to someone else. You are even worse than your mother." Ben sombers and waves his hand dismissively. "It's no matter though, both of them will die either way."

I push Cole behind me again and give him a look that I hope tells him to stay put. "Why are you here, Seraphine? Why do this to Ben?"

"I have spies everywhere, little mystic, you would be surprised how many people I already have under my control.

That could be a fun game, don't you think? How long it takes you to figure out who is mine. This one." He gestures towards his body. "Was an easy target. He left himself wide open when he showed up at that poor maid's house to deliver a present to her family."

My heart drops. Ben got caught while delivering the ring that I gave him for Alexia's family. Once again, another person's fate is on my conscious. If he dies, it will be on me and I will have to explain to yet another person that I am responsible for a loved one's death.

Ben slices his arm, drawing blood and my eyes follow the trail of blood as it drips to the ground. "Back to me, little mystic. I need your full attention." When I draw my eyes back to his face he smiles and again it is pure Seraphine, every ounce the evil person that she is. "Good, now pay attention. This is how this is going to work. You and your baker will come back to Myridia within two weeks time and surrender to us."

"You think it is that easy? I will never surrender to you."

"I think this next part will change your mind." He throws the knife in the ground right by Jordan's head, gauging my reaction. I stare back at him defiantly. "For every week after those two weeks that you defy our command, one of your friends will die."

"You don't have any of my friends. They are safely here, in Estera."

He picks up the knife and runs it along Jordan's cheek. Seraphine is enjoying herself. "Are they?" He quirks an eyebrow and doubt begins to creep in. "You didn't honestly think I revealed one of my spies just to talk, did you?"

"What did you do, Seraphine?" To my shame, my voice shakes.

"The vaekua you destroyed were only a distraction. My real targets were much more important than a few useless buildings in Estera. You will find that my creatures left with much more than they destroyed."

"Who did you take?!" Panic and terror are a living, breathing thing inside me.

"Every week you waste, you will lose someone you love."

"Seraphine, no! Stop this!"

"Time starts now, little mystic."

"Why are you doing this? You could have taken us while we were still in Myridia, why wait until now? Why do you have to involve these innocent people?"

Ben twirls the knife between his fingers, just above Jordan's head, and I watch every motion that it takes. One wrong move and it could fall and slice open his head. I curse Seraphine once again for taking away my wind element, I would send that knife flying into the nearest pile of rubble.

"Where's the fun in that, little mystic?"

"This isn't a game, Seraphine," I snap.

Ben's knuckles tighten around the knife and his eyes bore into me like daggers. "Oh, I know it is not game. Trust me, my people have lost everything and I will never allow that to happen again. Witches will rule this land from now until the end of time, I will guarantee it. Thanks to you, I now know exactly who my enemies are and where to find them."

Finally, it clicks into place. She allowed us to escape. She allowed us to get out of Myridia because she already had a spy among us. She wanted to find out where the mystics were and who was opposing her. I led her right to my people, I led her to Estera. She could have stopped us at any time but she didn't, she had a bigger scheme. Every step she has been a few steps ahead of me and continues to be ahead of me. How do I beat someone who always knows my moves? How do I defeat her when I don't even know who she has under her spell?

"I've been asked to tell you that Xavier is very much looking forward to having you back in his care. I believe the phrase that he used is, 'you are the air that I breathe and you are mine.' I don't think you will be able to get away from him so easily this time, little mystic. He is bent on having you again and never letting you go. We'll have such fun together, but alas, it is time for me to go. We'll be seeing each other very soon." Ben shrugs. "Or not, honestly either option is fine by me. But I know you will make the right choice. Until next time, little mystic, accept my parting gift."

Ben seems to sag as Seraphine's direct influence leaves his consciousness.

"Ben?" I tentatively murmur. Ben has yet to raise his head and is staring directly at the knife in his hand. His body is shaking and a low groan of pain escapes his lips. I try saying his name again and this time his head snaps up and his tear-filled eyes find mine.

"Maia, I'm so sorry. I have to do it, she told me I had to. I don't have a choice." His body continues to shake as he fights whatever command that Seraphine has given him. He raises the knife to his throat as tears fall down his face. He whispers something I don't catch and then slides the knife across his throat. Blood instantly begins to flow, covering his shirt and the ground around him. He falls to his knees and I rush to his side, catching him before he hits the ground. I cradle him in my arms, ashamed that I was not quick enough to stop him.

"Ben, no!" I push my dress against his neck, even knowing that it is too late. Seraphine's parting gift was punishment for escaping and to show me that she is serious. She will kill whomever she took if I do not go to her. She will take everything from me. I hold Ben as the blood flows from his neck and the life drains from his eyes. My tears mix with his blood, but there is no magical light that saves him like it did with Jordan. There is only the empty hollowness of losing a friend. The Prakera does not save him, I am not strong enough, weakened by my fight with the vaekua and the next second, he is gone. As I cry over his body I can't help but wonder how many more people I will say goodbye to before this is over.

Chapter 19

I SLOW MY PACE as we come upon the broken-in doors of the King's study. Cole—who has Jordan flung over his shoulder—is right on my heels. Cole drops Jordan to the ground as we both take in the carnage before us. The doors are off their hinges and all the guards that had been with King Erik are slaughtered, their bodies littered across the room. There is no sign of King Erik, Melinda, or Enora.

"Mother!" Cole bellows, eyes scanning the large space for any sign of her.

"Cole, I'm here, Son." Cole runs to his mother as she emerges from a small cabinet behind the King's massive desk. To my relief, Melinda crawls out after her; both are thankfully unscathed.

"Where is Father?" Cole asks, tucking his mother in the safety of his arms.

"They took him." She hides her face in his bloody and smoky shirt, talking quietly, and Cole lowers his face to hear her words. Her body rocks with silent sobs. I turn away, giving them privacy and hug Melinda in relief.

"What happened?" I ask her.

"We heard them coming, they had broken into the palace and we could hear their shrieks echoing off the vacant halls. Erik pushed Enora and I into the cabinet and told us to hide. It all happened so fast." Melinda shakes her head in disbelief. "Just as he closed the cabinet door, we could hear them break down the doors and then there were screams."

"So many screams." Enora whispers and Cole rubs his mother's back reassuringly. Sadness and anger storm in his eyes.

"The vaekua, they killed everyone and then they took the King."

"They took him alive?" Cole asks and looks at me over his mother's head.

"As far as we could tell. He was alive when they took him. Why would they take him?" Melinda replies.

I sigh. "It was Seraphine. Everything that was taking place on the edge of the city was a distraction. She sent her vaekua to distract us and then steal hostages right under our noses. We had a spy within our midst. He revealed to her all the information she needed to know."

"Who?"

I grab Melinda's hand, mine still covered and caked in dried blood; Ben's blood. "It was Ben. She got to him while he was delivering something to Alexia's family." I take in a sharp breath, fighting the tears that want to come. "I had asked him to do it for me. I felt so guilty that I had gotten her killed. She was their source of income, I had to do something. He was delivering something that could at least aid in alleviating their pain. Seraphine found him and put him under the control spell, but she altered it. He was her puppet this entire time and when he had served his purpose, she had him kill himself. He's dead Melinda. I'm so sorry."

Melinda drops her hand from mine and lowers herself to the ground, shock and pain firmly on her face. Ben had always been important to her. He was one of her first recruits to the Kamora and was clearly like a son to her. I want to comfort her but I do not know what to say or do because I am the cause of her pain. I am the reason Seraphine is hurting the people around me.

"Don't," Melinda says softly.

"What?"

"This isn't your fault, Maia."

"How did you know I was blaming myself?"

She offers me a sad smile. "Because you are so much like your mother and that is exactly what she would be doing, were she here. This is not your fault. This is all on Seraphine. She is bent on revenge and destruction."

"She is coming after me though. People are dying because of me."

"People are dying because of her greed and her madness. She may think she is doing the best thing for our people but she is only furthering their destruction."

"Princess Maia! Thank the ancient gods that I was able to find you. I thought that you had been taken as well."

"Malachi!" I greet the council member as he enters the destroyed study. His eyes survey the destruction around us and then finally settle on me. "Have you seen my brother, Malachi?"

Malachi wrings his hands nervously. "Those things took him, Princess. I thought surely they had taken you as well."

"Was anyone else taken? Were any of our people injured or killed?" I slip easily into my role, now that my brother is gone, I am now in charge of the Mystic race. I will make my parents proud.

"Several guards were killed while protecting him. The rest of our people are safe. You believe others were taken?"

"Yes. Malachi, I need you to go and do a headcount of our people. Find out who else may have been taken."

"Yes, Princess. I will report back to you as soon as I have the information. It shouldn't take too long; most the them are gathered in the council chamber." He bolts out of the room and only once he's gone do I allow myself to feel the pain of my brother's capture. Seraphine knew exactly what she was doing when she took him. Xavier, the swine, must have told her exactly who—

"No." He wouldn't, he couldn't have taken her.

I take off after Malachi, ignoring Cole's shout to come back. I catch up to Malachi easily but I sprint past him. I need to know she is safe. I need to know that Xavier did not betray me, yet again. The Mystic's part of the city is hardly damaged. The vaekua were not here for destruction, unlike other parts of the city. A few bodies are scattered upon the abandoned streets, but I barely spare them a glance; I have a single destination in mind. I burst into the council chamber room, startling several people and receiving a few annoyed glances. There are several hundred people in the small space and they are all milling about but I don't see a familiar mop of bright blonde hair.

"Layla!" I shout into the crowd. The room quickly slips into silence with a few murmurs as I continue to shout Layla's name. My cries are getting desperate with each passing second of no reply. Finally, a young mystic with shaggy black hair comes to my side.

"Princess Maia. My name is Zek." He rubs his hand on a large gash on his cheek, and stares at the ground. "I was with Layla. We were in her room when they came for her. We tried to fight them off but they were too powerful. They threw me through the window and before I could get back up to help her, they took her."

"Were they shadow creatures?"

"Yes, all but one. There was someone else with them. I don't know who he was, I've never seen him before. But he had magic, he is the one who threw me out the window with his powers."

I lay a hand on the boy's shoulder. "Thank you, Zek. You did everything you could to protect Layla."

I walk out of the council chamber room just as Malachi arrives. I instruct him to continue with the headcount and then I walk away, almost in a daze. I walk blindly in the direction of the King's study until finally anger breaks through the haze of my mind. I send a small energy blast into a nearby wagon, disintegrating it and then unleash a grief-stricken sob to the night sky, dropping to my knees. So many emotions and thoughts race through my mind. No matter what Melinda says, this is all my fault. I did this. I led Seraphine here. She is doing all of this because of me and my parents. The failures and mistakes of the past are shaping a tumultuous future of war and I don't know how to stop it. I don't know how to slow this downward descent. The world is crumbling around me.

Slow footsteps approach behind me but I don't lift my head from its place in my hands. I don't have the energy and I can't bring myself to care. The person stops behind me and I hear them drop to the ground next to me. The next thing I know strong, capable arms are enveloping me and pulling me into their safe embrace. My body relaxes instantly, I would know these arms anywhere.

"This isn't your fault, Buttercup."

I snuggle closer to his chest but don't reply. I feel like if I open my mouth the only thing that will come out is pain. Jordan rubs small circles along my back and murmurs things that I can't make out, but just his voice calms my racing heart. I don't know how long we stay like this; it feels like a million years as well as just seconds. I know I need to face my people, face the trials before me, but I can't bring myself to leave the safety of Jordan's arms. I'm so afraid that I won't be strong enough to face the turmoil ahead. I don't feel prepared, I don't feel ready. How can we defeat an army that can't be killed? How can we defeat her when she knows every move we are going to make?

I feel Jordan shift and he lifts my chin so that he can see my tear-streaked face. He kisses my tears away and then rests his forehead against mine, so that all I can see are his beautiful cerulean blue eyes. I get lost in their depth.

"It's going to be okay."

"You don't know that," I whisper.

"I do."

"How?"

"Because I believe in you. You wouldn't have been chosen to be the Aurora if you were not strong enough to handle it."

"I wish I had your confidence."

"You do. Things are just a little messy right now and the future seems more daunting than usual."

"I'm afraid, Jordan. Seraphine is so powerful, how can I possibly defeat her? I can't do this alone." Admitting those words aloud sends a shiver through me. It gives them life and fear starts anew.

Jordan takes my face in his hands. "You are not alone, Buttercup, and you will never have to face this all alone. You have me, Cole, Estera, and the mystics behind you; we are all here to support you. You will not face Seraphine alone, we will all stand by your side. Together we will defeat her."

"She's so strong."

"We are stronger. We are fighting for far more important things than she is."

"She took Layla and Kaden."

"We will get them back. We will get everyone back, whomever she took, together." He kisses my forehead and a sense of calm blankets over me. He's right, we are fighting for more important things than Seraphine. We have more to live for, more to die for. We will not be so easily defeated.

"Thank you." I wrap my hands around his that are still resting on my cheeks, turning my face to kiss his palm. Thoughts that I shouldn't be doing any of this with him, when I may have to say goodbye try to invade my mind, but I push them away before they take root. That is a worry for another day, for now I need him. "You always know the right things to say."

"I've had years of experience." He smirks and plants a chaste kiss on my lips. "But I mean every word. I believe in you and I know that you are strong enough to defeat her. She may have won today, but she will not win this war."

"Are you okay?"

"I'm fine. While we were fighting the vaekua Ben came out of nowhere and knocked me out. He caught me by surprise. I came to right after you left the study and Cole filled me in on what was going on and that's when I came to find you. I knew you'd be needing some extra support."

"I don't know who I can trust anymore. Seraphine could have anyone under her control."

"I know. We'll try and figure out a way to weed out people we can trust. Tonight, was just a setback. We will regroup and come back stronger than ever."

Jordan helps me to my feet and we begin making our way back to the study. We find Cole alone, collecting the dead bodies and gathering them to a central spot.

"Is your mother doing alright?" I ask, as we enter.

Cole nods. "She'll be alright. I took her to her rooms so she could get some rest. She's pretty shaken up, but she's strong. Melinda is staying with her, just in case though."

"Good. I'm—"

"Don't say you're sorry," Cole interrupts me with a smirk. "This isn't your fault. We knew the risk when we decided to align ourselves with your people. It was only a matter of time before Myridia attacked."

"We'll get your father back."

Cole stiffens at my words. "You are not giving yourself up to that witch."

"I think I may have a plan, but it will require time that we do not have."

Cole eyes the broken doors of the study. "Why don't we find a better place to talk. After what that witch said, I don't want anyone overhearing our conversation. We don't know who could be under her spell."

"I agree."

"I should meet with whomever is now in charge of the palace guard." He gestures to one of the dead bodies. "We lost the captain, so I want to ensure that we are properly protected in the event of another attack."

I nod. "I should address my people as well. I need to get a final count of who was taken by Seraphine's creatures. We can meet up later today once everything is settled."

Cole steps closer and gathers me in his arms, ignoring Jordan standing just a few feet away from us. Just like his brother, Cole is just a head taller than me and I fit perfectly just under his chin.

He tightens his arms around me and rests his cheek on the top of my head. "I'm sorry about your friend."

"Thank you. I just can't believe I never noticed a difference. I had no idea." I feel Jordan move away from us and he begins busying himself by taking over for his brother, gathering the bodies. His movements are stiff and jerky and I know that our embrace is the cause.

I pull away from Cole and put some distance between us. He seems confused at first until he sees my eyes drift over to Jordan. He looks between Jordan and I, and frowns. He closes the distance between us and says quietly so that only I can hear, "You know you will have to make your decision soon, especially now that we are at war."

My eyes follow Jordan's movements too afraid to look into Cole's eyes; too afraid of what I will see there. "I know," I reply just as quietly.

Cole is having none of my avoidance though and places a finger under my chin, guiding it back to him. His eyes are just as I feared, full of deep emotions. I see within his eyes, hurt, longing, determination, and many emotions that I don't want to put a name to, because one looks too similar to the way his brother looks upon me. His eyes dip down to my lips and longing comes forefront to his gaze and he runs his thumb along my bottom lip.

"Maia, I—"

I interrupt him before he can go any further. "Now is not the time for this conversation, Cole." I know I'm being a coward; he's right I do need to make a decision, but I just can't bring myself to do it yet. I need more time.

He drops his hand from my chin and nods, hiding his disappointment behind a fake smile. "You are right, of course." He bows. "Until later, Princess. Good luck with your people."

He disappears out of the study, leaving Jordan and I alone.

I stand before the Mystic people, all still crammed into the council chamber room. A nervous energy flows through the inhabitants of the space. Word has traveled that Kaden has been captured and their uncertainty is palpable. If what the council told me is true, there are some who doubt my loyalty to the Mystic race, so the fact that I am now in charge is probably sending terror through them.

Before addressing my people, I met with Malachi and he was able to give me an accurate count of how many people we had lost to either death or capture. Twenty Mystics were found dead, most of them soldiers and protectors. Six people are currently missing and we can only assume that they were taken by the vaekua. Guilt is a permanent emotion as Malachi lists off the names of the deceased and missing to the group of gathered Mystics. So many names, so many people that I never met and now never will.

"As you well know, the King and the young Mystic Layla have been taken by the creatures that serve the evil witch Seraphine. There are several people unaccounted for and we can only assume that they were taken as well. If you have seen any of the following people, please let us know. Council members Leon, Marcus, and Regan, and the warrior, Sage, are the mystics who are still missing." Malachi reports to the crowd.

Regret and sadness almost suffocate me at the final missing person. My last image of Sage was her walking away from me after I had to kill the vaekua possessing Myka's body. She had to watch him die and I kept his original death a secret from her. Her anger towards me was justified and now to make matters worse, she is a prisoner of Seraphine.

"Princess Maia, would you like to say a few words?" Malachi draws my attention back to the restless crowd in front of me. I nod and Malachi steps back with a bow of his head.

I sweep my eyes along the crowd and take in every face I see. Despair and fear seem to be the common emotion on most of the faces.

"Words cannot express how deeply sorry I am for the pain that has come down upon the Mystic people. I know that I am a stranger to most of you, raised among our enemies and ignorant of our ways. I am an outsider who brought pain and suffering to the safe haven that you called home. I understand that it is only natural for you to dislike me, even hate me. But I will tell you this right now—I am not your enemy.

I came to the Mystic City to find my family, something that I never had in the palace of Myridia. I had been raised to believe that I was the last of our race, the last of our people. Never did I hope or dream that what I was being told was a lie. Was I naive to believe their lies? Yes, I'm not ashamed to admit that I blindly accepted what I was told; but once I learned the truth about my parents and about what I am, I set out to right the wrongs that had been set in motion.

Hear me when I say, I did not know Xavier was working with his father. I did not know that Rolland and his army were following us to the Mystic City. I did not lead them there." I take a shallow breath, willing myself to believe those words as much as the people in front of me.

"Rolland is now dead and we are facing an even greater evil. The witch Seraphine has taken control of Myridia and has taken our King and others as hostage. She will stop at nothing to get what she wants. But we will stop her. With Kaden gone, it is now my duty to step in and take up the mantle of our people. I will not command you to stand with me. It is your choice, what you will do next, but if you follow me, allow me the chance to prove to you that I am the Aurora that my parents died for, I will not let you down. I will do everything in my power to ensure that nothing like what happened in the Mystic City or here will ever happen again. We will stand together as a strong race and we will face this uncertain tomorrow so that we may have a safe and secure future. We will not let Seraphine and her evil consume us. We will fight and we will win this war. I am Princess Maia, daughter of our beloved Alera and Gaven and I will defend you until my dying breath, that is my vow to you."

As I finish my speech I realize that the room is silent and that my skin is warm. I look down at my arms and I'm not surprised to find that they are glowing, actually my entire body is glowing. The Prakera brought to the surface by my emboldened speech and for the first time, in a long time I feel powerful and I vow to never allow myself to feel weak again. As the crowd begins to process their shock of seeing the Prakera first hand, applause spreads like a wildfire and hope blooms. I raise my chin with pride, embracing the person I need to be for my people; ready to face the impending war. I will defeat Seraphine, I will bring peace back to Myridia and all of Katear. I am the Aurora, chosen by the ancient gods and I will fulfill my destiny.

Acknowledgments

To all my readers, thank you for supporting my dream and allowing me into your hearts and minds. Your support means the world to me, and I'm humbled every day that people are reading my work.

There are several people that I want to thank individually for helping develop Mystic Turmoil into the book it is today. My amazing friends, Briana and Anna, who helped me brainstorm character and creature names for hours while at work, and also put up with me changing my mind over and over. I can admit that I did that a lot.

I cannot thank Mark and Lorna enough for all their help with designing the cover, and all the extra work they have done for me. The cover took lots of back and forth, and many hours of editing until it was perfect, and I appreciate that time spent. You two helped me through the process of Mystic Princess and, once again, you were invaluable when it came to Mystic Turmoil.

Once again, my book besties, Kim and Caitlin, who joined me on the entire journey of writing the book and gave me feedback every step of the way. I couldn't have written anything without the support of my parents and husband, who all encouraged me to keep writing even when I didn't feel like it.

After the love and support I received for Mystic Princess from my friends and family, I was so excited to write Mystic Turmoil.

This book is for all of you, and I hope you enjoy it as much as I thoroughly enjoyed writing it. It definitely turned into more than I could have ever imagined when I first started this adventure.

About the Author

Kelli Marie hails from Elgin, IL, where her love of books grew into a healthy obsession. Books have been a shining light through many dark times in her life, and it is her hope to be that light for others. Her favorite book genres are Young Adult Fantasies and Science Fiction.

Kelli Marie enjoys Star Wars and Harry Potter, and still believes she is meant to be a Jedi. She now lives in Tampa, FL with her wonderful husband, Nick, and their two cat children, Oreo and Goober. In her free time, you will find her at Disney World and Universal Studios, where she can continue to feel like a kid.

Made in the USA
Lexington, KY
11 September 2018